Exotic Worlds Sci-Fi Collection

by

Rafael Morillo

Exotic Worlds Sci-Fi Collection

A Compilation of Thirty Stories

By Rafael Morillo

Edited by: Kathleen Bosman

Cover Design by: Amnet Systems

ISBN: 979-8-9879325-0-6

Caribbean Lion Publishing

Dedication

I dedicate this collection to young people who are interested in science and technology. This is for young people who wish to make positive changes within their respective societies and desire to make this world a better place.

"'For I know the plans I have for you,' declares the Lord, 'plans to prosper you and not to harm you, plans to give you hope and a future'." Jeremiah 29:11

"May he give you the desire of your heart and make all your plans succeed." Psalms 20:4

Table of Contents

Exotic Worlds Sci-Fi Collection

A Compilation of Thirty Stories

By Rafael Morillo

Story I: A Starless Dream (Distant Future)

The light crept into his eyes as he slowly opened them and began preparations for his labor duties. The lands of this world were bathed in near-perpetual darkness except for the artificial lights found within the large domes that were constructed by the highest of human intellectuals. Marcus Johnson Alvarado enjoyed his duties, and during his leisure time, he found himself spending long periods alone with his thoughts. He was often curious about the nightwalkers that lived outside of the domes in the dark, frigid unknown. Marcus thought about their unsettlingly pale skin and abnormally small eyes which were less complex than the eyes of those who inhabited the domes. The nightwalkers had a heightened sense of touch, smell, and taste. The nightwalkers were considered inferior to the advanced human population in the domes and within the domes; darker shades of skin were considered a sign of higher beauty and intelligence.

Marcus Johnson had a naturally dark brown complexion while some of the scientists and leaders had lighter complexions. It was apparent that some of the elite members of society developed a complex regarding their complexion, so through science, they darkened their complexions slightly to distance themselves in appearance from the nightwalkers. Marcus Johnson Alvarado understood the reason for his complexion and facial features, and he traced his lineage to people who lived in the ancient islands of the Caribbean many ages ago. Marcus's parents informed him that his lineage belonged to the people of an island called Trinidad and a republic inhabited by a people known as Dominicans. The Dominicans were largely mixed-race people from a historical island that was divided into two nations.

Marcus was proud of his history and ancestry and sought to live a life that would bring honor to his family name. He belonged to a people once categorized as Latino in the ancient United States. The Latinos were part of the original builders of the domes, and currently, there were nearly 50,000 people with Latin last names and Latino ancestry within the domes. The overwhelming majority of the over five million people that lived in the domes of New Washington possessed Anglo last names.

Marcus enjoyed the artificial suns constructed in the domes, and sometimes, he suspected some jealousy from the elite members of society. Marcus was a hard worker, and he advanced quickly in the science of agriculture. As soon as Marcus learned to read, he developed an obsession with science. As a child, he quickly read the works of Gregor Johann Mendel, a scientist from an ancient land named Austria-Hungary. Gregor Mendel was called the father of genetics, and he was interested in the genetic codes that formed the rules of life. His love for plants and genetics quickly turned him to the study of plants and their genetic manipulation. Food was an essential part of life and was of primary concern as the colony had suffered major food shortages in the past. Some scientists attempted to vary the diet of the population by including wild, native vegetation from near the great sea in the east. Some of these wild fruits made most people violently ill, and some people suffered death. Marcus thought about studying the nightwalkers and their digestive system and methods of food preparation. Perhaps the secret to making wild plants more digestible existed within the digestive systems of the nightwalkers.

The nightwalkers had previously attacked the domed communities of New Washington, and although they outnumbered the population of the domed communities, the nightwalkers had been defeated. A major military offensive, led by leaders from the domed communities several generations ago, pushed the nightwalkers toward the caves near the sea. The domed communities expanded toward the mountains of the west while the nightwalkers lived near the sea and in the distant islands of the endless eastern sea.

The nightwalkers attacked numerous times in history but for several generations never attempted another invasion after the humans constructed a large electric border. The humans periodically patrolled the border areas to find any nightwalkers that may have made it through the borderlines. The description of their horrible alien appearance was often told to children to scare them when they misbehaved, and writers often depicted the nightwalkers as grotesque in appearance with a frightening and barbaric culture.

Marcus was a young man and was not assigned a wife yet. Usually, by his age, he would have a selection of possible female candidates that would have been suggested by his family members and approved by the Family and Marriage Council of his local community. The women would also be advised and would have to select from a chosen pool of men. Romantic love was encouraged, and new couples would undergo a genetic examination before final approval for marriage by the Family and Marriage Council. Thoughts of marriage and his future were put on hold because something had happened to his friend.

Marcus was not in the best of moods because on the previous day, he had been informed that his best friend Jacob had disappeared during his last patrol outside of the dome. Jacob had appeared anxious in the last few weeks, and he had been reprimanded several times by his superiors. Some people said that Jacob's curiosity might have gotten the better of him, and he could have encountered something deadly in the darkness. Jacob worked closely with the elite scientists and dome military to find various items for scientific study in unknown parts of the world. Marcus was eager to learn about what existed in the darkness, and he often spoke with Jacob about his experiences during his various duties.

Jacob had given Marcus a tiny smart chip just over a week ago and told Marcus to insert the chip into his small computer if something were to happen to him. Marcus continued to work; however, he felt sharp anxiety, especially as he began to read the secret documents contained in the smart chip. Jacob gave Marcus some instructions and various passwords to access secret files that revealed important information. It seemed that Jacob believed something terrible would soon happen to him, and he appeared particularly anxious the day before his disappearance.

As children, Marcus and Jacob had played basketball and baseball as well as various simulation games. Like most children, they were often curious about the dark world beyond the domes. The bitter cold and the alien lands that were enveloped in eternal darkness both intrigued Marcus and scared him. The residents of the domes were born, lived their lives, raised children, and died on this planet; however, many never felt truly native to this world. Parents often told their children that the nightwalkers and other monsters from beyond the dome would come and take them away if they misbehaved. Little was known about the nightwalkers, and parents usually depicted them as monstrous beings with pale skin and sharp teeth. As an adult, Marcus had learned that the nightwalkers had pale skin and walked upright and were humanoid in appearance with thicker bone structure and small eyes. It appeared that intelligent beings throughout the universe evolved similarly to humans, including the nightwalkers who were smarter than beasts but were not civilized like humans.

Jacob's family anxiously awaited information regarding his whereabouts. Jacob's parents demanded answers from their community leaders but received little information. The few people who were lost in the darkness never returned. People said that those who were lost far beyond the domes went mad after experiencing the bitter cold and the desolation of a world that no one had attempted to fully understand. Many people were curious about what lay beyond the domes, including Jacob, who was one of the few that had sought to explore the vast lands. As a young man, he had advocated for the exploration of the entire planet, despite the dangers that lurked in the shadows. Jacob quickly joined the exploration club and enlisted in scientific exploration duties in the darkness. Few were brave or crazy enough to join exploration teams, and few were like Jacob who was a curious and valiant soul. Jacob passed his examinations and physical assessments and upon completing his requirements and becoming an explorer, he was provided with the best technologies, which were unavailable to the average citizen.

Marcus was happy for Jacob and was interested in hearing his story but was soon surprised to discover that something horrible might have befallen his best friend. Marcus poured through hundreds of pages of classified information: Numerous animal and plant life that Marcus never knew existed. Deep-water fish of various colors, including green, yellow, blue, orange, and some multicolored. Some of the aquatic animals breathed from the atmosphere, like the aquatic mammals on

Earth, and could penetrate surface ice. After numerous generations of human presence, there was still plenty of mystery on the planet, including an abundance of fauna and flora yet to be discovered. Marcus's curiosity and fear heightened as he learned about the lands and water that existed in the darkness. He had learned that this planet was less than half the size of their ancestral home planet, Earth. This planet was similar to Earth in that it also had heavy metals inside its core, but it contained a little more radiogenic energy than Earth within its core, creating a slightly stronger magnetic shield.

Marcus read the various documents that Jacob had written, and he realized that Jacob had found information that the scientists had secret bunkers within the domes and one large bunker outside of the domes where several nightwalkers were held in captivity for further studies. Jacob never spoke to Marcus about his recent discoveries, but as he read further, he discovered that Jacob did indeed intend to inform him about what he had uncovered.

Marcus understood that he would have to move quickly before the authorities began to ask him and his family questions. Perhaps he was being monitored now?

The following day, a deputy from the local police department contacted him and asked him to report and meet with a police detective named Xavier. Marcus went home to his apartment and gathered his thoughts. He thought about the possible questions he might be asked, and he nervously pondered what Detective Xavier might know.

Later, Marcus entered a small vehicle that was paid for by the local police department, and he traveled to the city center at Justice Square. He entered the ten-floor Justice building and walked up to Detective Xavier's fifth-floor office. Detective Xavier was tall, pale, and middle-aged, and he appeared interested in speaking with Marcus.

Detective Xavier smiled and motioned Marcus to enter his office. "Welcome, Marcus. I am glad that we finally have a chance to speak. Firstly, I want to say that I am sorry that your friend Jacob has gone missing, and we are doing everything in our power to send expeditions to search for him. We believe Jacob is near the domes nearby. We believe that Jacob had an encounter with the native beings of this planet. Usually, they tend to be violent encounters, and these encounters are starting to become more frequent, just like the frequent violent encounters of generations past.

We have, unfortunately, lost contact with him, and we could no longer read his vitals. It appears his biometer malfunctioned or was damaged not long after he disappeared.

Marcus replied, "All of this seems rather strange. Jacob was very intelligent and aware of the dangers of this planet. He was more knowledgeable than most, and he also qualified to attend higher education and study the indigenous flora and fauna of this world. Jacob was always careful and aware of his surroundings, and I am at a loss as to how he could have disappeared."

The detective quickly replied, "I understand that you are sad and confused. The conditions outside of these domes are extremely hostile, and although we have lived on this planet for many generations, we have not yet been able to fully understand the lands and oceans of this world. Although the hostilities against the most advanced life forms on this planet have ended, minor acts of violence can occur randomly. Our surveillance systems are not fully effective, particularly a hundred kilometers beyond our frontier. Jacob was lost beyond our frontier on a sensitive mission. When we discover all the details about Jacob's case, we shall notify his parents and then you. We searched his apartment, and since you are a close friend of Jacob, we advise that you release any information Jacob may have given you in the past."

Marcus began to shake as anxiety gripped him, and he quickly got up and replied, "Jacob sometimes spoke with me about the weird fungi that he collected, but he did not give me any other information. If I find anything, I will return and release it to you."

Marcus left before his shaking worsened and his breathing became labored. By the time he reached his apartment, his heart was racing well above 100 beats per minute. When he opened the door to his apartment, he found his parents inside. His mother appeared nervous, and his father spoke with concern in his voice.

Marcus's mother Janet spoke first as she embraced him, "My son, I was so worried. We haven't spoken in person since the disappearance of your friend, Jacob. I understand you are hurting, like we all are, and I want you to cooperate with the investigation. Detectives are coming to our home tomorrow to speak with us and ask questions."

Marcus spoke with his parents for several hours and reassured them that he would cooperate with the investigation in hopes that it could lead to further information about Jacob. Before his parents left, his father quickly spoke to his son privately.

Thomas spoke carefully, "My son, I want you to cooperate with the investigations, and hopefully Jacob will be found. I understand that this may not make sense, but you must always think and maintain calm as this investigation moves forward."

Marcus interrupted his father, "Father, you are right! It does not make sense. Jacob revealed some information to me, and I also found some additional information regarding deeper government secrets."

Thomas interrupted his son and said, "My son, it is obvious to any person who has critical thinking skills that governments hide information from their populations. There is much to hide on this alien planet that we have made our home. Many generations ago, humans discovered simple alien life, and the government feared that it would destabilize societies on Earth. When we discovered this planet, we also discovered complex life. The discovery of this planet and its complex life also solidified the idea that advanced civilizations exist currently and did previously in our vast universe. The nightwalkers are considered intelligent beings although they are less intelligent than we are.

"Does our government know more about our planet than we do? Of course, they do, my son. Sometimes, governments do bad things to preserve peace, and sometimes, they hurt their people and justify it because they say it is for the improvement of society. We are from a proud Latino ancestry that persists until today. Even our people in the United States, so long ago, experienced various degradations, at times directly perpetrated by the government we sometimes fought for. There are some truths best left uncovered, my son."

Marcus quickly replied, "Father, I discovered that this planet has an abundance of life both on land and in the sea. This planet has more life than we are led to believe, and it appears our leaders are keeping us ignorant. A small organization within our government has traveled farther than what they report, and most of the planet and even part of the sea has been explored. Many of these organisms are similar to those of our ancient homeland. It appears there was a closer and long relationship between our government and the nightwalkers. We only know about the wars initiated by their random attacks, but Jacob left a file with the information he gathered, and it appears the nightwalkers are more intelligent than we believe."

Thomas had an intense focus within his eyes as he responded, "My son, there is more to this planet than is told. Our family members served on patrols in the past, and they shared stories about the nightwalkers before. There was much unrest during the early days of our colony, and anyone that could think critically understands that there are secrets our government hides from us. During our distant past, even before the time of the great wars on Earth, the elite of the United States hid secrets from the people. The United States degraded in the twenty-second century as the oligarchs increased their stranglehold on society and the lands burned from climate change and riots."

Thomas paused momentarily before he continued, "After several generations, the people of the United States began to experience some of the same ills that the poorer areas of the world had previously experienced. The US government made some adjustments to prevent increased turmoil as other nations, including China, became world powers. The US government implemented a horrendous foreign policy that was nearly as bad as the horrors of the nineteenth and twentieth centuries, and some activists spoke against the United States, leading to imprisonment and unspeakable horrors inflicted upon them and their families. In conclusion, son, sometimes, it is best to move carefully and not search for something that is not meant to be discovered. Sometimes, patience is required, and knowledge should be revealed at a later time."

Marcus reassured his father he would be careful; however, his curiosity burned within him as he waited for his parents to leave so he could continue to read the secret documents. He quickly inserted Jacob's file to try to consume as much information as he could. Marcus soon discovered the sad history of the first generations of colonists. Depression, alcoholism, and high suicide rates had plagued the colonies during the first generations, leading to several large-scale revolts led by various rebels that were labeled extremists, then imprisoned and executed. After the first ten generations, the population was sharply reduced by famine and disease, and a group of people living in a large dome named New Australia revolted. The people of New Australia were descendants of a select group of prisoners from the United

States who elected to travel to the alien planet instead of facing life in jail or the death penalty.

The original colonists departed from Earth sometime in the twenty-fourth century, with what was now considered primitive technology, toward a rogue planet that was heading toward the nearest black hole from our ancestral solar system. The elite class originated from scientists that were instructed on Earth to form a functioning government on the rogue planet. Most of the population was to be studied, and the information would be relayed to a secret scientific location within the United States. The descendants of the colonists would eventually be sacrificed after crossing the event horizon into the jaws of the black hole. The initial voyage took many thousands of years—using the primitive technology of the twenty-fourth century—from when the voyage departed the Earth from a secret facility within US territory.

What Marcus discovered next was truly shocking. The nightwalkers were human beings that originally lived within the New Australian dome that rebelled against the elites that governed New Washington. These humans were banished into the dark abyss and soon became nightwalkers. Some of the nightwalkers were currently being held prisoner in a secret facility underground near the main New Washington Dome. This secret was easily kept from the population as few people ventured outside the domes and only traveled out into the darkness to the smart roads to visit other domes.

There were two classes of nightwalkers. The smaller group was intelligent and maintained an organized society on the islands of the large ocean, and the others were said to live like animals in the darkness. Surprisingly, both groups of nightwalkers were humans that were among the original colonists that lived in New Australia.

The human rebels, now called nightwalkers, discovered that the elite were originally supposed to maintain the colony and monitor its inhabitants. The elite planned that their descendants would leave this alien planet while leaving the remaining inhabitants to die a catastrophic death as the planet passed through the event horizon of the black hole. A rebel leader named Elias discovered the truth, and he led an uprising within New Australia, which soon spread to the domes of New Washington and almost reached the dome of the elites in New Columbia. According to the files that Jacob left behind for Marcus, Elias and most of his followers were killed while the elites killed anyone who knew their secret. The remaining rebels were banished toward the eastern lands near the large, frozen eastern sea.

Marcus learned that the elites of New Columbia believed that the best access to the geothermal vents was near the small lakes near the western mountains, which is why the domes of New Washington were built near the western mountains. Through his files, Jacob explained that the nightwalkers discovered the largest hydrothermal vent on the other side of the world near an island archipelago in the eastern sea. The nightwalkers of these islands retained their complex communities, and they rarely interacted with the nomadic nightwalkers that roamed the vast darkness of the east.

The last entry that Jacob wrote detailed that he made contact with an intelligent nightwalker that had a complex name that Marcus could not pronounce. Jacob was trained to kill nightwalkers if he saw one because they were extremely hostile. Jacob hesitated because this nightwalker was calm and could speak broken English. The nightwalker pleaded for his life, and he informed Jacob that he and a few others were having talks with some elite officials from New Washington and New Columbia. The nightwalker said that the elites secretly captured the nomadic nightwalkers and performed experiments on them. He also said that they had special radioactive elements in large abundance that the elites of New Columbia needed to power the various spacecraft they were secretly constructing. The elites stated that they wanted to explore near space, however, transmissions were intercepted by the nightwalkers between the elites of New Columbia and the government of Mars. The nightwalker informed Jacob that, long ago, this rogue planet avoided what was believed to be certain destruction by swinging past the black hole in star system HR 6819, and the rogue planet was now returning toward the solar system of their ancestors.

The nightwalker revealed that humans had colonized their ancestral solar system with the largest colonies located on the Moon and Mars. The Mars colony eventually formed its government and has existed as an independent state for many centuries. The advancement of technology, particularly on Mars and Earth, also proved correct many theories from the greatest thinkers of our past. The Miguel Alcubierre drive, theorized by the Mexican theoretical physicist from the twenty-first century, was also proved correct. The improvement of the Miguel Alcubierre drive led to spacecraft that could fold space-time, causing nearly faster-than-light speed travel. It appeared that the few people on Earth that monitored activity on this rogue planet did not wish to communicate with New Columbia, however, the Martians agreed to reveal some of their technological advancements to help the elite of New Columbia and New Washington upon the rogue planet's entry into the Earth's solar system. It appeared the Martians were slightly more advanced than Earth and did not want to reveal their technology.

Marcus was shocked to learn some of the hidden truths of the rogue alien planet, and he feared that his friend Jacob was imprisoned and possibly executed. The last line of Jacob's message stated, "I was scared to reveal my encounter with this nightwalker, but it appeared a drone might have spotted my secret conversation. My team leader seemed anxious when he saw me, and it was odd that he had assigned me to a new mission at a new location. I am scared now, and if something does happen to me, I hope you can find me and alert our families and friends!"

Soon Marcus traveled to New Columbia in search of the secret location near the dome, using the coordinates that Jacob had left for him. Jacob had also written down a secret passcode he had stolen during his last trip to New Columbia. Jacob had revealed certain times when the patrols and drones wouldn't be nearby. Marcus planned to infiltrate the secret bunker and erase evidence of himself entering by manipulating the video recording. He raced deep down into the bunker until he heard noises and what seemed like a foreign language. Perhaps these beings could sense him before he could sense them. Marcus's heart raced as he inhaled the musky air, and his eyes opened in alarm when his nightmare became reality. What Jacob detailed in his writings was shockingly true! The nightwalkers were in cages and were being analyzed by the elites of New Columbia.

The nightwalkers were in a large lower room within a lab. They had pale skin and were slender with shrunken eyes. They shrieked even before Marcus entered the lab. The nightwalkers were usually found wearing furry skins from the various beasts that roamed the planet, but these nightwalkers were naked and on all fours within cages where they could not stand up. Marcus accessed some files in the lab computer that confirmed what Jacob had revealed in his writings. The elites were studying the nightwalkers and experimented on hundreds of them in attempts to genetically engineer humans that could survive in harsher elements. Some of the elites secretly genetically altered themselves to better survive in harsh elements. Now, most of the research was concentrated on developing advanced propulsion drives for the spacecraft they were planning to use to leave the planet and travel to Mars.

The humans that colonized Mars so long ago also appeared slightly different from their ancestors on Earth. The Martians had thicker skulls and eyes a bit larger than Earth's people, with brown and slightly orange skin. The files detailed a brief history of the rogue planet and its colonization by humans as it traveled toward a black hole in the triple star system HR 681, in the southern constellation of Telescopium. There were numerous attempts by the elites to re-establish communications with the United States. After several major wars and internal conflicts collapsed, the old United States, the elites of New Columbia, continued to attempt contact with the smaller and weaker Federated States of America. Marcus discovered that the elites also attempted to establish contact with the Latin American Union before successfully establishing friendly relations with Mars.

Marcus saved the additional information and located the computers controlling the cameras at the entrance and within the bunker. As he began to erase evidence that he entered the bunker, he heard a group of men entering the bunker. Marcus's heart raced, and he quickly sent all the information he and Jacob had gathered and sent a message to his father to spread the information if he were to go missing.

Two scientists walked in, and Marcus hid in a storage chamber, hoping to elude them. One of the scientists had a body-heat detector and discovered Marcus, so the scientist immediately called for security. Marcus attempted to escape the bunker, but one of the scientists attempted to apprehend him, and Marcus punched him twice, causing the scientist to fall backward. Marcus attempted to race out of the bunker, but he was met by an electric bat to his chest, causing blood to spew from his mouth. Additional security quickly rushed into the bunker, and one of the guards blasted Marcus with a high-intensity electrical beam that sent a strong signal through his central nervous system and locked his muscles, making him spasm and fall where he stood, causing him to fall sideways onto the ground.

Marcus woke up to security forces, scientists, and some members of the elite discussing his breach of the secret facility. He was restrained near the nightwalkers, and he realized he was now considered a sub-human just like the nightwalkers. Perhaps he remained alive because they wanted to confirm the information that they'd already gathered regarding his identity and his friendship with Jacob. Marcus mustered his strength and said, "Where is Jacob? What did you do with him?"

One of the men that belonged to the elite spoke, "My name is Preston Wright, and we know who you are, Marcus. We have been observing you and researching your close friendship with Jacob. We learned that you received information from your friend, Jacob, regarding our ongoing relationship with a class of nightwalkers that remained somewhat scientifically advanced. You also know of our development of spacecraft and contact with Mars. We have inherited the true governance of New Columbia, New Washington, and the large western region of this planet. We have ensured the safety of millions of people by maintaining the quality of life and safeguarding secrets that if unveiled could destroy our community.

"If we were to lose our society, we could be left to survive in the cold darkness, and most of us would devolve into these animals we call nightwalkers. We have not improved our memory-erasing technology, so every few generations, when someone discovers this sensitive information, we are sadly forced to execute them. You have seen a lot of our sensitive information, and we want to know if you will spread this information?"

Marcus understood that Preston belonged to the powerful Wright family—one of the three most powerful families on the rogue planet. Marcus replied, "What difference does it make what I tell you? You are going to kill me anyway, leaving me with no incentive for giving you the information you want."

Preston exclaimed, "Here is your incentive, Marcus. If you do not tell us who you sent this information to, we will give you a slow, painful death, and then we will kill your parents and other family members. We will fabricate a story about how you disappeared and how your family met an unfortunate demise. You made a grave error in judgment, Marcus, and we will give you some time to ponder your choices and thus the fate you wish for your family and yourself."

After what appeared to be an eternity, some elites and security re-entered the bunker. They appeared angry and desperate. Preston returned, and he loudly exclaimed, "You see what you have caused? This is the largest revolt in the history of our colony, and we believe you sent the information to your parents. Our relationship with the nightwalkers of the Eastern Sea has also worsened, and they may attack us during our moment of weakness. We shall stop this deadly revolt, and we will kill you and everyone you know!"

Tears spilled out from Marcus's eyes as security released him from his cage and were ready to beat him and torture him. The security took out their electric bats and began to beat Marcus as he fell to the floor. One of the men raised his bat to hit Marcus on the head when the first floor of the bunker exploded as the rebels reached the bunker. Marcus reached into the holster of one of the security guards and took his gun. It was an advanced magnetic gun that Marcus used, firing it into three of the guards, killing them instantly.

Preston's eyes opened wide as he nervously said, "I was never going to kill you, Marcus; we just needed information. I can spare your life and offer you a job where you can help us with the information you learned. After we quell this disastrous rebellion, I will spare your life."

Marcus smiled and replied, "You were going to kill me. I do not trust your words, and although I might die today, you too shall die, but at least I will live a little longer."

Marcus shot Preston in the head and aimed and fired at the other scientists as additional security guards rushed down the steps. Marcus released the nightwalkers who rushed toward the security guards, killing some of them. His heart raced, and he could barely breathe as adrenaline spread through his body. Some rebels also rushed into the bunker as Marcus aimed his weapon at the guards running down the stairs. He shot at them, and he thought dying in this way was better than being tortured and executed. Marcus overheard one of the security guards stating that the intelligent nightwalkers from the Eastern islands were approaching in large numbers.

Marcus realized that what the elites feared most was that these advanced nightwalkers would join the rebellion. It was a fear that had permeated the elites for generations. Marcus fired, and soon, he felt a sharp sting as he was also shot. He continued to advance as his heart raced. Marcus thought that perhaps he would die today, and then he smiled and remembered the quote his father had always said to him as a child: "A society grows great when old men plant trees whose shade they know they shall never sit in."

Marcus fired his weapon in the hope of leaving the bunker. He smiled as he saw the familiar domes again and the alien darkness he'd once feared but now embraced.

Story 2: Tears of the Horizon (Distant Future)

Time is relative and an important aspect of life. Time is infinite, existing even in a society that has lived on for millions of years and has discarded the frailty of simple biological life through the advancement of science and technology. Time passed slowly at times, and sometimes, it seemed as if time passed quickly. These days, there was always time to ponder and think about space and time. There was much to think about, and he enjoyed thinking about various subjects, including society and science, and often spent his time conversing with others who enjoyed similar subjects.

He was fond of philosophical conversations and deep space exploration, an endeavor that was of little interest to others in his society. The universe was immense, cold, and always expanding. He yearned to understand his inner soul, the souls of others, and find a deeper meaning to the purpose of existence itself. There were many mysteries within the simple things in life, and he enjoyed thinking of these secrets. He was admired by the individuals in his community, and he was a special being. His name sounds too complex for the human ear to understand, and his name could not even be attempted to pronounce by the human tongue. We can simply call him by a name that he recently adopted, Strawberry Fields. His family name was important for numerous generations because his family members made notable improvements to their complex society, including the founding of this colonial society that eventually became semi-independent.

Individuals in this society were naturally born as either male or female. Some individuals sought to switch sexes or live as hermaphrodites. Due to the extreme lengths of time that individuals lived, experiments with sex and gender roles were common. Many individuals changed their perspectives throughout their extended lives and experienced their worlds and reality from different points of view. Their parent civilization called themselves what would roughly translate into English as "The Observers." The concept of individuality was nearly erased within the Observer civilization. Strawberry's society, however, focused on individuality, a concept that the Observers largely discarded long ago. These worlds where Strawberry lived were left untouched by advanced technology, and the flora and fauna that made up this complex ecosystem were allowed to flourish with minimal disturbances. There were still vast mysteries in the universe left unresolved, and some even returned to faith as a guiding light.

This semi-independent civilization was spread among three planets and five moons within a binary star system. This society was among the few that separated from the main, greater civilization that focused on collective consciousness and their goal of expansion throughout the cosmos. Although communication could be performed visually, vocally, chemically, and through the mind, Strawberry's society focused more on individualism, and thus, certain methods of communication were limited, allowing for greater privacy. Communication was encouraged with the native animals within Strawberry's society, however, the natural course of this ecosystem was not to be altered. Nature could be harsh, but it had an order, and it was beautiful in its ways.

After almost 1,000 revolutions around this binary star system, Strawberry Fields did not wish to exist anymore. It was a serious decision, and Strawberry's wishes were eventually respected and accepted by his parents and family members. It was a privilege to cease to exist in Strawberry's society because members of the parent civilization were not allowed to do so without making the case that the ending of their existence would benefit the greater civilization. Strawberry Fields felt deep sadness and joy, a perplexing feeling with pangs of melancholy. He believed he had experienced all that he desired to experience, and he understood the loss of a family member or friend was deeply felt by those who continued to live as long as they chose to live.

Strawberry Fields lived well in a small apartment, within a tree canopy overlooking a large waterfall. He farmed and hunted his food and enjoyed his simple lifestyle. This society was great for individuals who desired to leave the advanced cybernetically-enhanced collective society of their parent civilization. They did not want to manipulate nature and enhance their bodies with technology. Strawberry Fields said his final goodbyes to his family and friends, and he soon departed as the two suns began to set on the distant horizon.

The spacecraft quickly lifted from the ground, through the pink clouds, through the atmosphere, and into space. He ate some plants that he gathered before his voyage which slowly began to induce an altered mental state that altered time and the space around him. Strawberry Fields lived on the closest planet to the binary star system, which created its near-year-round tropical weather. This darkened Strawberry's skin similar to humans that lived near Earth's equator. Strawberry Fields observed his home and his planet and the two stars of similar mass dancing almost perfectly in an ellipse around their common barycenter. Perhaps there was a more intelligent being, a creator, that constructed the great wonders of the cosmos.

Strawberry Fields belonged to possibly the most advanced civilization in this universe after the fall of the advanced intergalactic civilization called the "Great Ancients." The Great Ancients had empirical desires but soon collapsed due to internal conflicts and rebellions against their rule as their grip over their colonies weakened. Currently, the second most advanced civilization was called The Exploiters. They belonged to large soft-bodied liquid breathers with radial muscles, large tentacles and large heads, and who had copper-rich protein hemocyanin that made their blood blue. The Exploiters expanded to other galaxies and appeared to have aspirations similar to the extinct society of The Great Ancients and were kept under supervision by The Observers. The third most advanced civilization were primates that called themselves humans, who currently lived on their home planet of Earth and expanded to the Moon and Mars.

The Observers only made contact with The Exploiters to avoid confrontation. Humans were left alone to continue their development in the relative safety of their solar system. The Observers only planned to interfere with human civilization if they could not learn the error of their ways and stop the devastating rapid warming of their planet. They would also interfere if the humans could not advance technologically and travel to other star systems before the death of their star. Humans were also considered an underdeveloped society because they still suffered from wars and great civil unrest. The remaining life in the universe was less advanced or simple life forms.

Strawberry Fields thought about the advancements of his civilization and the return to a simpler life, focusing on the self. His spacecraft was now leaving his binary star system as the effects of the mind-altering substance began to gain a stronger presence in his consciousness. He thought about the ancients and their immense knowledge and their ability to manipulate black holes and space-time. They were able to enter alternate dimensions. The Observers studied alternate universes, however, after so long, they still had not been able to reach the level of knowledge The Great Ancients had attained. Although The Observers were not as advanced as The Great Ancients, they'd learned to extract energy from black holes.

Strawberry's society was harnessing energy from a nearby black hole, and this was the same black hole where Strawberry Fields was now heading. Strawberry Fields marveled at the beauty and great destruction that the black hole possessed. He thought about all that was great and all that seemed insignificant. His society was far advanced, however, his particular society learned from less advanced societies. The humans valued their individuality and at the same time valued their bonds to one another. Strawberry looked at his tanned brown hands and understood the similarity between himself and the humans. They were slightly larger than the humans and walked on two legs like the humans, with the only difference being that his people had four arms. It was an adaptation to the high gravity in their ancient homeworld. Unbeknownst to the humans, members of Strawberry's community were able to learn about human culture and its history. Their various ancient civilizations included those of Sumer, Egypt, Persian, the Mali Empire, Rome, the Incas, the Aztecs, and the Apache. Strawberry enjoyed certain societies including those called the Tainos from the Caribbean islands of the Greater Antilles.

Strawberry enjoyed the society of the United States which was the latest great power on Earth, although now they no longer were. He enjoyed the music, especially the experimental music. He called himself Strawberry Fields after listening to Elton

John and *The Beatles*. Strawberry laughed as tears came to his eyes because he understood that you can learn from even lesser civilizations as well as organisms that could be considered less intelligent. An ant on Earth belongs to a Eusocial society, a concept that The Observers were trying to recreate. Eusociality was ideal for The Observers, however, this type of society could also lead to the possible downfall of The Observers. Perhaps learning from the mistakes and improving upon the accomplishments of other societies was best. These would be questions for those of this generation and the generations to come to answer.

The starship slowed down as it approached the event horizon of the black hole. Strawberry Fields was close to losing consciousness as the herbs took full force within him. Strawberry's community was known as The Seekers, and he was proud of what they had accomplished. He programmed a small computer bio-stick and linked it to his brain. The bio-stick recorded his conscious mind and subconscious mind and relayed the information to his home to be shared with his family and friends. The bio-stick helped Strawberry replay the most joyous moments of his life and together with the mind-altering substance he consumed, would give him one last beautiful experience. Some would call that a type of Nirvana. Time slowed down, and he slowly observed his death as he passed the event horizon into certain death. He played reggae music, including some Bob Marley, as he felt a strange but comforting mix of melancholy and happiness. The spacecraft began to strain under increased gravity as his tears fell from his eyes and his smile was as large as it had ever been. Then there was darkness and silence.

Story 3: Foreign Affairs (22nd Century)

Simon Ortega was elated to finally purchase his first home in an upper-middle-class neighborhood in Charlotte, North Carolina. It was February of 2190 when, at the age of twenty-five, Simon moved to North Carolina, escaping the high-cost apartments of Queens, New York. Simon Ortega planned on purchasing a home for his parents Julio and Maria and providing them with an early retirement from their blue-collar jobs. Simon's family arrived in the United States from the Dominican Republic in the mid-twenty-first century.

He was happy to move to North Carolina where his girlfriend Rania lived. Rania was a Palestinian-American who was studying journalism at the Hussman School of Media and Journalism. Rania was completing her senior year at the University of North Carolina at Chapel Hill and was ready to move to Charlotte and live with Simon. Rania's grandfather Farid moved to Florida from Palestine before the two-state solution came to fruition and the state of Palestine was fully recognized as an independent state in the mid-twenty-second century. The State of Palestine was now becoming an advanced nation, and Rania's family sometimes returned for family events. Rania's father Ismail moved to North Carolina as climate change eroded the coastlines of southern Florida.

Rania's parents were happy with Simon even though he was not a Muslim. Rania suggested that Simon explore the Koran but never insisted that he should convert to Islam. Simon respected Rania's culture and religion and enjoyed the peace of mind she brought him. He had a few days of vacation at the same time she had spring break, and he invited her to see his new home. Simon had last visited Rania at her school in Chapel Hill the previous week and spent some time with her and her friends. She was excited to see his new home and chose to visit her boyfriend instead of going to Mexico for spring break.

Simon was elated to earn enough to provide a better life for himself and his family. Over half of the United States lived in poverty as the oligarchy increased the power and wealth of the elites. Few jobs lifted working-class people toward upper-middle-class status, and it was nearly impossible to become wealthy when a person came from a lower class. Although Simon received substantial pay and benefits, his career was becoming increasingly stressful. Simon was asked to routinely work ten and twelve-hour shifts. Sometimes Simon would work up to fourteen hours piloting multiple vehicles or avatars.

Simon studied Computer Science in college, and he was recruited to work as a contractor with the United States Air Force, performing reconnaissance missions on both the Lunar and Martian colonies. He was interested in astronomy and space exploration, and he was eager to excel in his career. The government agreed to pay most of his loans, and by twenty-four, Simon became a lead pilot operator and among one of the best in the country. He trained and initially worked in Nevada before he applied to work at a recently constructed secret facility in North Carolina. Simon controlled androids and drones on the Moon and Mars. The missions were pre-planned, and Simon spent most of his time researching sensitive information and creating scripts that were sent to the drone before the actual mission would take place. If an error occurred, often an intelligence officer on the Moon or Mars would override the pre-planned scripting. NASA had several large Lunar Bases and a few Martian bases. The corporations aided NASA and also advanced their space missions to the Moon, Mars, and other planets and satellites within the solar system.

Simon was happy to spend some days with his girlfriend, and he woke up early to begin breakfast before her arrival. He was cooking the typical Dominican breakfast, *mangu* or mashed and boiled green plantains, fried white cheese, fried salami, and some eggs over-easy, the way Rania liked them. Rania was driving her used electric car that she bought during her freshman year. Simon was thinking of purchasing a new car for Rania and decided that he would instead purchase a new electric car battery for her upcoming birthday in June.

The morning was cool and rainy, and Simon knew Rania would drive slower due to the road conditions. The drive from Chapel Hill to Charlotte was just over two hours, and Rania left her dorm room. Later, she called and informed him she was less than ten minutes away. Simon served breakfast and set it on the table just as Rania arrived and parked her car in the driveway. Simon poured some *morir soñando* with crushed ice into a big glass for his girlfriend. She enjoyed *morir soñando* and was previously introduced to the famous Dominican drink made of orange juice, evaporated milk, cane sugar, and vanilla extract when she began dating Simon three years ago.

Simon opened the door and gave Rania a passionate kiss, which brought a wide smile to her face and initiated a girlish laugh that indicated that she was in a great mood. Rania had light brown skin and black hair. She was tall and just two inches shorter than Simon who was just over six feet in height. Rania was often confused for a Dominican woman, and Simon's friends mistakenly spoke to her in Spanish when they were first introduced to her. He loved her perfume and her white dress, which had designs of flowers with bright colors. She had an athletic physique with a slim waist, lush eyebrows, and long, jet-black hair that reached below her shoulders. Her eyes were almond-shaped and beautiful, and her lips were a lighter shade of brown. Rania came from a conservative family, and Simon found comfort in her views and strong morality.

Simon proudly proclaimed, "*Bienvenida a mi nuevo hogar, mi amor.*"

Rania smiled and replied, "*Shukran jazilan.* Thank you for inviting me to your new home. Wow, Simon, I must say this is a very large home. I am proud of you, Simon. You see, hard work does pay off!"

Rania was impressed with the home, and Simon promised to give her a tour after breakfast. She looked at her plate and asked, "Is this beef salami, my love?"

Simon laughed and replied, "Of course it is, Rania. You think I would serve you pork?"

"So how are things at school?" Simon asked.

Rania replied, "I am so excited to finish school. I already applied to work for a few environmental news sites, and I received two offers. I think this will be a great opportunity for me to use my skills and bring attention to the climate change issue. The United States has taken steps to slow down climate change, but there are still many politicians and companies that are excusing the companies that are causing pollution through fossil fuels and illegal waste disposal. They are causing so much harm."

Simon was impressed with Rania's passion and morality, and it made him more self-reflexive. He had slowly lost respect for himself due to his inability to stand up for his beliefs. He felt a pang of depression and hurt return and fought hard to keep it hidden. He brushed some of his darker thoughts aside and resolved to remain positive while his girlfriend was spending time with him. His joy returned after breakfast when he gave Rania a tour of his house, and he thought about a possible future with her.

The home was painted blue and white with two stories and a large basement area that Simon planned to use to design computers and also to relax and play billiards. The first floor had a large living room, a kitchen and dining room, and another large room facing the backyard where Simon would spend some time at night watching the stars in the night sky as he pondered his future. There were three bathrooms, and the master bathroom was located on the second floor where he planned to purchase and place a large smartbed. There was a large jacuzzi where he planned on spending time with Rania, talking about their lives and future aspirations. The three-car garage had two car battery chargers and some car maintenance equipment that Simon recently purchased for his new electric sports car.

Rania was impressed with Simon's home and suggested different furniture or paint colors that he could use to add some style. After speaking about her interior design ideas, Rania turned her attention to her boyfriend's well-being.

She was curious and asked, "I understand you are working five days and sometimes even six days a week now. Are you getting adequate rest? I think you should focus on yourself and get some rest sometimes. I know you are getting paid a lot of money, but if it is causing you stress, perhaps you should take a pay cut and work shorter hours. Do you still want to make your job a lifelong career?"

Simon tried to keep a happy façade as he slowly replied, "My job has provided me with a middle-class lifestyle, and if I continue to advance in my career, I may even retire early. Early retirement and an upper-middle-class lifestyle are goals that over seventy percent of the US population will never be able to reach. My occupation is important, and I have a lot of responsibilities. It is a serious classified job that I perform for the US government. I control androids and drones and perform surveillance on the Moon and Mars to protect US assets and provide security for high-ranking US officials and US allies. The job is vital and stressful, and my goal is to complete my contract and possibly move into another career field. Perhaps I can get into the health industry and fix and operate hospital drones."

Rania smiled and said, "Success in life is not just about how much money you earn, my love. If you are facing hardships or you are facing turmoil, you should search for a solution, and if you need me, I will be right here to support you."

Simon smiled as some of the weight he'd felt the past few years lifted with Rania's words. He'd started drinking heavily a year before, but he'd hidden this from his family and Rania. His life was good, and he was successful, however, reality did not fit how Simon wanted his life to truly be. He desired something more, a change in his life. Part of this positive change would include Rania.

The couple spent the week going to various events in North Carolina and danced to new and classic music until late at night. They also spent some time looking at furniture and electronics for Simon's home. During his time with Rania, Simon noticed his nightmares were less frequent, and he experienced improved sleep.

He wanted to become a better man for his family, Rania, and himself. Marriage was rare in the United States, and it was strange to see a married couple in their 20s, however, Simon was sure that Rania was the woman he wanted to spend the rest of his life with, and he planned to take Rania on a two-week vacation in Las Vegas, Nevada to visit the flagship Atari Hotel.

That summer, Simon and Rania traveled to Las Vegas and stayed at the Atari Hotel. They danced at various clubs. The clubs, restaurants, rooms, and game rooms had various themes based on Atari's classic games and some of their current games. Simon particularly enjoyed the large arcades filled with numerous Atari games from the twentieth century. Simon enjoyed various classic games including *Asteroids*, *Centipede*, *Missile Command*, *Enduro*, *Combat*, and *Pole Position*, while Rania's favorite was *Ms. Pacman*. The temperature was hot, and the skies had shades of orange due to the large wildfires that made large parts of California uninhabitable. Despite some of the weather issues, the air conditioning and large pools at the hotel helped guests remain comfortable.

Simon felt at ease with Rania, and he openly spoke to her about starting a life together in the future. He was delighted that she also shared the same thoughts. Simon had slowed his drinking and informed his colleagues that he would not join them and their usual drinking after work. He now understood the importance of moderation and the lessons that his father Julio had instilled in him and the behaviors that Rania wanted Simon to improve upon. Once, Simon had felt weak in character and sometimes less than a man, especially as a Dominican man. Strength, strong moral character, and self-respect were instilled in Dominican boys as virtues to strive for, and he felt he'd failed to reach them, but slowly, he was regaining his sense of self-worth.

One night after Rania fell asleep, Simon woke up in a panic and full of sweat. He'd had a nightmare again. This time it was about one particular mission that threatened to pull the fabric of his very being. Simon remembered the first time he was involved in several missions where he was ordered to neutralize terrorists that were threatening to harm US colonies. He remembered a particularly horrific mission on Mars.

His thoughts were transported to the frigid and dead Martian landscape. Sheltered behind a secret facility in Nevada, Simon felt the frigid Martian air and then saw the sharp orange shades of the Martian soil. He remembered the strike and the six people who were killed. Among the dead was a small child who lay on the ground in one of the large central domes belonging to the allied UAE and Chinese colonies near the US Martian colony. The child's right leg was severed, and he writhed on the ground while he bled from his femoral artery. Simon switched his high-quality camera to the infrared camera and watched as the child's body turned cold. For over four additional hours, he was forced to observe and gather additional intelligence. Simon was later informed that some of the victims were not involved with any terrorist groups, particularly the young child. Simon continued to work after the tragedy and performed additional missions where he was ordered to strike adversaries, however, that particular incident hurt him deeply.

Simon looked at various rums in the bar of his hotel room and thought about having a drink, but he restrained himself. He decided he would speak to his supervisor and finish the remaining year of his contract. He'd apply to work for the health industry in North Carolina, delivering medicine by drone. His supervisor informed him that he would be possibly selected for a multi-year contract in a secret Lunar or Martian Colony where he could perform missions in real-time, but he declined. He decided his service had ended and he chose his sanity over money.

Simon and Rania danced and listened to music until late that night, and soon Simon fell asleep first. Later in the night, he woke up suddenly, and he breathed deeply as he dried the sweat from his face. Rania woke up and noticed the anxiety within Simon. She kissed him tenderly on the lips and said, "My love, I will always be here to bring you peace. Follow your heart, Simon, and I will be with you along the way."

Simon kissed Rania as he reassured her that he was alright. He smiled as he blinked a tear from his eye. He thought about converting to Rania's beautiful religion of Islam, and he decided he'd propose to her later that year. Perhaps they would have a Christian and Palestinian wedding. They would invite their families and start their life together. He thought about his father's words about honoring his duties, but he also questioned when he thought something wasn't right.

Simon could not change the past, but he could learn from his mistakes and become a better man. The bad choices he had made and those he would make would always be part of him, but he had a chance to do good, as well. Perhaps, one day, he'd be able to explain to his parents and Rania the source of most of his pain, but that would be a conversation for another time. It felt like a weight lifted from his shoulders as he embraced Rania and closed his eyes. *May Allah forgive me,* Simon thought as he slowly drifted off to a deep, dreamless sleep.

Story 4: Exotic Pandemic (22nd Century)

Irfan Persaud enjoyed his well-earned role as a scientific advisor to the government of Trinidad and Tobago. Irfan was able to propose solutions that helped avert catastrophe in Trinidad as the world continued to endure a global pandemic that now entered its twentieth year. The pandemic began at the end of the twenty-first century, during the spring of 2095, and continued until the current year of 2115. The United States suffered over twenty million deaths, the nation's highest number of deaths by raw numbers, and the highest percentage of deaths among the leading nations of the world. Scientists had never seen a virus like this but because of its similarity to other coronaviruses, it was called pseudo-coronavirus X, or as most people called it, the new plague.

The United States was no longer a world power and was reduced to a regional power while China, Russia, and Unified Korea controlled Asia and Eastern Europe. Canada was now the leading North American nation, and Mexico now rivaled the United States. Latin America was largely successful in keeping deaths at a low level and their economies stable. The damage of climate change, coupled with deforestation and pollution, increased the potency of the pandemic and crippled most nations. In the Caribbean, the island nations of Trinidad, Cuba, and the

Dominican Republic managed to survive economically and were able to mitigate the spread of the virus. Latin America managed the pandemic well, and many Latin American nations were able to avoid a catastrophe through various government programs.

Irfan Persaud had become a leading immunologist ten years before and was also a leading bacteriologist and virologist. Irfan Persaud had an interest in viruses and how they spread, and as a teenager, he began studying devastating pandemics of the past, including the Covid-19 pandemic that began in early 2020. Irfan's efforts during the pandemic made him a global celebrity. Irfan, alongside his wife, Aarushi Persaud, an epidemiologist with the Ministry of Health of Trinidad, was able to reduce cases in Trinidad and Tobago to among the lowest levels in the world. The virus was a respiratory-enveloped RNA retrovirus with high variation, leading to high mutation rates, making it difficult to stop the pandemic. The virus progressed to infect the microglial cells of the nervous system of the host but did not cause death immediately. Instead, the virus was a progressive disease that increased its control over time. Many perished early during their infections while others lived longer and became ghosts of their previous selves.

Irfan worked tirelessly to learn the various mutations of the pseudo-coronavirus X. The virus appeared like a coronavirus, however, scientists could not determine if this virus originated from an animal. The virulence of the virus increased in combination with other diseases, which are far more frequent currently because of the negative impacts of climate change. The origins of the virus remained a mystery, and scientists continued their research in attempts to bring an end to the crippling pandemic. At first, scientists believed it was an ancient virus that emerged from the thawed permafrost regions of possibly Canada, Greenland, or Siberia as these areas had unleashed some ancient viruses and bacteria that were returned to the world and brought pain and death after millions of years. Eventually, Irfan Persaud and several scientists were the first to confirm that the pandemic originated in the Arctic Circle and began to spread throughout Northern Canada.

Irfan secretly believed that the pseudo-coronavirus X was extraterrestrial after observing its mutation patterns within the first eight years of the pandemic. His closest friends insisted that he should refrain from writing a paper regarding his beliefs on the alien origins of the virus. After he became famous for his handling of the pandemic in Trinidad, he kept his opinion a secret while continuing his research. Irfan studied various meteor strikes that occurred shortly before the beginning of the pandemic. In the search for the origins of the virus, several expeditions to northern Canada were started, and a few expeditions to locate the meteorites that had broken away from the main meteorites were organized, however, the expeditions to locate the other meteorites ended.

The pandemic began in the northern regions of Canada in one of the northwestern islands of Nunavut Province. Most scientists agreed that the virus spread mainly toward Manitoba and Ontario provinces before crossing into Michigan and New York, where it quickly spread throughout the United States. Canada was devastated for the first five years, and Latin America for nearly ten years, however, the United States suffered the greatest casualties throughout the twenty years of the deadly pandemic. In nations like the United States, with a large number of cases, the youth who recovered from the disease were now suffering from long-term issues with their nervous system causing high suicide rates and an increase in crimes.

Irfan spoke with leading astronomers in Canada and discovered that several years before, a large meteorite crashed in northwestern Nunavut Province in 2093, just two years before the pandemic began. After several expeditions in the Nunavut Province, they were still unable to find several of the large pieces that broke from the main meteorite as it exploded in the atmosphere, and to Irfan's dismay, these expeditions were largely abandoned as various scientists gave up interest in his search.

Irfan was at his office in the Port of Spain, Trinidad, after having a meeting with the vice-president. The streets of Port of Spain were slightly busy today, and most people wore a facemask or air-filtration unit. The facemasks were creative: some of them had the Trinidadian flag; some had people and characters from pop culture; others wore their favorite candidates during election years. Irfan was one of the leading voices that advocated for additional protection in public soon after the pandemic began many years ago. Irfan believed he could finally end the pandemic, but now the virus appeared to be mutating, once again, into a possibly worse version.

Irfan enjoyed success, but secretly, he spent many sleepless nights wondering if he would not be able to solve the next mutation. He had nightmares of Trinidad falling into despair like the people in the United States where further complications were becoming a reality. People who were now suffering from advanced nervous system issues were acting more erratically. It was as if the virus was controlling them. Irfan wanted to travel to the United States and study some of these individuals. Numerous nations banned travelers from the United States, however, Irfan was allowed to travel to the United States to pursue and enhance his research.

Irfan called a leading geneticist from the Dominican Republic named Esperanza Molina. Irfan met Esperanza Molina about ten years ago when she was regarded as the next great scientist. She was the best student of the biotechnologist and humanitarian Dr. Radhames Lopez, who'd helped improve the standard of living in the Dominican Republic for over six decades. His advances in genetics influenced Esperanza Molina and her studies on bacteriophages, virophages, and genetic editing. At the age of only thirty, Irfan believed Esperanza would now surpass her mentor.

Esperanza Molina believed she was close to a breakthrough and could deliver the final death blow to the pandemic. She'd previously spoken with Irfan and stated that she developed a genetically engineered virophage. Irfan was skeptical that she could develop a successful virophage, but he was hoping Esperanza would prove him wrong.

Irfan could hear the excitement in Esperanza's voice when she reached him through his communicator. "*Amigo*! Irfan, I have great news! The virus I engineered appears to be effective against the virus! There have been a few successful genetically engineered virophages, but the one I and my team created appears to kill the virus and the patients appear to make a full recovery within a month, depending on how early we can administer the virophages. I think you have done a great job over the last fifteen years, but I think if we work together, we can finally put an end to this pandemic and apply this technology to stop future pandemics. We can work together and find the best way to mass-produce this biotechnology for distribution throughout the Caribbean and the rest of the Americas. You should come to the Dominican Republic and visit my home in Azua so that we can discuss the next steps we should take."

A rush of excitement flooded Irfan's body, and he instructed his assistant to close his office door as he replied, "Do you believe that your virophage can finally put an end to this pandemic? I sure hope you are correct, my friend, because an end to this pandemic will revitalize the world. We will be able to make our people healthy, improve our economies, and strengthen our societies. I will be happy to visit the Dominican Republic if you can further explain your findings."

Esperanza calmly replied, "Engineering virophages has come a long way in the last few decades. Since the discovery of the first virophage, named *Sputnik,* in a cooling tower in Paris, France, in 2008, the studies of virophages and their application advanced throughout the twenty-first century. My teacher, Dr. Radhames Sosa, was an expert in many areas of biotechnology and the synthesis of functional RNA and DNA and inserting cellular agents to mitigate and stop various diseases. Building on the work of my mentor and working on this problem since the beginning of this pandemic, I was finally able to synthesize DNA and build a synthetic virophage that could enter the virus and wait until the virus enters the cells of the host's respiratory system. Once the virus enters the host's cells, the virophage activates and gathers the ribosomes and other cellular material that the virus takes from the host and uses it to replicate itself and turn off the virus's replication ability. It soon synthesizes an enzyme that breaks up the virus. The virophage is not harmful to humans and soon exits the body after the infection is over. We experimented on various animals, including birds as well as a few patients who were paid large sums of money to partake in this experimental treatment. I believe if I expand my team of scientists, we can mass-produce this virophage and implement your policies to reduce further infections and put an end to this pandemic."

Irfan visited the Dominican Republic and stayed in the country for a month as he observed Esperanza's research. By the following year, in 2118, the virus was eradicated in the Dominican Republic, Haiti, and throughout the Caribbean. In 2119, the synthetic virophage was shipped to Africa and the Middle East, and Asia, where the pandemic finally ended. Under popular pressure in the United States, the government mass-produced the synthetic virus and provided it to the people of the United States against the desires of powerful pharmaceutical companies. The synthetic virophage was named *Virocido X* or Virucide X and made Esperanza Molina a wealthy woman, mostly due to foreign sales. Virucide X was made free to all Dominican citizens and all working-class people of poorer nations.

By late 2120, the pandemic was officially over with few advanced cases of neurological disorders in the United States and Russia. Esperanza Molina, at only thirty years of age, received global acclaim. Irfan Persaud also solidified his legacy within his field, and many asked him to run for President of Trinidad, which he politely refused. Esperanza Molina turned her attention to developing technologies to create other synthetic bacteriophages and virophages as well as other applications to stop various forms of cancer. A system of delivering breathable virophages and bacteriophages was also being developed. The Dominican government also studied the potential uses of bioweapons by bad actors and several ways of defending against these types of attacks. The science of genetic engineering would advance further as kids became interested in it, creating another generation of advancement in health and science.

One night, after Irfan and his wife, Aarushi, returned home from Diwali celebrations in 2122, Irfan received a message on his telecommunications device. Aarushi was driving Irfan's new electric car because Irfan was slightly inebriated from the night's celebrations. When they arrived at their home, Aarushi prepared rice, plantains, beans, and pepper sauce, with curry chicken. After the meal, Irfan washed it down with some beer and rum. His wife sat next to him on their second-floor balcony in their beautiful home as they enjoyed the cool breeze of the Trinidadian night.

Later at night, both went to bed, and Aarushi said, "We are truly blessed, Irfan. Our son and daughter graduated from university and are both married to beautiful people. We have made progress with biotechnology and now pandemics like these might be a thing of the past to be studied by historians. I'm so happy we have another chance to rebuild our country, and the world has a second chance. I'm glad that you have found success and happiness, and tonight you can finally sleep peacefully."

Tears fell from Aarushi's eyes, ruining her eye makeup and darkening her brown skin. Her long, black hair fell on Irfan as she kissed him. Irfan was satisfied this terror that had gripped the world was over, but the origins of the virus eluded the best minds on Earth and his theories on the matter troubled him. Irfan tried to forget these thoughts when he received a message from his friend and a Canadian astronomer named Oliver.

Oliver was breathing heavily as he said, "Irfan, you won't believe what happened last week! An Inuit fisherman discovered a piece of the meteorite that fell in Canada in 2093. We thought we had discovered all the pieces. This one landed several miles south of the main meteorite in Nunavut Province, and an astrobiologist discovered that it contained organic material. It appears that this material is not from Earth, and we found evidence of possible viruses within the meteorite, which we are currently analyzing further in Ontario. I understand you have revealed your theories to me in the past, and I will inform you of any additional discoveries we make."

Irfan's heart raced, and his voice awoke his wife from sleep. His wife inquired about the call, and Irfan said he would let her know in the morning, attempting to inform his wife with a calm mind. He kissed his wife and closed his eyes, and a smile formed on his face as he chuckled to himself. He attempted to sleep but would only fall asleep later in the night.

"The rising sun may bring some more blessings, God-willing," he quietly mumbled to himself as his eyes slowly closed.

Story 5: Jehova's Studio (27th Century)

Jamal Jacobs was skilled in his work. He was able to push the human body to reach new heights and also able to work fast and accurately. Some said Jamal was blessed by God, or perhaps it was just his hard work, intelligence, and recent genetic modifications. Jamal could now be considered a trans-human, a status only the elites had attained. He was one of the few black trans-humans in the world as most of the trans-humans were wealthy white, elite men in Western countries and a few wealthy individuals in Asia and Africa. Only the wealthiest people could afford safe genetic modification, and most modifications were legally allowed for wealthy business owners and politicians who chose to live for long periods on Mars and the Moon.

Jamal was earning a lot of money pushing the boundaries of science and sometimes secretly modifying his wealthy patrons beyond the legal limits. His work would have been considered illegal centuries ago, but now, in the year 2675, these modifications were legal for the wealthy who influenced the government of the United States. Jamal did not hold a license to perform these complicated modifications, however, his abilities rivaled the best in the field. Jamal's abilities provided him with a large income, and he made sure to hide his wealth to avoid police investigation and possible incarceration.

The United States was now a smaller decentralized country consisting mostly of the Northwest, Midwest, and what remained of the Northeast that had not been submerged underwater due to climate change. Much of the southwest and West Coast was now under the direct and indirect control of the Mexican government. The Southeast consisted of Georgia and Northern Florida while the Southern Floridian islands belonged to the Confederation of Antillean Nations or simply the Antillean Confederation, which consisted of the union between Cuba, Puerto Rico, and the Dominican Republic.

The oligarchy of the United States pushed the nation into World War III in the late twenty-third century to protect US corporations and secure the US dollar. The United States was further weakened after World War IV in the late twenty-fifth century, which led to the first major loss of the United States and witnessed China and Russia solidify their power and influence. The United States nearly collapsed after internal turmoil and extreme political polarization that led to rioting by mostly Caucasians who belonged to a broad alliance of anti-government groups, right-wing libertarians, and far-right groups. A new conflict was brewing with the progressive coalitions of black people, whites, Asians, and Latinos against the mostly white far-right minorities and the oligarchy, which was close to fully losing power. The power base of the United States was located on the liberal and progressive East Coast, while the wastelands of the Midwest were now ruled by local state governments and local right-winged militia groups. The Northwest was also led by progressive local governments that formed an alliance with the East Coast and were now attempting to remove the oligarchy and restore democracy.

Jamal Jacobs was not politically active, but he supported the policies of the president and the progressives that were finally able to consolidate power and who now attempted to strengthen the United States and unite the country. Jamal kept his political views private and avoided speaking about politics publicly, especially when he was working with conservative clients in the Midwest. Jamal rented an apartment at the Old Market Lofts where he kept his equipment and would carry out his operations in a laboratory in a home that he and a biohacker named Wesley shared. Jamal would travel throughout the Midwest, staying in different hotel rooms, but he rarely visited the East Coast where there were stronger regulations and a stronger central government presence. Jamal enjoyed the East Coast, but he preferred Omaha in the Midwest which was one of the few multicultural cities in the Midwest. He also enjoyed the company of Canadians and other foreigners who visited and lived temporarily in Omaha.

Jamal's current client was David Preston, the twenty-year-old grand-nephew of the conservative tech tycoon, Maxwell Preston, who was the owner of Preston Enterprises, a large tech business on Mars and a major competitor of the Tesla Martian Company. Maxwell Preston was ninety-four years of age and with his genetic enhancements, he was expected to live to over 200 years of age. As usual, Jamal only asked for minor information from his clients and agreed to keep information regarding their enhancements a secret. Jamal was not overly concerned if his clients were discovered, however, as the wealthy were usually able to circumvent the law.

Jamal visited David Preston at his home in Omaha, Nebraska, after David invited him. David lived in a large three-story home in the neighborhood of Skyline in Omaha. Jamal had altered David's genetics, giving him slightly better strength, a higher red-blood-cell count, and further developed his regeneration abilities. This was Jamal's final visit, to perform several diagnostic tests to confirm that David's body was functioning properly. Clients usually did not invite Jamal to their home, and Jamal preferred it that way, but David and Jamal were almost the same age, and David insisted he visited him at his home.

The house was modern, with a colonial style that gave it an elegant look as you approached it. The house was a smarthome controlled by a quantum computer, and David pre-programmed each room to adjust its color and light intensity as soon as he entered it. David gave Jamal a tour of his home, spending most of the tour in his weapons room, showcasing his collection of advanced weapons that were banned on the East Coast but which the wealthy collected in the Midwest due to relaxed gun laws. The basement had a virtual gaming center and a billiards table, and when David invited him to a game of pool, Jamal happily agreed, excited to display his skills. Jamal was good at the game of eight-ball, and he often played whenever he visited the Dominican Republic.

David set up the billiard balls, and right after Jamal broke and began the game, he said, "I just want to say thank you, Jamal. You have dedicated most of your time to me for almost an entire year. I believe these enhancements will help me adapt quickly to life on Mars. It is an amazing gift you have, Jamal, and I never asked you how you became so scientifically gifted. Did you go to school or were you born with your talents?"

Jamal sunk a few balls and before he took his next shot, he replied, "My family is poor, and I had a hard life in Camden, New Jersey. I was raised by a single mother, and she could not afford to send me to school. I don't know much about my father, and I rarely visit him in Baltimore. My interest in school came from my older cousin, Hakeem, who was an academic and obtained a full scholarship to study biology at M.I.T., and he would lend me his school software when I was in junior high school. I realized I could understand some of the mathematics and genetics. By my sophomore year in high school, my grades drastically improved, and I was comprehending graduate-level subjects on genetics and chemistry. I did two years at a local community college but had some personal issues and never completed my degree. Maybe in the future, I will return to school and find a good career."

Jamal sunk the 8 ball and won the first game rather quickly, and David began to rack the balls for the second game as he replied, "You are making more money doing what you do now! Why waste your time with school? I went to school, but I didn't need to go because I already have a job lined up as a supervisor for one of my family's robotics factories on Mars."

Jamal replied, "Not all of us are fortunate to be born into a successful family, David. I saw friends that were talented in the arts and sciences, and they never had a chance to make it because of the conditions we were born into. My cousin was a rare exception, and I consider him a genius who was fortunate enough to remain disciplined and stay away from the daily troubles in our community. I was born with a talent, but I also worked hard to learn from all the advanced science software my cousin gave me."

Jamal only had two billiard balls on the table to sink while David had six remaining on the table. David shook his head and replied, "I respect your discipline. You should stay in the Midwest and earn more money rather than staying on the East Coast and suffering through regulations and working side jobs where you are not allowed to let your genius blossom. You can enhance professional athletes, for example—some of the elite athletes pay a lot of money, especially the foreign athletes."

Jamal replied, "I thought about enhancing amateur and professional athletes, but athletes are strictly monitored by the US government, and it is very risky. I guess I can work with foreign athletes, but I don't want to work with famous clients. I think working mostly in the Midwest makes it easier for me to work to my full capabilities, however, I think some of the problems we have on the East Coast are worse in the Midwest. Poverty is worse in some places here as well as the pollution in the poorer areas."

David Preston changed the conversation as Jamal won the billiards game and invited him to visit a few clubs in the Old Market in Omaha. Jamal was relieved to discontinue the conversation due to his negative views on the politics of the Midwest. It appeared that parts of the Midwest, including Kansas City, had regressed to the early 1900s as deregulation led to increased pollution and the return of preteens into the labor force. The level of pollution in the Midwest angered Jamal because local politicians hadn't learned from the climate emergencies of the previous centuries that had led to worldwide devastation.

Later that night, after Jamal returned to his apartment, David picked him up, and they went to a few clubs at the Old Market and enjoyed the Omaha nightlife. It was a clear night in November, just a week before Thanksgiving. Centuries ago, Omaha would be bitterly cold during November, but nowadays, the weather was rather mild and would only get colder at the beginning of December. The factories near Omaha were filled with workers old and young. Many were teenagers that were desperate to earn money to support their parents and siblings. The US government had little power in the Midwest but promised to re-establish regulations to keep young people from suffering from mandatory work and low wages. The clubs that David and Jamal were going to, most of the public could not afford to go to. Jamal could afford to go out on the weekends, and people like David could go every day if they chose to do so.

Both young men dressed nicely, in button-down shirts, slacks, and shoes. David was more stylish with a button-down shirt, that gradually shifted colors, and pants that reflected his Midwestern upbringing. It appeared that David cared more about the new Midwestern fashion trends than Jamal did. On the East Coast people adopted a more European style of dressing and some adopted more Caribbean-style clothing, and David preferred Eastern fashion styles. They entered a bar full of mostly young white people from the local area. David had a new Ford electric sports car. It was a sleek, black car with two blue stripes running on the sides of the vehicle. It was a smart car that could be programmed to drive on its own. David enjoyed flaunting his wealth which was a luxury that Jamal could not enjoy due to the nature of his work.

They entered a high-class club full of upper-middle-class and wealthy young people. David's friends arrived around midnight, including David's best friend James Donnelly who went simply by Jim. Jim was a tall, slim young man with brown hair, a small mustache, and an interesting goatee. Jim said hello to David and Jamal as he ordered some drinks for the entire group of eight young men. Jim appeared nice at first but soon revealed himself to be mercurial.

Jim introduced himself, "My name is James; I'm David's old friend. I'm happy to finally meet you. David has mentioned you a few times before, and he says you are a talented man."

Jim appeared pleasant and quickly became angry when his drink was not prepared to his liking. Something was unnerving about Jim that Jamal had seen in certain types of people with bad character.

Jamal smiled and said, "Thank you, Jim. Honestly, I am just a hard worker, and I try to do the best that I can."

Jamal remained at the club with David until a little after two in the morning before Jamal informed him that he would be returning home. David promised to sign a few documents ending their agreement before Jamal left the club and boarded a cab home.

Jamal preferred to listen to retro reggae music or Dominican music and usually frequented those clubs back east or whenever he visited his friend Jeremias in the Dominican Republic. Jamal and Jeremias had become friends when they met at Rutgers University in New Jersey at a genetics event, and their friendship strengthened when Jeremias invited Jamal to the Dominican Republic. There, Jamal started dating Jeremias's sister Magdalena. He quickly fell in love with Magdalena's intelligence and kindness as well as her rich caramel complexion, almond eyes, and long, black hair.

When Jamal returned to his apartment, his friend, Wesley, informed him that he believed he was hacked and some of his procedures and client information might have been compromised. Jamal asked Wesley to quickly join him at the apartment for a full explanation, and they promised to return to their laboratory the next day.

Wesley was nervous as he exclaimed, "Jamal, someone or some group has been viewing your files for several months now. I am certain it is not the government, but it is going to take some time to find the location of these hackers and what they are using our information for. I pray it is not an international issue or we may be facing a long jail time."

Jamal's heart raced, and he regretted his work in the black market. He should have quit earlier and used his money to complete a degree program and become legitimate. Jeremiah had constantly advised him to seek a legitimate career path, particularly if he desired to marry his sister in the future. Jeremiah belonged to a conservative Dominican family who were also Jehovah's Witnesses. Jamal fought back tears, and after his anger subsided, the anxiety consumed him. His fears would intensify several weeks later when he and Wesley discovered that David had allowed James Donnelly and a group of hackers to steal his information. It appeared James Donnelly was sending Jamal's information to a secret research division of a far-right white nationalist group named the Sons of Old America. They were using Jamal's information to learn new ways of genetic engineering in hopes of creating a white super race. The white nationalist group hoped to take over the Midwest and soon overthrow the government in Washington D.C.

Jamal and Wesley destroyed their laboratory and all their hardware and software. Jamal only kept a few important notes regarding his genetic research, and they quickly moved out of their home. Jamal subsequently cleared their apartment in Omaha and moved out. Wesley fled to Europe, and Jamal returned to a low-income apartment building in Philadelphia near his hometown of Camden, New Jersey. Jamal attempted to find the whereabouts of David and Jim Donnelly, however, they must have suspected that they were discovered. Jamal believed that David left Nebraska and possibly moved to Idaho.

Jamal spent his free time visiting the historical sites in Philadelphia. He saw the founding fathers and wondered how they would view the current fractured nation of the United States which nearly fell to a powerful oligarchy and was a shell of its former greatness. It appeared that the Midwest would split from the United States, and Jamal feared for the non-whites and the poor living in those regions. He felt sick because he believed he'd unintentionally aided a far-right nationalist group due to his greed and personal shortcomings. He was guilty of being born with nothing and seeking wealth in a land full of poverty and pain. Jamal felt he should have made some money and invested in furthering his education as his girlfriend suggested. Now, because of his greed, he would surely end up in prison.

Jamal spent increasing amounts of time in Jarabacoa, Dominican Republic, where he stayed near the home of his friend Jeremias and Magdalena. He was able to finally gather information on David and Jim Donnelly, and he soon discovered that Jim Donnelly's uncle, Oliver Donnelly, was a high-ranking member of the Sons of Old America. Jim had applied some of Jamal's techniques in the genetic enhancement of several young extremists in their group. They were engaged in minor terrorism throughout the Midwest and were planning larger terrorist activities in various federal buildings throughout the East Coast. Jamal soon let Wesley know that he would contact the US government. Wesley reluctantly agreed with Jamal, and Jamal contacted the US government.

The following year, in December 2676, Jamal was enjoying a beautiful Sunday night with his girlfriend and her family. In the Dominican Republic, he felt more comfortable spending his money, and he purchased a flying electric vehicle which he placed under Magdalena's name. The couple had just returned from their short stay in Puerto Rico, using the Antillean Skyway that connected Cuba, Puerto Rico, and the Dominican Republic. The skyways were only used by citizens of the three Spanish-speaking nations, so Magdalena flew the vehicle back toward the Dominican Republic.

The couple spoke frequently about Jamal's future and the future of their relationship. After his ordeal was over, Jamal would ask permission from the US consulate so that he could move permanently to the Dominican Republic, and he promised his friend Jeremiah and Magdalena he would create a new life for himself in the Dominican Republic. At Magdalena's family home in Jarabacoa, Magdalena and Jamal discussed their future together.

Magdalena embraced Jamal as she said, "I tried to advise you to leave that life. You made your money, but it is not worth getting involved with dangerous and powerful people. Usually, it is the people without power who are the ones that pay the price. You decided to cooperate with the authorities, and I think you made a wise decision. If these extremists in the United States were to inflict terrorist acts using your techniques, you could be implicated and could face a long prison sentence. I hope that you can explain what happened and clear your name."

Jamal fought back tears as he replied, "I was poor growing up, and I sought fast money. I wanted the easy money that the drug dealers and illegal tech merchants had. I finally made my money, and I should have quit this work before I got into serious trouble. Wesley and I became greedy and wanted even more money. I told Wesley that I would contact the F.B.I. and I found, out not long ago, that Wesley left England and reported to Washington D.C. I think that I might get the call soon to return to the United States. If I am incarcerated, I will promise to use my time to go to school and learn Spanish so that I can live with you here in the Dominican Republic."

Jamal and Magdalena kissed, and she promised she would wait for him. Jamal sometimes used the small translator chips that tourists used, but if he wanted to live in the country permanently, he desired to fully learn the Spanish language. Jeremias interrupted the couple and called them to join the rest of the family as dinner was placed on the table. Jamal began to walk toward the dining room before he was interrupted by a phone call.

A young man from the F.B.I. was calling from an encrypted line. Jamal answered the phone and the voice responded, "Hello, Mr. Jamal, I hope that your vacation in the Dominican Republic has been pleasant. We want to discuss a potential deal that you may accept, and you could do less than two years of prison time. You have to fully cooperate with the ongoing investigation and release all your research and the names of your previous clients. You broke several laws, but they are not serious. We stopped various neo-fascist groups in the Midwest, and we need you to testify against David Preston and James Donnelly. We will also have enough evidence to move against these far-right organizations and the various conservative politicians they fund throughout the Midwest. After you complete your time in prison, you may leave the U.S., however, you will continue to remain under probation, and we can extradite you if you break any foreign laws. Your identity will be kept secret, and we will discuss further considerations regarding this agreement once you report to Washington D.C."

Jamal thanked the agent and breathed a sigh of relief. Jamal understood that he and Wesley could help bring an end to the Sons of Old America and the Patriotic Worker's Party, so the US government could regain control of the Midwest. Most importantly, he could finally start a new life and regain control of his life. Wesley also discussed the possibility of leaving the United States for Jamaica. Jamal desired to return to the Dominican Republic and apply for a job in biotech. When Jamal would later return to the Dominican Republic, Magdalena expected she would be certified as an elementary school teacher. It would be a great start for the couple.

Magdalena walked to the balcony where Jamal stood silently and said, "Is everything alright, *amor*?

Jamal replied, "I received the call we have been waiting for, Magdalena. The deal is not as bad as I thought. I just have to cooperate and serve a year or two in prison. You can visit me whenever you wish, and I'll gladly move down here after I finish my time in federal prison. I'm going to finish my final payments on my apartment, and after I pay back whatever damages I owe, I will leave my mother some money and use whatever I have left to purchase a place down here."

Tears fell down Magdalena's eyes as she kissed Jamal passionately. Jamal enjoyed the cool Dominican breeze on his face as his heartbeat slowed back to normal. His hands were not shaking as much anymore. Jamal embraced what was to come, and although he was ashamed of his past, he smiled because he now had a new future to look forward to.

Story 6: Diplomatic Immunity (25th Century)

Raul Mendez was on his fifth trip to a specialized lunar base housing the top scientists from Earth. Raul was visiting representatives from an alien civilization that had arrived from within the Milky Way and had constructed a diplomatic office on the Moon. Ten years ago, during Christmas of 2390, representatives of an alien civilization had arrived in the solar system and landed on the Moon. Many people hoped that this sudden contact with intelligent life would unite mankind. Unity was needed after the last world war in the twenty-third century. The war pitted the United States, Israel, Saudi Arabia, and Canada against the Central forces that included China, Russia, and various Middle Eastern nations. The conflict left most of the United States, China, and Russia in ruins and the entire Earth awash in various degrees of nuclear waste.

Latin America, Southeast Asia, Northern Europe, the Middle East, and Eastern Africa became regional areas of affluence, power, and a good standard of living. During the first years of the alien arrival, various leaders advocated for a possible war against the aliens, fearing that they had come to invade Earth, however, the aliens, although having advanced technology, made it clear to world leaders that they did not intend to engage in warfare with the nations of Earth. The aliens stated that they wanted to help humans dispose of the lingering nuclear fallout and help improve human technologies in space travel and nuclear waste disposal. The aliens wanted to occasionally visit Earth to study ecology, human history, and society.

The aliens revealed that they lived in a multi-planet civilization located in a region within the Perseus arm of the Milky Way Galaxy, however, they did not reveal the specific location of their star system and promised to reveal their specific origins after further concessions were made, allowing the aliens to research the animals of Earth. Various nations sent their diplomats to speak with the aliens who called themselves, *an-enkt-Aat*, which roughly translates into English as the explorers. The names of the aliens were hard to pronounce, and soon they were called the Perseids by most people due to the location of their civilization within the Milky Way Galaxy.

The Perseids were hideous to look at, however, Raul Mendez was accustomed to their appearance and mannerisms. They appeared to be a kind of fungal and animal hybrid. They had different colors with irregular spots of different shades on their skin. The Perseids communicated with each other chemically, and they could exchange complex information simply through touch, however, they could also communicate verbally and were able to learn various human languages within a few weeks. They usually kept most of their body covered in an exoskeleton and rarely revealed their full form to humans.

Raul Mendez was traveling aboard the Dominican space shuttle, *Quisqueya Cinco,* toward the Latin American lunar colonies where a group of Perseid diplomats lived. He remembered the first two years after contact with the aliens when various nations sent their diplomats to gain knowledge from the aliens regarding their intentions and to prevent other nations from gaining information that could give them increased power. The relationship between the diplomats improved as well as their relationship with the Perseids. The Perseids soon asked to speak with select diplomats, including Raul Mendez who became one of their favorite diplomats.

Raul Mendez was now a sixty-year-old man, with vast experience during times of conflict and peace and with a wealth of knowledge regarding Perseid science and culture. Raul remembered his humble beginnings in Puerto Plata, the Dominican Republic, and his interest in culture and politics that led him to learn various foreign languages, including, Mandarin, English, Arabic, and Korean. His knowledge of history and global affairs provided him with a successful career in diplomacy. His most recent accomplishment was that he had seemingly gained the trust of the Perseids, thereby gaining access to sensitive information, and became the most important diplomat on Earth.

Raul was happily married to Gloria, and they had two grown children named Miguel and Luis, who were both in the tech industry. Gloria advised Raul to retire from diplomacy upon the arrival of the Perseids because she feared her husband would get sick with the same radiation poisoning that people experienced after coming into close contact with the aliens. Unexpectedly, Raul's health improved after several years, and he appeared more youthful. Raul's doctor said his body was more youthful, and he observed that Raul had more vigor.

It was later confirmed that Raul had developed a type of radioactive immunity, which appeared to confirm the hypothesis of radiation hormesis. He developed this enhancement of his physiology after several years of meeting and spending time with the Perseids. The first few visitors who spoke with the aliens died months after their encounters, and scientists were baffled by the reasons why some people like Raul experienced improvements in their health while others rapidly became sick and perished. Scientists discovered that the Perseids had natural agents that caused cancer in humans. The Perseids produced what appeared to be a more aggressive form of aflatoxin, which led to the development of advanced spacesuits for those who met the aliens. Several diplomats developed some immunity and Raul developed an advanced immunity where he could spend limited amounts of time with the Perseids without his spacesuit, although he usually maintained his spacesuit during prolonged meetings.

The aliens helped improve human spacesuits to help mitigate the impact of cancer-causing agents on the human body. The Perseids possessed a deeper knowledge of radioactivity and quantum physics. It was a deeper knowledge that Raul slowly acquired after years of talking to several Perseids. He learned about the Perseid culture and was allowed to learn some information on Perseid history. Raul also discovered that some of the Perseids were curious about relationships with humans and were interested in forming deeper chemical connections with humans which gave them a certain pleasure that could be similar to sexual enjoyment.

The Perseids were searching the galaxy for radiation-rich worlds and radiation-emitting bodies, particularly neutron stars and magnetars. During their exploration, the Perseids discovered simple life in other areas of the galaxy, however, humans were the first complex civilization they had discovered. Raul was able to discern the private perspectives and opinions of Perseid officials as he acquired a deeper understanding of Perseid language and began to discern their emotional changes through their chemicals. It was unexplainable the insight that Raul now possessed, and he attempted to describe this feeling to the leading Dominican biologist and mycologist, Dr. Carmela Vargas.

Dr. Carmela Vargas studied Raul's physiology and the changes he'd undergone during his diplomatic missions with the Perseids. Raul was initially nervous when his body began to change but discovered that he was not ill and surprisingly, his health improved. Raul discovered that he was able to comprehend the Perseids and understand their perceptions, which improved his understanding. As the starship, *Quisqueya Cinco,* landed on the Lunar Pad near the Perseid domes, Raul thought about the meeting that would occur later with one of the Perseid diplomats. The shuttle shined bright with its white and grey exterior, and the large flag of the Dominican Republic on the left side of the shuttle confirmed that Raul had arrived.

About eight Earth hours after Raul's arrival, he was invited to speak with two Perseid diplomats. After years of working with the Perseids, he was accustomed to their appearance and the slightly fragrant smells they emitted. The larger Perseid's name was hard to pronounce, however, Raul called him Rayma. Perseid language used similar pronunciations as the Romance languages, which enabled Raul to learn and speak their language with greater ease. Rayma greeted Raul in his best Dominican Spanish, "*Mi amigo, estoy alegre que regresaste.*"

Raul replied, "Yes, Rayma, I am happy that I returned here to see you once again. I am here to discuss our plans for the acquirement of the new technologies you promised our governments on Earth. We will also need instructions on the science and operation of these technologies and help in bringing a few potential conflicts on Earth to an end. The Dominican government, as well as the other Latin American governments, want your aid in helping diffuse any remaining tensions on Earth. We are also looking for defensive capabilities and enhanced radiation cleanup technologies. The Dominican government would also appreciate these technologies for the Dominican Republic to conserve the safety and environment of the Caribbean Islands."

The Perseids looked at each other as their chemicals spread through the room. Raul did not have his spacesuit on as he was now mostly immune from the cancer-causing radiation that the Perseids emitted.

Rayma replied, "We have attempted to speak to the diplomats of all the nations, and we believe that we can help bring peace on Earth. We can help you with the technologies you ask for, but what use would it be if the nations of Earth continue to engage in warfare? We are visitors to your star system, and although we have tried to bring peace to Earth, we have observed that much apprehension and hate remain toward our people by many people of Earth. This is to be expected as human history is full of wars ignited by your different cultures, beliefs, faiths, and even the colors of your skin. You have gone to war because of politics, land, and resources, so it is natural for you to be afraid and have hatred and reservations for a civilization completely alien to those on Earth."

Raul took a moment before he replied, "You are our guest in our solar system, and we have much to learn from each other. Your people have learned far more about our people than we have about yours. Our leaders have worked hard to calm the fears of our people and to accept the reality that we are not alone in the universe and that life and possibly other advanced civilizations exist within our galaxy and in the universe. We would like to know more information about the other advanced civilizations and the kind of simple life your people have discovered to advance our knowledge of the universe. Another subject that the Dominican government desires to speak with you about, is the possible study of your physiology. We are using some fungi that were discovered in Chornobyl, Russia, that act as natural radiation shields in space. Your people are structured like the fungi we have on Earth, but your people thrive under harsher radioactive conditions, and we would like to study your anatomy and physiology further. Perhaps we can exchange some biological samples so that you can learn more about us and we can learn more about you?"

The meeting continued for several days until Raul and the Perseid diplomats reached a small agreement. The Perseids promised to provide the Dominican government with technology to improve radiation shielding and cleanup as well as advanced information regarding genetic engineering. The Perseids also promised to speak to other nations to help bring peace to any remaining conflicts around the world. Some nations had not yet learned from the nuclear conflicts of the past that turned the middle eastern deserts into glass and rubble and plunged the world into a nuclear wasteland in the twenty-third century. Raul desired to help mitigate any further conflicts on Earth and at the very least, gain some advanced technology through his negotiations.

An Earth week later, and just two days before Raul was scheduled to depart, some of the Perseids were having a party with some of the humans. Raul felt uncomfortable during his visit and had disturbing dreams about devastating conflicts on Earth that would once again plunge the Earth into nuclear devastation. In the dream, Latin America and the Caribbean were spared the direct devastations experienced by the other regions of the world, however, radiation sickness reached lands that were untouched by direct warfare. Raul woke up abruptly, and he was covered in sweat and breathing heavily. Anxious, he almost called his wife, Gloria, but felt a strange presence nearby. He left his room and walked down the hallway and observed other Perseids sleeping but felt the presence of another Perseid awake and in an excited state.

Raul was aware that some Perseids secretly engaged in sexual activities with humans who were also somewhat immune to the radioactivity. A Perseid named Mandu was known to engage in sexual activity with humans and was responsible for causing several deaths among the human diplomatic population during the first years of contact between Perseids and humans. Some of those diplomats carried the radiation to Earth and killed their spouses and other members of their families while some of the humans who were in close contact with the Perseids developed varying levels of immunity. Raul was able to understand the Perseids through radiochemical communication, and during his return to the Perseid lunar base, he realized that his communication abilities had improved.

Raul became increasingly anxious and feared that his new abilities would be noticed by the Perseids. He approached a few doorways that were unlocked and walked down a large staircase built to accommodate the large lower pods of the Perseids where he found the Perseid named Mandu appearing to be comatose with two female humans who were in a state of ecstasy and didn't notice Raul nearby. Raul could feel the thoughts of excitement, anger, anxiety, and fear that coursed through Mandu's body. Most of the fear within Mandu was regarding humanity and their possible attack upon the Perseids. It confirmed what Raul already pondered about the Perseids. The Perseids lived in constant fear of a unified Earth attacking the Perseid lunar base, if humans discovered their intentions.

Raul quickly looked throughout the chamber for any documents to confirm his beliefs. He soon located Mandu's access card to his private quarters, and he quickly entered and gathered some documents he could find, as well as some written notes in the Perseid language that he could read. Raul exited Mandu's private quarters and entered his entertainment chamber where he now lay with his two companions, one wrapped around him, and the other in another bed. Raul collected any information regarding the two female diplomats and took a small biological sample from one of Mandu's smaller tentacles, and dashed out of the chamber.

The following day, Raul and his crew departed the Perseid Lunar base and returned to Earth to the Dominican Republic in their space shuttle, *Quisqueya Cinco.* Upon Raul's return to the Dominican Republic, he traveled to the Dominican Space Center in Santo Domingo and presented his observations regarding the Perseid's plans. Raul also supplied Perseid tissue samples to the laboratory of a leading biologist and mycologist, Dr. Carmela Vargas in San Cristobal.

Several months later, the Dominican government deciphered the various Perseid files that revealed that the Perseids were secretly meeting with officials from various antagonist nations, including Pakistan and India, and attempting to cause a renewed division and civil war within Unified Korea. The Perseids desired to initially conquer Earth just as they had previously conquered other planets with less advanced life forms. The Perseids soon realized the civilizations of Earth had advanced technology and armies that numbered many millions of men. They learned about the long history of warfare on Earth, and they desired to initiate another world war and then capitalize on the destruction and division to conquer Earth and the human colonies on the Moon and Mars. The Dominican government quickly spoke with other Latin American governments, and soon, the governments of the rest of the world were notified, leading to a large allied force that planned an attack on the Perseid lunar base.

Raul realized his diplomatic skills would not lead to any peace between Earth and the Perseids after the Perseid plans were uncovered. He'd risen to fame when he'd previously negotiated peace treaties that ended a possible civil war within Haiti and because of his work with leaders that led to peaceful terms between China and the Philippines. Raul's diplomatic skills included a successful peace treaty between the state of Palestine and Israel, but now a war between Earth and the Perseids was unavoidable. The Perseids were late in realizing that the nations of Earth were mobilizing an attack on their lunar base, but they managed to send distress signals to their home planet, asking to quicken reinforcements.

Raul and Gloria were at home, watching anxiously with the rest of the world, as the allied attack upon the Perseids soon resulted in a resounding defeat for the Perseids. The Perseids unleashed their superior weaponry, but it was too late. Over 10,000 soldiers, mostly from various Latin American nations, died in the battle while nearly all of the 1,500 Perseids perished, except for seven Perseids who escaped the battle and four Perseid hostages, three of whom were taken to Mexico and one to the Dominican Republic for interrogation and to further the studies on Perseid anatomy and physiology. The nations of the Earth soon improved their technology and prepared for possible retaliation from the Perseids, which might arrive at a future time.

With enhanced technology, the nations of the Earth had a good chance of winning a second war with the Perseids. Raul pondered about the possible second war along with the rest of the world, but he was comforted in the rapid technological advancements now found mostly in the Dominican Republic and Latin America. He later retired from diplomacy with full honors and full of joy that the Earth achieved world peace at least temporarily, but he was saddened that these dire circumstances were needed to bring about positive change on Earth.

Story 7: Fantasy Planet (29th Century)

Back on Earth, it was currently the year 2861. The Dominican astrobiologist and astrobotanist, Julia Matos, was asked to join an elite team of international scientists to reach a certain strange planet in an alien star system many light-years away. The star system was located within the Norma Arm of the Milky Way Galaxy. The colonists were mainly sent by the Latin American Union through their united Latin American space agency. The mission was led by various nations, including Mexico, Chile, Argentina, Ecuador, and Colombia. The planet was discovered in the year 2712 by Mexican astronomers, and the planet remained a Mexican government secret for several years. The scientists were amazed when they observed the abundance of life found within the planet, and soon the planet was named Tōnacācihuātl, after the Aztec and Meso-American goddess of fertility and creation. The planet had a satellite similar in size to the Earth's moon which was soon named Tezcatlipoca after the Aztec god of night and sorcery and the patron deity of Aztec kings and young warriors.

Various geologists estimated the age of Tōnacācihuātl as roughly 10 billion years old, over twice the age of Earth. Although life was found in abundance, it was odd that humans were now the apex predator on the planet. During the first expedition to

Tōnacācihuātl, the explorers introduced various plants and animals from Earth that survived and flourished on Tōnacācihuātl. Some of the chickens, pigs, and dogs escaped human captivity and surprisingly reproduced with native plants and animals on Tōnacācihuātl, creating fertile hybrids that became beasts of burden for the human colonists and also a source of nourishment. Scientists marveled at the biodiversity of Tōnacācihuātl and the abundance of life. Scientists were also perplexed regarding the lack of civilization on Tōnacācihuātl despite the planet existing over twice the amount of time as the Earth, leading numerous xenoarcheologists to launch a search throughout the planet for signs of ancient civilizations.

Soon the Mexican government disclosed their findings to other Latin American nations, and they began to plan a secret mission to Tōnacācihuātl. The first mission in 2725 sent a group of twenty scientists to examine the planet to confirm that it was indeed habitable. The Mexican government improved their Annihilation Drive, which used the violent interactions between matter and anti-matter, to power their starships from their Lunar Base toward planet Tōnacācihuātl. Using the annihilation drive and the cosmic gravitational superhighways, the Mexican government was able to lead Latin America in deep space travel. To the astonishment of the scientists, humans could live on the planet's surface without the need for a spacesuit. Conditions on this planet were far superior to the deteriorated conditions of Earth.

The second mission sent a colony of over 500 men and women, which included scientists, military personnel, engineers, and people of many different trades to help establish a human society. Young men and women were encouraged to visit this new planet and were promised biotechnological enhancements that could prolong their lifespan to an average of over 200 years if they agreed to live on the planet for a prolonged amount of time. These enhancements were only available to the wealthy on Earth, and many working-class young people volunteered for the mission. Scientists on Earth studied these enhanced humans and were surprised that the human body improved after a prolonged duration on the alien planet. Later, missions to the alien planet became a united effort through the Latin American Space Agency.

Julia Matos had previously traveled to the Moon, Mars, and various space stations, however, her mission to the mystery planet had been her first voyage outside of Earth's solar system. She'd heard terrifying tales of the dangers that lurked outside of the solar system. They were similar to the stories shared by explorers sailing to unknown lands on Earth many centuries before. The vast ocean and unexplored lands led to fantastical tails of mermaids, sea monsters, and strange lands filled with dangerous beasts.

Julia Matos had arrived over one Earth-year ago at the mystery planet, and she searched for any negative aspects of the planet and any drawbacks for prolonged stay by humans. Upon her arrival to the planet, Julia Matos felt the richness of the alien air in her lungs and how energetic she felt as her circulation improved. Scientists were on the planet continuously studying the various habitats and food on the planet and the improved physiology of the settlers. The first children that were born on the alien planet were observed to have superior health when compared to babies born on Earth. Several generations had been born on this alien planet, and most of the colonials were the great-grandchildren of the original adventurers that arrived over 120 Earth years ago.

The Mexican government initially forbade unprotected sex within the colonies to prevent humans born on an alien planet, however, after many years of intense debates, the Mexican government allowed the formation of families in the colonies. Some of the crew that arrived felt disturbed about living on an alien planet despite its superior conditions and returned to Earth, however, most people desired to stay rather than return to an Earth suffering from centuries of destruction by climate change and violent conflicts. The official language was Spanish, and most colonists spoke predominantly Mexican Spanish and a mixture of South American and Caribbean Spanish.

Julia Matos made many discoveries on a planet that appeared to be a living, breathing organism. She wondered if there were other planets like Earth or Tōnacācihuātl within the galaxy. It was rather odd to Julia that humans could thrive on an alien planet filled with a variety of animals, plants, fungi, and micro-organisms, all of which appeared to benefit humans. This conundrum frustrated Julia and drove her to work harder, which amused her friend Enrique. Enrique Salazar was a respected young Colombian chemist who joined Julia and her crew and their journey to planet Tōnacācihuātl. Enrique enjoyed the journey into the ocean of stars and often compared their adventure to the stories of Jason and the Argonauts. Enrique was having fun, and he found it perplexing that Julia was the only person who did not enjoy the benefits of the alien planet.

Julia was building a team to travel to distant parts of Tōnacācihuātl to analyze the various ecosystems. She invited Enrique two days before the expedition. Enrique laughed as he said, "This planet is full of abundance and pure joy and reminds me of the land of Colchis, the home of Medea. This is our own *Argonautica,* my friends. This is the land of Colchis, and we have found our Golden Fleece! We simply have found an oasis in the vast desert of a cold and dead universe."

Julia noticed that the fauna and flora vastly changed as they moved farther from the human colonies. It appeared that the region surrounding the human colonies in the southern mainland of the planet was adapted to provide optimal conditions for human society. It was hard to notice anything strange on this seemingly perfect planet. Julia investigated the various plant life and wild animals near the colonies and far from the colonies, and began noticing increasing differences in the flora and fauna and the environment as she increased her distances from the colonies.

Julia's ongoing research and theories in Tōnacācihuātl caught the attention of a leading theoretical physicist named Carlos Puyucahua. Carlos was a respected physicist from Ecuador and a proud man of Quechua ancestry. At the age of ninety-five, Carlos had recently been widowed after his wife Josefina passed away, so he said goodbye to his children and grandchildren and embarked on one last adventure to Tōnacācihuātl over ten Earth years ago. Carlos was now over 105 years old but looked like a man of sixty due to his rejuvenation during his stay in Tōnacācihuātl.

Julia and Carlos led a small group of scientists to observe plants at various distances from the colonies. After about 100km, the plant life and the various alien animals that inhabited the plains and forests began to change slightly. One of the plants that grew in abundance near the colonies was blue cotton which produced whitish fruits similar to berries as well as tubers rich in starch with a slightly sweet taste. Many plants on Tōnacācihuātl were similar to various plants on Earth, and scientists observed how their nutritional values increased slightly through the first few generations of human inhabitants on Tōnacācihuātl.

All plants on Tōnacācihuātl emitted various chemicals and transmitted messages to other plants and animals, however, Julia observed abnormal activity in certain plants after about 100km from the nearest human settlement. Julia cut some of the plants and quickly transported them back to a lab in one of the settlements. These plants, through their flowers, appeared to have an advanced form of quantum computing that transmitted messages about the human settlements through the atmosphere of Tōnacācihuātl toward Tōnacācihuātl's moon and possibly another unknown location.

It appeared that some of the plants gathered information from the plants near the settlements and transmitted it toward the Tōnacācihuātl's moon, Tezcatlipoca, now commonly called Tez. Some of the plants could be described as organic computers that operated like quantum computers with molecular qubits that received and transmitted information into space. Carlos believed the information was packaged and translated and transmitted possibly toward an alternate dimension. The mathematics, biology, and quantum physics needed to construct a planet like Tōnacācihuātl were beyond the comprehension of the most intelligent human minds, if this planet was indeed artificial. Carlos became obsessed with the possibilities of Tōnacācihuātl and the advanced alien civilization that constructed it while Julia's fears deepened. Julia believed the aliens may have allowed past civilizations to thrive on their artificial planet until it was time to perform more direct experimentation and possibly attack their homeworlds, and she feared for the fate of Earth.

Julia's discoveries motivated over 100 xenoarchaeologists to lead several teams in an exploration of large regions of the planet for evidence of intelligent life and past civilizations. A planet-wide search began for evidence of any past civilizations that may have inhabited Tōnacācihuātl. Researchers also hypothesized the reasons for Tōnacācihuātl and the purposes of the architects. Soon Carlos confirmed some of Julia's hypotheses. The plant life was far more intelligent than previously thought.

Physicists also observed variations in gravitation in areas near the colonies and other regions of the planet. When the colonists first arrived on the alien planet, the gravitation force was about eighty-eight percent of Earth's gravity, and currently about ninety percent of Earth's gravity. Gravity toward the opposite side of the planet, in the other large land mass in the eastern hemisphere, was currently at about eighty-five percent of Earth's gravity. It appeared the planet changed its gravity to help the colonists adjust to the planet.

Three regions in Tōnacācihuātl were discovered with different weather and ecosystems, which appeared almost foreign to the planet. These regions also contained what appeared to be the ruins of ancient civilizations. In the north, an ancient civilization was discovered, belonging to beings that looked like furry primates that walked on all fours and preferred colder weather and higher elevations. In the large archipelago, near the equator of the great ocean, the ruins of a civilization belonging to amphibians were discovered, and in the southern jungles, the ruins of a civilization belonging to what resembled reptiles on Earth were found and were biologically constructed with opposite chirality. The plants and animals found near the ruins were also the mirror image of all life found on Earth, and their food and plants were enantiomers of all that was found on Earth and the other regions of Tōnacācihuātl.

Julia theorized that Tōnacācihuātl was constructed for research and experimentation by an advanced and ancient civilization. Planet Tōnacācihuātl was a galactic zoo, and perhaps there were other zoos in other galaxies. Carlos Puyucahua theorized that Tōnacācihuātl was constructed by an advanced multidimensional civilization, and the planet was designed to accommodate intelligent civilizations that mistakenly or purposefully visited Tōnacācihuātl. It appeared that other civilizations that had lived on planet Tōnacācihuātl left the planet, leaving behind their technology. It was unknown if they left peacefully or were removed by the advanced civilization that constructed the planet.

Carlos theorized that some of the animals on Tōnacācihuātl were also gathering data on human anatomy and physiology and transmitting signals out of the planet toward an unknown location. Julia's theory was discussed within the scientific council and the governing council, and the theorized civilization responsible for the construction of Tōnacācihuātl was soon called Species X, then later commonly called the Architects. Soon, the information regarding the various theories relating to Tōnacācihuātl was publicly announced.

Governor Emiliano Palacios made a public announcement relating to the possible dangers of humans establishing permanent settlements on Tōnacācihuātl. The governor announced that he would communicate with the Mexican government on how to proceed with the long-term plans for the colonization of Tōnacācihuātl. Governor Palacios began to organize starships for those who desired to return to

Earth, including colonists who were born on Tōnacācihuātl. The Mexican government soon agreed to repatriate natives of Tōnacācihuātl back to the country of their ancestry or their preferred nation in Latin America. Most of the natives of Tōnacācihuātl decided to remain on the planet of their birth while a minority decided that they would return to their ancestral planet. Some of Julia's crew decided to stay on Tōnacācihuātl into the near future, including her friend Enrique.

A year later, Julia and most of her crew prepared and prepared to return to Earth. Most of her belongings and research materials were packed on the starship, and she enjoyed her last two days on Tōnacācihuātl, speaking to her friends, including Enrique Salazar, who decided to stay on Tōnacācihuātl. Julia was invited to a large outdoor festival with music, dancing, and all the food a person could eat. Enrique was in a jovial mood, and he was dancing and laughing with a beautiful young sociologist from Honduras named Sofia. Sofia was athletic with dark eyes, long, jet-black hair, and beautiful dark brown skin. Enrique preferred women with brown skin and dark black hair, and he was interested in Central American women, so Julia did not interrupt her friend's dance. Enrique could dance *punta* very well and impressed Sofia.

After the dance, Enrique noticed Julia and walked over to her while drinking a glass of *Agua Ardiente.* He offered Julia a glass, but Julia refused the Colombian rum. Enrique smiled and said, "You know you can't convince me to return to Earth with you, Julia. I cannot go back to an Earth destroyed by humans for so many centuries. We polluted the Earth since the nineteenth century and only began to attempt to reverse the negative impacts of climate change in the last several centuries. I would like to stay here in Tōnacācihuātl a little longer until I decide what I want to do. Part of me wants to go to Earth, but I feel at home here."

Julia smiled and replied, "I understand our failures on Earth and your preference to remain here. I want to remind you of the potential dangers of remaining on this alien planet. The civilization that modified this planet is far advanced and may pose, not only a danger to our colonies here but a danger to mankind on Earth. We discovered some ancient civilizations that traveled here and met their demise, and the ruins were mostly sanitized, so we are not sure if there were wide-scale massacres or if those alien beings were collected and transported to another world, or if they left on their own. It appears that our discoveries are mostly limited to what the Architects wanted us to see. We have to be careful while we continue to study this planet and the civilization that created this paradise of a world."

Julia and Enrique walked toward a table full of food and liquor as Enrique replied, "I am having a lot of fun here, and I feel much healthier. Perhaps the Architects responsible for this planet mean to do us harm, or perhaps they are so advanced that they view the smartest among us similarly to how we view chimpanzees and will not harm us. Perhaps they are collecting data on other civilizations to improve their civilization or they mean to build a coalition with Earth and other alien planets. Whatever it may be, I am pretty sure they will not make contact with us for many generations or perhaps never at all. I shall return at a later time if I decide to do so, but for now, I'd rather live here and eat, dance, and make discoveries as my body revitalizes itself. Although we have made progress in reversing the negative impacts of climate change, the Earth remains heavily polluted, and I'd rather stay here and add years to my life."

One of the colonists, named Gloria, who was born in Tōnacācihuātl, overheard the conversation and encouraged Enrique to remain in Tōnacācihuātl. "My father is from the nation of Uruguay, and my mother is from Costa Rica, and they were also born on Tōnacācihuātl. I only know of Earth from computer images, videos, and direct communication with my extended family members. We speak Spanish in Tōnacācihuātl, and many still believe in Christianity, but we do not have a full understanding of the politics and the intricacies of Earth. All I know is the settlements here on Tōnacācihuātl, and although the announcement by Governor Palacios did strike some fear within me, I am anxious about returning to my ancestral homeland on Earth. Additionally, I am not sure if I should return and live in Costa Rica or if I should live in Uruguay; I only consider myself a native of Tōnacācihuātl. Someday, I will return to Earth, but I need some time to think about my future and if I want to start a family here or on Earth."

Julia got up to dance a *bachata* song with Enrique as tears forced themselves onto her cheeks. Enrique, with his breath full of Colombian rum, reassured Julia about his decision and blessed her voyage back to Earth. Carlos Puyucahua was also in attendance, dancing with the young ladies and appeared more energized and youthful. Despite the ancient ruins discovered on the planet and the potential implications of staying long-term on Tōnacācihuātl, Carlos and many others had decided to remain.

When Julia got tired and went to her quarters to sleep, Carlos called out to her, "I wish you the best, Julia, on your return voyage to Earth. I have decided to die on Tōnacācihuātl because there is little left for me on Earth. My lovely wife passed away, and my children are grown and doing well. They understand and respect my decision to remain, and I hope you do, as well. I hope that I go to paradise and see my wife and loved ones in paradise, but for the time being, I will enjoy life in this manufactured paradise. I will not bring children onto this world because I am not sure what the fate of humanity is here, however, I know that all I will know is bliss until my last days."

Julia returned to her quarters and rested before she boarded the large space shuttle with most of her crew and some others that decided to return to Earth. The Mexican government and other governments planned on examining the plants and animals of Tōnacācihuātl as well as the hypothesis that Tōnacācihuātl was a large laboratory constructed by an advanced alien civilization. Soon other governments would also discover the existence of Tōnacācihuātl, leading to larger conversations regarding humanity and the existence of other advanced civilizations within the Milky Way Galaxy.

As the shuttle began to rise above the land and through the atmosphere of Tōnacācihuātl, Julia Matos thought about her friend Enrique and his love of Greek Mythology. Perhaps Enrique and the human settlers who chose to stay would become like the lotus-eaters—the race of people living on an island dominated by the lotus tree whose fruits and flowers were a narcotic that caused the inhabitants to sleep in peaceful apathy. Or maybe the human settlers were correct and maybe she was in the wrong. The Universe was vast and full of mysteries, and Julia eagerly awaited what the scientists would discover about Tōnacācihuātl and the cosmos. For now, she desired to return to Earth and her homeland, the Dominican Republic. She thought about her experiences in Tōnacācihuātl as she looked through her window and out into the dark expanse of space.

Story 8: The 4-Train Paradox (21st Century)

Felix Lopez remembered when his understanding of the world changed. It was the day when he accidentally discovered that a person could skip through space and time. Last year, during the weekend of Thanksgiving 2035, he became drunk in downtown Manhattan with his friends. He began his evening at a hookah lounge in the Lower East Side with his childhood friend, Jose. Felix and Jose were current sophomore students at Lehman College in the Bronx, and the two spent many weekends together downtown. The two friends met up in the afternoon, then later met with the rest of their friends and went to several clubs downtown. At about 1 a.m., Felix and Jose decided to head back to the north to the Bronx.

The two friends got on the uptown D-train and transferred to the 4-train at 161st St and Yankee Stadium. Jose got off at his stop at Burnside Ave, and Felix remained on the train and said goodbye to this friend. Shortly afterward, the conductor asked all passengers to exit the train and wait for the next one. Felix could barely walk, and he got on board another train before everything became black. That was the last thing he remembered. He didn't remember the next stops, and he missed his stop at Kingsbridge Avenue.

Felix awakened at the final stop in Woodlawn and somehow ended up near the local park. It must have been early morning when he woke up, embarrassed at his level of drunkenness the night before. He tried calling his girlfriend, Valeria, but she didn't pick up the phone. Felix remembered being discovered later that morning by an angry, older black man with gray hair, named Robert Jacobs, who asked him for information and tried to force him back into the train station. Felix remembered seeing people early that Sunday dressed differently and talking differently.

Felix walked to Mosholu Parkway toward his previous school, DeWitt Clinton High School, the school his father, Manuel, and his Uncle Esteban had also previously attended. It was lunchtime when he noticed many of the students wearing baggy clothes in a style from the past. He then noticed some members of the Clinton baseball team, including a man that appeared like a younger version of his brother Esteban Lopez. When he noticed his family's last name on the back of the young man's jersey, it made him realize that he was indeed his uncle. His father would have been in middle school when his uncle attended Dewitt Clinton. Felix was shocked when he realized that he was somehow in 1994. His uncle made eye contact with him, and he turned away and headed for the bushes across the street from his school and vomited.

When Felix stood up, he was approached by a strange tall, black man with gray hair who introduced himself as Robert Jacobs. Felix explained his confusion and his belief that the present date was October 1994 when he noticed Halloween signs near the local stores and heard various rap songs from *Ready to Die* by the Notorious B.I.G, the hit song *The Most Beautifullest Thing in This World* by Keith Murray, and songs from the album *Hard to Earn* by Gang Starr. Robert Jacobs confirmed Felix's suspicions and informed him that the train he accidentally boarded was a time transport-vehicle. Felix had traveled backward in time in a machine disguised as an uptown-bound 4-train, and Robert Jacobs was the conductor.

At first, Felix was frightened, but later, he was able to grasp the basic physics of the time-traveling train, and Robert Jacobs soon invited him on his frequent time-traveling missions. Robert Jacobs explained the purpose of his research and also warned Felix that there were other time travelers, some friendly and some potentially dangerous. He warned Felix pointedly about a Jamaican woman, named Alice Nicholson, who traveled to the past and posed a serious threat to Robert. Felix pondered what would happen if they were to encounter Alice and what actions Robert would take. Felix believed that Robert would kill Alice if he could, and Robert would change the conversation whenever Felix desired to learn about the mysterious woman.

Felix enjoyed learning about time travel and witnessing history through his own eyes. He wrote some of his experiences down but made sure to keep his escapades a secret. He kept his time-traveling secrets from everyone because he would be labeled crazy and also because he feared that the police or a federal agent would discover what he was up to. He didn't inform his parents or his girlfriend, Valeria, about some of his activities late on Saturday nights or random days of the week. Valeria was a beautiful Dominican woman from Santiago with light caramel skin, jet-black hair that went down below her chest, and bangs that danced over her beautiful hazel eyes. Valeria also had a temper, and it was often difficult for Felix to explain his whereabouts when he would spend hours away during his trips through time.

Felix became interested in visiting the future, and after several months, he managed to convince Robert to visit different periods in the future. Robert was far more interested in visiting the past, particularly the 1980s. During the trips to the 1980s, Robert usually demanded that Felix stay behind near the train at Woodlawn station. After a short period, the train would slip into a kind of space-time fabric that would envelop it, rendering itself invisible to everyone except Robert and Felix. Sometimes, Robert would allow Felix several hours to visit certain locations of interest but advised him not to make contact with any of his family members as any encounter could result in drastic changes to his future.

The Saturday night after Thanksgiving, Valeria was away at her parents' apartment in Hollis, Queens. Felix had declined the invitation to go with her, saying he would be with his friend Jose. He decided to stay behind after he was urgently notified by Robert earlier in the day to meet him at the Bedford Park Boulevard station by 2 a.m. It was a cold Thanksgiving weekend as Felix walked briskly toward Lehman College and to the train station. There, he waited for about fifteen minutes until he noticed the approaching 4-Train and Robert in the conductor's booth. The few people at the train station were teenagers and young adults, most of them drunk and oblivious to this time machine parading as a 4-Train. No one noticed Felix as he entered the train and then entered a temporary bubble in time and space.

The 4-Train zoomed quickly toward Woodlawn Station before time seemed to stand still, and they were once again transported back in time. Robert Jacobs smelled of alcohol, and his eyes were bloodshot. He gifted Felix some clothes from the 1980s and exclaimed, "We are in September of 1987, Felix! The time has shifted toward the early afternoon. You do not have to guard the train and look for anything suspicious. You can have fun today, but remember to return within ten hours."

The weather was nice and warm, and people were out in the streets. The album *Bad* by Michael Jackson was recently released, and he could hear many of the tracks at the local parks and on the streets of the Bronx. Felix walked down Jerome Avenue, passing the armory on Kingsbridge, and observed teenagers wearing Adidas and breakdancing on the corners of Aqueduct Avenue and 192nd Street, and some were doing the same in St. James Park. Some of the young men were walking with their boomboxes and Jheri curls.

Felix made it a routine to travel to Fordham Road and observe the way language and styles changed depending on the different periods that he and Robert traveled to. As he walked down the street, he observed a group of beautiful young ladies talking about a recent movie called *La Bamba* and how handsome Lou Diamond Philips appeared in the film. A young Puerto Rican girl, who was with the group of young ladies, made eye contact with Felix and smiled at him. The girls were near Woolworth's on Fordham Road, and Felix walked toward the entrance just as the ladies decided to enter, as well. She had shorts on, exposing her long, athletic legs that descended from her small waist and curves. Her light skin was tanned a darker shade of brown, he presumed from her time outside during the summer. She looked attractive, and Felix was very tempted to say hello to her. He'd never engaged in any romances during his visits to alternate points in time, however, he felt a small conversation with this beautiful Boricua would be okay.

The beautiful Boricua introduced herself as Cristina, and she later informed Felix that she was attending Bronx Community College. They both struck up an interesting conversation, and Felix followed her and her friends, who walked down Morris Avenue and into St. James Park. Cristina gave him her phone number, and

Felix almost pulled out his new cell phone. Imagine the shock on Cristina's face if she would have seen a small cell phone from the year 2036. Felix's heart raced as he thought about the possible mistake he'd made. Robert constantly warned Felix to keep all present-day technology on the train during their travels through time. Cristina kissed Felix on the lips, leaving Felix wanting. Several hours later, he said goodbye to her and her friends and boarded an uptown 4-Train.

The trains were full of graffiti, and the smell of the Bronx summer air filled Felix's nostrils. When he reached Woodlawn Station, it was late afternoon and Robert soon appeared. He was in a joyous mood, and he was almost manic. They quickly entered their specialized train and were transported to the present. Felix questioned Robert to discern the reason for his glaring happiness, but Robert only said, "I am beginning to understand time travel more deeply, and I made some significant discoveries today. I will make sure to explain these discoveries to you in a few days."

Felix was excited to hear about Robert's discoveries, but several weeks passed, and Felix couldn't reach Robert Jacobs. Felix couldn't visit his home because Robert had never revealed where he lived and had rarely discussed his personal life with Felix. It was finals week during December, and Felix decided to take a break from studying late one afternoon as the sun set on the horizon and the sky began to darken. Valeria remained inside cooking Dominican-style rice and beans and goat meat. Felix drank a few shots of scotch to warm himself up a bit, then put on his coat and boots and walked outside toward the Jerome Park Reservoir. He decided to take a left and walk down the street until he reached a small park area near the old John Peter Tetard Junior High School. Felix looked out into the horizon as light snow began to fall again, deepening the snow already on the ground. He thought about Robert and wondered if he'd fallen into some trouble when he felt the presence of someone behind him.

To Felix's horror, it was Alice Nicholson, the woman that Robert warned him about, looking straight at him with a .38 Smith & Wesson Special in her hands. She did not aim the weapon at Felix but made sure to let him see that she was armed. Her face was focused on Felix, and she broke the silence as she exclaimed, "Yes, I am Alice Nicholson. Judging by your frightened look, I gather that Robert Jacobs must have told you vicious lies about me. I am armed because of the stories that Robert has filled your head with. Robert Jacobs is a dangerous man that has used you to attempt to kill me and others. You are a pawn that he used to lure me to you, and perhaps after my death, he would find a way to kill you."

Confused, Felix managed to say, "What have you done with Robert?"

Alice replied, "I incapacitated him and left him imprisoned in the past, just as he attempted to imprison me over five years ago. I managed to escape but was stuck in the past and suffered nervous breakdowns due to time sickness. Robert failed to inform you that it was I who developed time travel, and with his help, we created a capsule that could travel through time using an abandoned train car. The train car appears as a regular train in your time, but it can travel through space.

Alice paused before continuing, "Your friend, Robert Jacobs, has severe mental sickness that has intensified with his numerous travels through space-time. It is a phenomenon that I call time sickness. During your brief adventures with Robert, you probably thought about reversing certain aspects of your past. Perhaps you want to change a bad grade or reverse your chances with a girl you liked or change some choices in your life. As you get older, you'll see that you will look back on your life differently. You will think about all the choices you wished you would have made. Robert was a gifted man who was socially awkward as a child. Through science, he was able to find an identity and he advanced quickly through school. In 1980, I met Robert in my Physics college class at Fordham University. I was a young professor from Jamaica and was thirty years of age at the time, while Robert was twenty."

Felix calmed down and sat on the park bench while Alice sat next to him as she continued, "Robert graduated and soon pursued his doctorate in engineering, and I soon included him in some of my research. In 1982, Robert married a young lady from the Bronx, named Julie, and they had a baby called Simon in 1984. To make a long story short, Robert ignored the fact that Julie suffered from depression and abused crack cocaine. Julie began to steal money from Robert, and they constantly had fights due to her drug addiction. In the summer of 1985, she was unable to pay back money to a local crack dealer, which led to her killing. Their baby was also accidentally shot in their apartment on Webster Avenue near Fordham Road. The crack dealer was later fatally shot in 1990, and the killer of his wife and baby son was arrested in 1987 and killed in Rikers Island in 1989."

Felix replied, "What happened to Robert after that?"

After a brief pause, Alice responded, "Robert fell into a deep depression and went into debt, so I decided to help him. I loaned him some money, which he later paid back, and soon he decided to get into education. He became an engineering professor at Queens College in 1996. We continued to work together, and by 2020, I was able to develop a way to bend space and time and travel vast distances, which led to the possibility of time travel by 2025. Robert helped me build the time-travel capsule, which we camouflaged as the 4-Train, and we bravely tested our system through the manipulation of gravity and the strong and weak nuclear forces. For several years, we traveled to the past as far back as the late 1800s, not knowing the negative impact of time travel through the phenomenon I called time sickness."

Alice paused for a moment before she continued, "It appeared to hit Robert quickly, and all of his old demons came back. He drank and abused drugs for the first time, and his mind unraveled. Through his notes, I found out that he'd attempted to travel back in time to reverse the events that led to the killing of his wife and son. He planned to travel back and stop his wife from abusing drugs, but then when he failed, his attempts became more blatant and violent, including the killings of the drug dealer, the perpetrator, and the perpetrator's family."

Felix was shocked as he replied, "I find that hard to believe. Robert appears fine, and he was even happy the last time I saw him."

Alice shook her head. "Robert is a broken man. He was happy because he discovered the origins of his wife's killer when he last traveled in time with you in 1987. The killer came from a broken home and was in the foster care system before getting involved in gangs. Robert bribed a lawyer in 1987 who revealed court documents stating that the killer's parents were from Virginia, and his mother took him to the Bronx in the early 1960s. Robert was attempting to go back to 1962 and kill him and his mother or possibly travel to Virginia and murder the killer's parents before he was born. But what I found out was that we can't change the past to alter events in the future. What has happened appears to be set within this dimension, and any changes would slightly bend the timelines but will self-correct to keep the events that are already set from changing."

Felix was confused and said, "I do not understand?"

Alice slowly replied, "If something already occurred and you travel back in time to change what has happened, time and space will find a way to correct the disturbance. One way or another, Robert's wife and son will die. If Robert tries to kill the perpetrator's parents, something will happen—either his gun will jam, or an event will stop him from killing them.

Felix was confused as he asked, "What about the future—how does it relate to our present?"

Alice thought for a moment before continuing, "The future has its complexities. If you travel to the future, you may see various possibilities for your future. I am not sure if those possibilities exist in other dimensions or if they are simply different possibilities that you can change in the present. I do not advise spending too much time observing the future. If you are a Christian, you will understand that God gave us free will. In the present, you have the possibility to change the future. When you travel to the future, you will observe different possibilities of your future each time. There is a chance you will witness a future very close to the one you will live in. The question I ask is, do you want to know exactly what will happen to you in the future? If you encounter a future you do not wish to have, you may attempt to alter your life in the present and possibly enter a psychological downturn caused by obsession and anxiety. You will possibly have a psychotic break from your present reality."

The sky darkened as Alice continued, "Robert's numerous attempts to change his present have somehow become ingrained into his consciousness. His mind has merged various timelines into his subconscious. It is something I cannot fully explain, biologically or theoretically, yet, but it has resulted in a form of what I call extreme time psychosis. I have not published my research, but it would be interesting to see what psychologists say about this. Robert was trying to kill me for several years, and I was able to follow you. I paid that Puerto Rican girl in Fordham Road to insert a small tracking device into your wallet. I was able to hear your conversation with Robert, and the chip that was planted on you was able to receive information from Robert's computer. I tracked him down when he traveled back in time by himself to 1986, again, where I was able to knock him unconscious and tie him up in a secret location."

Nervous again, Felix asked, "How can I trust you, and what happens now?"

Alice smiled and replied, "I will give you the information you need. I have my computer files and Robert's records. As for Robert, he had a massive breakdown once he realized that he no longer had control of my time travel machine and when he realized he could never change the past. I will bring him back to the present and report him to the police. I will stay in communication with you to make sure he does not try to contact you again. As for me, I am eighty-sixed years old and suffering from time sickness. I have merged with my present self but have already developed sudden mental problems, which my children have noticed. My husband Patrick passed away eight years ago so I spend most of my time alone. I don't think I have many years to live. I gathered you are a Physics student, so I will turn over my research paper and my technology to you. Just be careful what you share with the public. This technology and knowledge can be dangerous in the wrong hands. Now is the time we say goodbye, Felix. You have the chance to learn from the mistakes of others and make the most out of your life. You have gazed into the deeper realms of our reality, which only a few have seen throughout the history of humanity."

Felix hugged the woman and slowly walked home as tears fell from his eyes. The cold wind pierced his skin as he saw Alice disappear into the darkness like a dream. Once home, he hugged Valeria and they kissed as they sat down to eat dinner. Valeria asked him where he'd been, and he simply said that he went for a walk. Felix finished his dinner and played some music as he continued studying for his finals. He enjoyed classic progressive rock music and played the album *Close to the Edge* by Yes. It was an album that calmed his spirits and made it easier for him to study.

On New Year's Eve, the local news reported that an older black man committed suicide by jumping in front of a 4-Train at Woodlawn Station. Felix soon discovered the man was Robert Jacobs. After months of investigations, it was concluded that he was a lonely and disturbed man. Detectives found drawings and random writings about time travel in his pockets. Few people went to his funeral, and Robert was quickly forgotten but was always remembered in the minds of Alice and Felix.

Felix completed his B.S. Degree in Physics and was later accepted to Cornell University for the PhD Physics program. Valeria traveled with him after she completed her B.S. Degree in Biology, and they lived in Ithaca until the completion of Felix's studies. His interest in Physics blossomed, and he soon applied his knowledge to the mysteries of time travel and its uses for space travel through the manipulation of space-time. Alice passed away soon after Felix began his doctorate studies, and he privately continued his research in time travel. One night, Valeria questioned Felix about his strange behavior in the first years of their relationship in the Bronx, and Felix informed her about some of the details. He decided to tell her about his experiences with time travel at a later date. What he experienced was inconceivable for Valeria and the world, and it was even unimaginable for Felix.

Story 9: The Gems of Deminán (22nd Century)

Ramiel Moreno was a shy kid from Barahona, Dominican Republic. His teachers often spoke about his great potential but complained about his lack of attention during class. Ramiel was about to begin his senior year of high school at the age of fourteen at the *Centro Educativo: Politécnico Cruce de Palo Alto.* He was an introspective teenager, and after taking special examinations, his teachers recommended that he skip several grades and start the senior year of high school. His teachers soon spoke to Ramiel's parents about his possibilities in higher education.

Ramiel often spent his leisure time walking by himself through the *conucos* and rivers instead of playing baseball or basketball like most teenagers. He was not interested in video games and preferred to study animals and nature. His grades were highest in the sciences and particularly in Biology and Physics. Some of his teachers began to call the young Ramiel a genius and a child prodigy, which filled his parents, Juan and Susana Moreno, with admiration and anxiety. They were proud of Ramiel's achievements and potential and were nervous about how their son would handle the mountains of expectations held by Ramiel's teachers and their community. Juan encouraged his son to be more sociable and tried to include him in family activities to make him more well-rounded and boost his confidence.

It was the summer of 2109, and the temperature was over 110 degrees Fahrenheit. Despite the establishment of anti-fossil fuel policies in many countries, the summers continued to be abnormally hot. The Dominican government launched numerous progressive measures in the mid-twenty-first century, including using green energy to provide the majority of power in the nation while phasing out gasoline vehicles by the late twenty-first century. The Dominican government fostered electric and hydrogen-powered car companies that provided jobs for thousands of Dominicans, including Ramiel's father, Juan.

Juan Moreno constructed engines for various Dominican companies, including Dominican Luxury Motors, which provided upper-middle class and wealthy Dominicans with luxury electric and hydrogen vehicles. Juan's technical abilities and work ethic provided a good upper-middle-class lifestyle for his family. Juan's wife, Susana, was an elementary school teacher who instilled discipline and a love for learning in her two sons. Juan and Susana encouraged their children to excel in school, and their oldest son, Ramsés, was an accomplished student, interested in public service and was currently studying Chinese Language and Literature at Shenzhen University in Shenzhen, Guangdong, China. With Ramsés living in China, Juan could focus his attention on his more introverted younger son, Ramiel.

Juan and Susana thought it would be a great idea for Ramiel to spend some time with his great-aunt Epifania. Epifania was now over 100 years of age, and she had outlived all five of her younger siblings, including her youngest sibling and Ramiel's grandfather, Jenocrates, who passed away in the previous year. Epifania worked as a geneticist for over fifty years at Quisqueya Genetics in Santo Domingo and married her coworker and prominent geneticist Raul Montesinos, who advanced the field of genetic engineering in the Dominican Republic. Epifania divorced Raul when she was thirty-five years of age and never remarried, preferring to live a life of travel and leisure. Epifania had one son from her marriage to Raul, named Nicolás Montesinos, who lived in La Romana and had a family of his own.

Ramiel spent about a month of his summer vacation with Epifania, and he learned more from her life in the few weeks than he had ever known before. Family and friends visited Epifania's mansion and two-acre estate throughout the summer as she gifted many of her possessions to them. Many of the visitors commented on Epifania's beautiful estate overlooking Neiba Bay and the Caribbean Sea. She had a beautiful garden with birds and a large aquarium in her home. She had a luxury electric vehicle and an electric sports vehicle within her large three-story mansion. In her large home, she had numerous pictures detailing her travels to many nations, including China, Japan, the Philippines, India, Ethiopia, France, Italy, Germany, and Norway. Epifania also traveled to the Coyolxauhqui Base, the Mexican Lunar Base, on her sixtieth birthday, which inspired her to help raise funds and gather public support for the first Dominican Martian probe mission, which landed on Mars in 2105.

Unlike many of his family members, Ramiel didn't ask Epifania for any gifts and didn't expect anything. One Saturday afternoon, when it was just the two of them, Epifania decided to reveal an important possession that she planned to give Ramiel as a gift. Epifania went into a private room on the third floor, reached into her safe, and pulled out a beautiful gem, roughly the size of two fists. The gem was a light green octahedron and was made of diamond. It was a splendid gift for such a gifted and selfless young man.

Epifania walked downstairs as her gracious white dress flowed in the Dominican wind and her majestic long, gray hair danced on the horizon. She had deep and rich brown skin with indigenous eyes, and high cheekbones giving her face an Asiatic look that other members of her family, including Ramiel, also shared. She brought Ramiel a cold drink of *morir soñando* and joined her grand-nephew in her backyard overlooking the beach. Ramiel enjoyed the cold orange juice and milk drink, and as he took his first drink, Epifania handed him the mysterious crystal.

She smiled and said, "My dear grandchild, I must admit I am proud of your intelligence and the potential that you have. Because you have always been kind to me and others and you have a curiosity for the world around you, I have decided to gift you my most prized possession. I have an interesting gem that I have kept in my possession since it was given to me as a young woman. I now believe I should entrust you with this ancient gem so you also might see different perceptions of time and space."

Ramiel was speechless but managed to reply after a long pause, "Who gave you this gem, and when was this gem constructed? What brilliant mind created this?"

Epifania replied, "This gem was created here on our island in the region called Jaragua which is now Barahona. The ancient people created this gem, and it passed to our other native ancestors which the Spaniards called the *Tainos.* This marvel existed for thousands of years before the birth of Jesus Christ. The concept and construction of this marvel occurred through various gifted minds throughout many generations. Much of our world and universe remains a mystery for us today, and although we have learned much since ancient times, we have also lost other ways to look at our reality."

Epifania paused and allowed Ramiel to think about what she said before she continued, "Time and space are important concepts that have been discussed for countless generations. Ptahhotep said, 'Follow your desire as long as you live and do not perform more than is ordered, do not lessen the time of the following desire, for the wasting of time is an abomination to the spirit.' The ancient Vedic texts of the Hindus discussed the repeated cycles of creation, destruction, and rebirth, of the universe, with each cycle lasting 4,320,000 years. The Incas called time and space *Pacha.* What I have learned is that time can be considered linear or circular, and I have come to know that there are other forms of time. My sadness is that I do not have another lifetime to observe and learn."

Ramiel listened closely as Epifania continued, "The ancients, the Macorix, and the Tainos wrote down information regarding these gems and that soon the gem would come into the possession of those considered wise. Some of these wise men were advisors to various caciques on our island. These wise men pondered about space and time through their observations of the sky and our beautiful lands. They found interesting patterns in nature and found and developed these crystals that displayed a repeated pattern in space and time."

Ramiel was astonished, and after a long pause, he responded, "I am amazed, *Tia* Epifania. I read about the concept of time crystals in various scientific papers from the early twenty-first century. How were these gems and concepts discovered so long ago?"

Epifania laughed as she said, "My dear grand-nephew, many confuse technology with wisdom. Many people in history were just as wise as people today. You can even argue some people of the past were wiser in certain aspects. Only now has the Dominican government and society returned to pursuing policies to conserve nature and promote education and upliftment. Our ancestors, including the Tainos, respected and understood the importance of the environment and our role on Earth.

We now enjoy high-quality universal healthcare and green energy, and our lands are once again filled with animals and plants in a healthy ecosystem. We are now an example for other nations in our fight against climate change, and yet, we are only building from the knowledge of our indigenous ancestors."

Ramiel asked, "What should I do with these gems, and where do I learn from the countless Wisemen who came to possess this marvel?"

Epifania responded, "Were we created to understand quantum mechanics or to understand how nature works on a microscopic level? I believe we were created to explore the world around us and work together as a community. We were given basic senses to survive on Earth and coexist with nature as well as the gift of imagination. We build upon the foundations of philosophers, messengers, and teachers from the past. There have been teachers including Zarathustra, Siddhārtha Gautama, Jesus, Muhammad, and the Great Peacemaker. There have been great minds including Imhotep, Chanakya, Isaac Newton, Albert Einstein, and Stephen Hawking. There have also been great teachers and leaders including Simon Bolivar, Maximo Gomez, Ramón Emeterio Betances, Gregorio Luperon, and Anacaona, one of the most celebrated ancestors in our land. I saved the teachings of numerous scholars in chemistry, mathematics, biology, and physics, within various smart chips, including the works of modern scientists relating to time crystals. I also have some personal research and discoveries I have made throughout my life stored in smart chips and written in my journal, which I will give to you today."

Epifania reached into a folder she was carrying, which contained her journal and various smart chips, and she handed them to her eager grand-nephew. After a brief pause, she continued, "The ancient people of these islands, later called the Tainos, understood the importance of living in harmony with nature. Our ancestors maintained their childhood curiosities even as adults and studied the nature around them and simply used the materials that our creator placed on Earth to understand nature from a more complex perspective. Wise men searched for the hidden mysteries of the universe, and soon science and beliefs intertwined. The Tainos lived in harmony with the environment in Ayiti, Cuba, and Xaymaca. After the arrival of the Spaniards in 1492, and the West Africans they brought around 1501, we soon became a society at war that intermixed, and later created our own identity as Dominican people. We struggled as a people but just several decades ago, we made many technological advancements and a more democratic government that increased harmony with society and our environment. We are learning what our indigenous ancestors already understood. We are learning to advance as a society while respecting the precious ecosystem that sustains us. Our history and culture are also recorded in interesting ways within this gem. It is believed there were other gems like the one now in your possession, and these gems came to be known as the gems of Deminán."

"Deminán Caracaracol, the creator and ancestor of our native people?!" questioned Ramiel.

Epifania answered, "Yes, Deminán Caracaracol, the one believed to have created man and the Caribbean islands. Some of our ancestors who came into contact with these gems believed they were created by the first humans, and soon they believed Deminán influenced wise men to create them and record information and time. This is the belief system of our ancestors before the Spaniards arrived and brought the enslaved Africans to our land. Atabey is the supreme goddess of our indigenous ancestors, representing the Earth Spirit and the Spirit water, lakes, streams, the sea, and tides. Yúcahu is the god of creation, the sky, the sea, peace, and harvest. The gods of our natives are directly intertwined with what people experience on Earth, for example, Guabancex can cause the violent winds and storms of the Juracan. These violent hurricanes have increased in ferocity and frequency due to human-caused climate change. Our ancestors respected the environment, and only now has the Dominican social democracy increased regulations on the corporations that hurt our environment and advocated with other nations to reduce pollution in the world."

Ramiel was astonished at the information Epifania was relating to him and replied, "*Tia*, this is a vast ocean of information, and I am honored to receive this gift. I will do my best to learn and use this information to improve my life and the lives of our society."

Epifania stood from her seat, kissed Ramiel on his forehead, and said, "Our family has substantial indigenous ancestry, and it manifests in our appearance. We have a strong connection with our ancestors and their culture. I learned much from a lifetime of learning from this gem and the information from our ancestors. I must also warn you to not only focus on intellectual pursuits but also focus on yourself and having a healthy social life. I was a child of great potential like yourself but also isolated myself. I was a loner like you up until middle age. My husband divorced me, and I admit, most of the problems were of my own doing. I learned later to free my inhibitions and engage with my family and friends, and although I never married again, I did meet other partners, including my longtime partner, Antonia, who was with me until her passing ten years ago. I learned to be closer to my son and my family, and it has enriched me more than all of the mysteries of the universe I have uncovered. I am overjoyed that I found a worthy candidate for my precious gem, and I am proud that it is you, my grand-nephew."

Tears flowed down Epifania's eyes as she embraced Ramiel. The sky was beginning to darken, and the air cooled slightly as they heard the Caribbean waves crashing on the shoreline. Epifania gave a small portion of her wealth to Ramiel's father and promised to purchase a new Chinese electric sports car for Ramiel upon his graduation from high school. Ramiel wondered how he would use the gem and if he would make a discovery that could improve Dominican society and the world. Ramiel was once again full of motivation and imagination, and he promised to follow Epifania's advice.

Epifania was there to see Ramiel's graduation from high school. Ramiel soon began his freshman year of college in Santo Domingo. He made friends in college and continued to maintain the friendships he had in high school. Ramiel remembered Epifania's advice and formed a close bond with a young lady from San Cristobal named Faustina. Faustina attended Ramiel's high school and was attracted to his intelligence, and she planned on pursuing mathematics. Ramiel enjoyed her free spirit and her patience in teaching him how to dance salsa. He was inspired in his young life and was determined to live a life of curiosity and healthy relationships with his family and friends. During his second year in college, a professor inquired which degree he wished to pursue. Ramiel smiled and said, "Physics and Quantum Biology."

Story 10: Ātman of Harlem (21st century)

Rakeem Jackson found luck for the first time in his life. For most of his life, he'd only known pain, suffering, and misfortune, and at twenty-five, he believed he had lived the troubled life of a man of fifty. Rakeem did not know who his father was, and his mother, Janet, had troubles of her own. Rakeem grew up in the Harlem River Projects with his mother and two older brothers, Rashad and Malik. His oldest brother, Rashad, was shot and killed by a Puerto Rican teenager from Spanish Harlem, and Malik recently moved out and lived in Kingsbridge Heights in the Bronx after impregnating his Salvadorean girlfriend, Rosa, from the Marble Hill Projects.

Rakeem was the youngest, and he found himself in trouble with the law at a young age. He ran away from home after dropping out of high school in his sophomore year. Rakeem was homeless, living on the streets for several years, and was involved in several robberies. One robbery resulted in the death of a young father in Hollis Queens at the hands of another man that had connections with Rakeem. Rakeem was falsely accused and was arrested and accused of manslaughter at seventeen. After serving a year in a juvenile facility, he was found not guilty and soon returned to the streets.

Rakeem sold synthetic drugs briefly but succumbed to drugs himself as he looked for relief from his sad existence. The drugs Rakeem sold were illegally imported through the Chinese black market into the United States. The United States banned illegal substances arriving from China, and the Chinese communist government banned them within China, however, many new synthetic variants escaped the arms of justice, and the products continued to be shipped into the United States as addiction rates continued to rise into the late twenty-first century. Drug abuse, suicides, and overdoses were at an alarming rate in the inner cities and the Midwest as income inequality and the unemployment rate continued to rise.

Rakeem received fentanyl-related precursor compounds that he used to chemically produce various synthetic drugs under the instruction of a drug dealer, Richard Smalls, who went by the name Harlem Rich. Harlem Rich was a friend of Rakeem's older brother, and he ordered the killing of the perpetrator that killed Rashad. Harlem Rich felt obligated to take Rakeem under his wing but grew frustrated with him as he began to slip into drug addiction.

Things became even worse for Rakeem when he was discovered in the subway at Chamber's Street in Lower Manhattan by a young member of the Hare Krishna movement named Brian. Rakeem was slumped on the floor near one end of the platform at around 2 a.m. and would have been an easy victim for some local teens if it wasn't for Brian and his fellow devotees.

Rakeem was recommended to enter a homeless facility by a Hare Krishna, and later he began to spend more time with them. He soon met a young Bangladeshi-American woman, Salma Hasan, who encouraged him to rid his body of illegal drugs and read the *Bhagavata Purana* and the *Bhagavad Gita* for guidance. Salma had disobeyed her parents after she'd failed to marry Asir, a man they chose for her. Salma was against arranged marriages, and although she respected Asir's work ethic, she detested his jealousy and greed and was not attracted to him. Asir became verbally abusive toward her, and Salma quickly ended their relationship against the wishes of her parents.

Salma Hasan's parents Prabir and Indrani arrived in the United States in the early 2040s, and they lived in Queens, New York. They grew up together, and soon, their families arranged their marriage, and they married after they graduated from New York University. Prabir became a lawyer and Indrani a teacher, and they instilled discipline and the importance of education into their two sons and only daughter Salma. Salma was studying at Queens College and was interested in becoming a social worker where she could help disadvantaged youth like Rakeem. During her freshman year at Queens College, she became involved in the Hare Krishna movement and soon met Rakeem.

Salma was astonished by Rakeem's life story and his determination to improve his lot in life. She and her roommates agreed to temporarily take him in and help him study for his G.E.D. After a year of studying, Rakeem received his G.E.D., and he was able to leave his life of crime although he occasionally struggled with relapses that he tried to keep from Salma.

Rakeem continued to struggle with depression, and he soon gained the attention of local researchers who asked him and other local youths to attend a medical study for anyone above eighteen years of age. Rakeem was given an experimental empathogen developed by a laboratory. He was paid 5,000 dollars to participate in the secret study held at NewYork-Presbyterian Lower Manhattan Hospital and was given the money, which he saved to help Salma with some of her expenses as well as to help pay for college.

By the winter of 2085, Rakeem learned the teachings of Krishna and soon joined the International Society for Krishna Consciousness. Rakeem also found that his depression almost completely disappeared, and he became healthier. He cut his small afro and cut his hair short and neat and began to read science books with the encouragement of Salma. Rakeem's emotions improved and his self-respect and confidence increased. Most notably, his empathy for others increased substantially, and he understood that his previous life of crime and self-harm not only hurt him but also his friends and family who deeply cared for him. Rakeem contacted his mother and began helping her with her bills. He also began to speak again with his older brother, Malik, and his former girlfriend and now wife, Rosa, and congratulated them on their young daughter, Valentina.

In the summer of 2086, Rakeem was preparing to enroll in the Borough of Manhattan Community College with the help of Salma. Salma had grown fond of Rakeem, and he was able to sense her growing feelings toward him which encouraged him to ask her to be his girlfriend. At first, she said she was unsure, but after Rakeem began his first semester, she said yes.

Soon, several community activists spoke publicly regarding the illegal actions committed by researchers using poor minorities as test subjects. Rakeem learned he was one of the subjects that were given false information about the studies he was subjected to. The studies not only used various empathogens but also manipulated his genes to induce positive feelings. The studies were used to develop drugs and genetically altered soldiers to improve morale on the battlefield and to help decrease veteran depression and suicides. Most of the people who participated in the studies suffered genetic problems while only a few, including Rakeem, experienced a positive outcome.

A settlement was later reached, and Rakeem received roughly ten million dollars. Doctors desired to study Rakeem's physiology because he was the patient with the most positive outcome from the unlawful trials. For the first time in his life, Rakeem did not have to worry about what he would do the next day. He no longer worried about survival, which was the sad reality for a majority of US citizens.

One Saturday morning, Salma asked Rakeem, "What will you do with all your wealth?"

Rakeem smiled and replied, "I have been given the curse and the gift of heightened empathy in this cold world. I only knew darkness, with only glimmers of hope, until I met you. I feel I not only have a purpose for my own life, but I also have a higher purpose to help other unfortunate souls in my community. This is also another opportunity to start my new life with a solid foundation, and I hope that you can join me in our new life."

Tears began to fall down Salma's face as she simply replied, "Yes, my love."

By the summer of 2088, Rakeem had earned an Associate Degree in Science from the Borough of Manhattan Community College. He learned chemistry during his time as a criminal under Harlem Rich, and now, he planned on applying his knowledge to study chemistry. Rakeem learned how to mix chemicals to produce various synthetic drugs, and now, he advocated against illegal synthetic drug use. He declared his major as Chemistry and desired to pursue work as a clinical chemist and was accepted at Columbia University.

After the killing of Harlem Rich by a rival gang member in 2089, Rakeem began advocating against gang violence, drug abuse, and the illegal trafficking of drugs into the United States. He funded various community programs for troubled youth in

Harlem and the greater New York City area, and spoke publicly against illegal clinical trials that targeted poor minorities. Rakeem also supported affordable education and healthcare for the poor and used the teachings of Krishna to help his community. Rakeem graduated from Columbia University in 2090 and pursued a post-graduate degree in Chemistry as he and Salma looked for homes in the suburbs of New Jersey to start a new life together.

Story 11: Horn of Africa (23rd Century)

It was hard being a black man in the US Midwest in 2253. Ronald McCormick was another poor black man from Kansas City, Missouri. He was an only child raised by a single father who passed away from cancer when Ronald was only ten years of age. Ronald was raised by his Jamaican grandfather, Francisco McCormick, who instilled in him the value of hard work and education. Ronald excelled in school and received the highest scores in Mathematics and Computer science. He completed school at Metropolitan Community College but didn't have enough money to pay tuition at a good university. Ronald applied for several scholarships but didn't have any success, and he did not want to go into student loan debt. There were few opportunities for Ronald in the Midwest, and he wished to start a new life elsewhere.

Despite much progress in the previous centuries, the Midwest fell under the power of far-right politicians and the companies that supported them after another world war that economically devastated the United States. Poor whites in the Midwest experienced crippling economic anxiety and increasing unemployment as synthetic drugs began to increase the incidence of overdoses. Far-right politicians used white fear and anxiety to turn conservative whites against the extensive Latino and Asian populations which also controlled congress. Far-right politicians and right-libertarians controlled the Midwest, and racism reared its head once again at the black minority.

The progressives were able to bring some positive changes in the late twenty-first century, including the passage of Universal Healthcare, however, they were defeated by the liberal government of President Samuel Alvaro which brought the United States into a proxy war against Russia and China. It was argued that the United States needed to stop the Chinese from expanding in Africa and Southeast Asia, however, that war was highly unpopular in the United States, and the corporate elite of the United States was directly challenged by a majority of voters.

The white minority was currently concentrated mostly in the Midwest and Northwest while the nation's power continued to be in the Northeast. Most of the white population identified as liberals and moderates, however, far-right politicians received nearly all of their support from corporations and radical whites who felt they had lost their country. The current leaders of the United States were President Julio Matos and Vice-President Rajat Singh, who were both Social Democrats that supported left-wing candidates in the local Midwestern races. Ronald McCormick was involved in local politics and was advocating for progressive leaders in Missouri, including the young Marxist leader, Dr. Julio Vargas, who was running for Senator of Missouri.

Ronald McCormick thought about moving from the Midwest to Florida or the Northeast, but the cities were too expensive for him. He was working in a small software company, fixing software for quantum computers. His life was one of struggle since he was a child, and as a young man, Ronald sought to unwind. Ronald sometimes went to local bars and clubs to enjoy the nightlife and meet new people. A few months before, Ronald went to a local Ethiopian restaurant and bar after his friend Chris convinced him to go. Shortly after, he met a beautiful, young Ethiopian woman named Aida there, who introduced him to her younger sister, Zala. Ronald was stuck by Zala's beauty and asked if he could buy her a drink.

Ronald was entranced with the various beautiful Habesha women. Most of the women were Eritrean and Ethiopian and some were Somalian, and they all had beautiful faces and smiles. He was entranced by their beauty, but particularly by

Zala's beauty. Zala was tall, almost six feet in height, and close to Ronald's height. She was of brown complexion with long, jet-black hair. She was twenty-two, the same age as Ronald, and she was also attracted to him, so she invited Ronald to dance *eskista* with her. Zala laughed when Ronald had trouble executing the rhythmic soldier movements required in traditional Ethiopian dance, but she respected that he tried.

After speaking with Zala for a couple of hours, the conversation turned to current events, and Ronald could not help but ask, "Your culture is very interesting, but why is there a conflict between Ethiopia and Egypt, even as European influence has weakened the last fifty years?"

Zala was impressed that Ronald was well-informed regarding foreign affairs, and she replied, "Ethiopia and Egypt have a history of conflict. From 1874 to 1876, the Ethiopian Empire and the Khedivate of Egypt went to war, which resulted in victory for the Ethiopian Empire. The Khedivate of Egypt was part of the Ottoman Empire at that time. Emperor Yohannes IV helped bring Ethiopia into the modern age. During the first Italian-Ethiopian War, Emperor Menelik II defeated the Italians in 1896, and the Ethiopians, under Emperor Haile Selassie I, alongside allied forces, were able to defeat Benito Mussolini and the Italians during World War II. Emperor Haile Selassie I attempted to bring reforms, including a progressive tax, but the Ethiopian nobility opposed it."

After a brief pause, Zala continued, "After Ethiopia's involvement in larger global conflicts, our conflicts continued with Sudan and Egypt. After the construction of the Grand Ethiopian Renaissance Dam in Ethiopia in 2030, the Egyptian government launched a war against Ethiopia, leading to Ethiopia's victory over Egypt in the late twenty-first century. Since then, we have had minor conflicts and now maintain a fragile peace. Some of the droughts in Egypt have caused problems again, and the Egyptian government is trying to start ethnic conflicts in Ethiopia to weaken us. Hopefully, the Ethiopian government and Egypt can agree so that we can unify and share in our African abundance."

Ronald interrupted before Zala continued, "Haile Selassie, yes I think I know who he is. My grandfather, Francisco, was born in Jamaica, and he became a Rastafarian at a young age. He always talked about Rastafari, and he spoke about how Haile Selassie was the second coming of Jesus Christ. He also spoke about Marcus

Garvey who promoted Pan-Africanism and was seen as a prophet in the Moorish Science Temple of America and Rastafarianism. When I was a little boy, my grandfather spoke about Marcus Garvey and his visit to Harlem, New York, and his influence on black culture. Sometimes, he also spoke about Africa and particularly Ethiopia."

Zala smiled and replied, "I am a Christian, and in Ethiopia, we also have a long history of Islam and Judaism. In 1948, Emperor Haile Selassie gave 500 acres of land at Shashamene, about 150 miles south of Addis Ababa, to black people from the West who had supported him in his struggles against Mussolini's Italy. The first settlers that arrived in Ethiopia were African American Jews, and they soon moved on to Liberia or Israel. Later, in 1963, a dozen Rastafarians settled in Ethiopia, and the numbers increased after Emperor Selassie visited Jamaica in 1966."

Ronald enjoyed his conversations with Zala, and soon they became a couple and spent much of their free time together. Zala was completing her studies in Agricultural Engineering at Kansas State University and planned to return home to Ethiopia. She convinced Ronald to apply for a work visa in Ethiopia for a lucrative program and career in quantum software engineering in the various green energy careers in Ethiopia and the Horn of Africa. Zala encouraged Ronald to take an examination for an Ethiopian engineering company that would help him gain a work visa. Ethiopia was becoming a regional power in East Africa and the Middle East and was seeking young talent within Ethiopia and throughout the world. Many of the smartest young people were leaving their native lands to work in Ethiopia.

In the spring of 2255, Ronald McCormick discovered that he'd passed the exam and was eligible to travel and move to Ethiopia to participate in a paid one-year schooling in quantum software before beginning his career in developing software to help deliver green energy efficiently to Ethiopians and the people of East Africa. Ronald also enrolled in school to learn Amharic and Egyptian Arabic during his time in Ethiopia where he planned to join his girlfriend, Zala, and her sister, Aida. Ronald promised to start a life for himself and his girlfriend in Ethiopia and also purchase a retirement home for his grandfather, Francisco, in Jamaica.

Later, Ronald's candidate Dr. Julio Vargas successfully defeated his far-right rivals and became the junior senator of Missouri, leading to numerous progressive victories in the Midwest and the promise of greater unity in the United States. Ronald was happy to see that the United States could find a better path once again in domestic affairs and foreign relations.

Before Ronald left for Ethiopia in the fall of 2255, his grandfather, Francisco, blessed his trip, saying, "My only grandchild, you have made it out of poverty and struggle and made a new life for yourself. I am overjoyed you have chosen an Ethiopian woman as a partner, and I hope that you two find happiness in the future and have a large family. I am glad that you chose to start a new life in Ethiopia, a land of high importance for us Rastafarians. You can visit me in Jamaica whenever you like, and I hope that Jah blesses you and Zala all the days of your life."

Story 12: Martian Emancipation (25th Century)

Mario Cruz was released from Martian prison after serving almost a full Martian year. He was accused of being part of a large-scale rebellion that caused damage to some of the Martian factories. For many decades, there have been strikes due to unsafe working conditions and low pay. Many workers said that working conditions on Mars in 2432 were worse than the conditions faced by workers during the Industrial Revolution on Earth during the 1800s. Mars displayed the worst aspects of corrupt capitalism that crushed the rights of laborers who toiled under the red haze of Mars far from the safety of Earth.

Space became the new domain of the elite capitalists with limitless possibilities, while on Earth, the new progressive government of the United States had largely cut back on the excesses of the elite and was actively removing the remnants of the US oligarchy. The progressive government reversed the policies of the oligarchy that previously wreaked havoc on the populace of the United States during the last five centuries. When over eighty percent of the US population fell to the lower middle class and poor class status in the twenty-third century, numerous politicians, advocating for progressive taxation and the end of corporate control of congress, began to win throughout the United States.

The US colonies on Mars were the first Martian colonies to allow Martian births while the colonies of the United Arab Emirates, China, and the European Union did not allow births. Most of the early Martian births belonged to the Latino and black communities which comprised most of the labor force for the US Martian colonies. Some of the births on Mars belonged to immigrants who were promised US citizenship if they agreed to serve four-, five-, or ten-year labor contracts on Mars.

The main US Martian colony was located at the Martian lava tubes near Arsia Mons, close to the Martian equator. The colony now approached one million people. Most of the colonists were laborers who worked in a variety of fields, including construction, computer technicians, agriculture, and sanitation. Construction included myco-architecture that used fungi. Most of the poor laborers survived on meals provided by insect farms while some could afford food produced through cellular agriculture. Water was mostly produced by melting Martian ice and was provided to all taxpayers, but workers received a weekly portion of water that they could not exceed. The Martian Ice and Water Company controlled most of the water manufacturing that supplied the US colonies.

The elite of Martian society was able to afford Earth vegetables, fruit, and processed meat that arrived through thousands of transport ships from Earth. They also could afford specialized seeds and seedlings that could produce crops on Mars. The process of terraforming Mars now included large reflectors in space that focused solar rays toward the Martian surface while various greenhouse gases, including water vapor, carbon dioxide, and methane, were continually produced. Other Martian colonies proposed sharing and partially socializing the terraforming technology to speed up the terraforming process to help create a more habitable Mars. The US Martian elite considered these proposals, however, they desired more of the funding to come from the US government while minimizing their tax rate and maintaining their increasing profits.

Mario Cruz belonged to a Puerto Rican family from Ponce that advocated for the independence of Puerto Rico. Some of his relatives were key figures in the independence movements which led to the establishment of the Republic of Puerto Rico at the beginning of the twenty-second century. Mario Cruz learned from his father, Luis, the important history of Puerto Ricans who fought for independence, and working-class issues both in Puerto Rico and in the mainland United States. Mario learned about historical figures, like Ramón Emeterio Betances and Segundo Ruiz Belvis, who were abolitionists and the architects of the *Grito de Lares* uprising against Spanish rule in Puerto Rico in the nineteenth century. He learned about men like Pedro Albizu Campos and the activities of the Young Lords in New York City and as a teenager, he learned about the Black Panthers, Martin Luther King Jr., and Cesar Chavez.

Mario advocated for increased radiation protection, higher wages, safety regulations, and the expansion of robots and androids for various duties. The European Space Agency used robots for most of its labor. His hard work and discipline earned him a position as lieutenant to the Mexican labor leader and activist, Julio Cesar Gonzalez, who was the most famous labor figure on Mars. Within two Martian years, Mario began to form the largest union in the US Martian colonies, which caught the attention of business leaders and politicians in the United States. Mario was scheduled to openly advocate for the formation of the United Martian Laborers Union in the US Congress. He was also instructed by Julio Cesar Gonzalez to petition the US government for the formation of a democratic Martian government to help enforce additional regulations for the safety and well-being of all people within the US Martian colonies.

The director of the US colonies on Mars was supported by the Martian elites and by the conservative minority in the United States. Director Hampton was appointed by the various company owners on Mars just as the previous directors were. The Martian colonies were pitched to be egalitarian and the best form of meritocracy during the early twenty-second century but quickly devolved into the worst forms of hyper-capitalism by the twenty-second century. The directors were from wealthy families, and they grew wealthier by turning a blind eye toward the degradation of daily life for the poor laborers. The laborers were initially promised wealth and adventure but soon discovered that although they earned more money than in the poor nations of their origins, their daily life and safety had significantly worsened.

Conditions in the factories on Mars were worse than in Industrial Age Europe and the early twentieth-century United States. Society on Mars was now defined as a kind of neo-feudalism by some political scientists. The Martian elite influenced Martian politics and controlled most of the lands and housing units of the laborers. Life for Martian laborers was becoming increasingly worse and more dangerous. The decreasing standard of living caught the attention of the US press and soon spread throughout Latin America and the world. The large working class supplied by mostly Latin American immigrants was now beginning to decrease, and the various Martian corporations attempted to speed up work production as they searched for other exploitable workers on Earth.

As Latin American nations made significant progress in standard of living, education, and environmental protection, fewer Latinos traveled to the United States, and by the early twenty-fourth century, fewer Latino laborers arrived on Mars, and increasing numbers of laborers arrived from less developed African and Southeast Asian nations. The Martian elites became increasingly worried as the United States government became increasingly progressive, leading to the election of the social democrat and biologist President Marcos Alvarez. The Martian elite became increasingly brutal as they feared their power was now threatened. Previous rebellions were suppressed through corporate propaganda and secret assassinations, however, if the US government and activists became involved, labor reforms would soon come to fruition.

Most of the laborers demanded direct democracy and an expansion of the Martian council. The fight against the Martian elite was now supported by a majority of the people in the United States and Latin America. The Mexican government was in the beginning stages of creating a Martian colony, and they invited Latinos to work in their colony, which put additional pressure on the Martian elite as they searched for new exploitable workers. The Mexican government became an enemy of the Martian elite when they publicly spoke against the abuses the Martian elite had committed and began to support Julio Cesar Gonzalez.

These developments further threatened the elites, and assassinations of labor leaders had increased within the last fifty Earth years. Some of the rebels were violent anarchists, however, the majority of the assassinated labor leaders had been falsely accused of violent acts. Most of the assassinations were portrayed as accidents by various liberal and far-right governments that received bribes to keep silent. This quickly ended during the current administration, however, Mario's life was threatened, and he was advised to promptly leave Mars for Earth.

Mario Cruz quickly called his girlfriend, Anusha, as soon as he was released from prison. Anusha was from the Indian state of Kerala, and she'd earned a special visa to work on Mars as a software developer on a short-term contract. Mario was born in Puerto Rico and qualified for a special visa because Puerto Ricans born in Puerto Rico no longer qualified for US citizenship after the independence and the Republic of Puerto Rico were declared. Mario had met Anushka eight Earth Years before when they were both twenty years old. Mario was quickly attracted to her dark brown Indian skin, long, jet-black hair, and enchanting eyes. Anusha fell in love with Mario's work ethic and strong moral character, and they soon began a relationship before they traveled to Mars.

Anusha was relieved to hear her boyfriend's voice, and between anxious gasps, she exclaimed, "Mario, *mi amor*, please leave on the next shuttle to Earth. I asked a few of my coworkers to hack into the computer system, and we discovered plans to destroy the current labor movement on Mars. You were listed among the names to face serious repercussions if you remain on Mars. Your leader, Julio Cesar Gonzalez, is to be assassinated but we don't know in what way they are planning on killing him. Some secret US government agents are supporting the Martian labor movement, but I am not sure if President Alvarez will publicly call for regulations on Mars and the formation of a new Martian government. We are already receiving information from the Indian government to leave Mars as soon as our contracts are completed. I beg you, my love, to leave as quickly as possible, and I will meet you in Puerto Rico when I return to Earth, *amor*."

Mario replied, "I will inform Julio Cesar Gonzalez and my friends in the movement to be careful. I wish to stay, but I fear you are right. It is too dangerous for me on Mars, and I do not want to go through another trial that will cost me too much. The union members promised to support my lawyers, but I believe my life is in danger, and I will leave it in the hands of the people and president of the United States."

Several months later, Mario returned to Earth where he was met by the US media, which asked him numerous questions. He learned that the labor leader, Julio Cesar

Gonzalez, was assassinated, and the new leader of the Martian labor movement was now the Filipino sanitation activist, Roberto Acuña. Mario was soon advised to travel to Washington D.C. on a direct invitation from President Marcos Alvarez. Mario Cruz was provided security and lawyers with the help of the government. His immediate family members in Puerto Rico were also provided security with the permission of the Puerto Rican government. Mario was to testify against various Martian companies and scientists after President Marcos Alvarez publicly spoke against the Martian companies and declared the formation of a new Martian government.

President Marcos Alvarez was provided information regarding scientists and their illegal experimentation on laborers to study the long-term impact of life on Mars and the medical concerns caused by births on Mars. These studies were to be used to help develop long-term medications, new genetically engineered solutions, and biotech to aid the elite to comfortably live long-term on Mars. An investigation was launched into illegal experimentation on Martian laborers and their offspring on Mars. Sealed documents would be opened, and those responsible would be punished. President Marcos Alvarez was aware of the shameful history of the United States and its experimentation on vulnerable communities, and he desperately sought to create a new progressive United States through his domestic and foreign policies.

President Marcos Alvarez and Vice-President Rashida James supported the Martian labor movement. President Alvarez was of Mexican ancestry and sympathized with Julio Cesar Gonzalez. The Alvarez administration formed a coalition administration that appointed progressive members of other parties, including the Socialist Alternative leader and economist, Sonia Singh, as Labor Secretary, and the Dominican-American leader of the Green Party, Julieta Hernandez, as director of the Environmental Protection Agency. President Marcos Alvarez understood the ideas of compromise and coalition building, and he was supported by most US citizens against the Martian elite and quickly ordered government agents to leave for the U.S. Martian colonies. President Marcos Alvarez revealed to Mario that he would publicly speak against the Martian government and establish a functioning democracy and appoint a governor on Mars that would remove the power the Martian elite had established during many generations of corruption.

In 2345, Mario became a celebrity in the U.S. and amongst Martian civil rights movements. In San Juan, Puerto Rico, Mario was asked to make a public statement. He became a labor leader in Puerto Rico and was engaged to Anusha who moved to Ponce, Puerto Rico, where she planned on building a new life with her future husband. During the *Grito de Lares* celebration in San Juan, Puerto Rico, Mario addressed a crowd of people who came to see him speak. After several important Puerto Rican politicians and celebrities spoke, Mario was called to address the crowd.

A smile appeared on his face as he slowly began to speak. "I am happy to stand here with my fiancée, Anusha. Without her, I would not have survived my adventures on Mars. She is from the beautiful and ancient land of India. The land that some of the European explorers believed they had reached when they settled in our brother nation, the Dominican Republic. I have learned much from her, and she and her coworkers helped in our labor struggle on Mars."

The crowd cheered, and after a brief pause, Mario continued, "I remained strong during my imprisonment because I am a strong *Boricua*, and my *Boricua* people are strong. I have the blood of fighters running through my veins. Puerto Rico was once a colony of Spain and then became a territory of the United States for many generations before we finally declared our independence. We had freedom fighters who fought against the United States, and we also had Puerto Ricans who fought with the United States against their enemies and enriched her culture. The United States had a long unfortunate history of imperialism in Latin America, but now the United States has started a new chapter and has begun a new relationship with Puerto Rico and Latin America. The administration of President Marcos Alvarez has embraced economic rights throughout Latin America, and we now have an opportunity to use our resources to uplift our people without the need for warfare. It is this US government that I became enamored with, and it is this US administration that offered me and my coworkers help and brought freedom to Mars. Perhaps, in the future, Puerto Rico and other Latin American nations will develop their respective space programs after our necessities are fully met. Education, hard work, and a great society will help Puerto Ricans and the nations of the world as we reach out into space as brothers and sisters."

The crowd erupted in applause as Mario Cruz passionately kissed Anusha. Anusha waved to the crowd, and they cheered "*Otra*! *Otra*! *Otra*!" and Mario gave the crowd what they wanted and kissed his fiancée again. He did not wish to return to Mars, but perhaps his children and grandchildren would experience a more welcoming Mars, full of opportunities based on merit. History was now written, and hopefully, people would learn from it. Mario looked into Anusha's eyes and was convinced that she was the woman he would marry and start a family with. A joyous feeling enveloped his spirit as he looked toward the Puerto Rican horizon and the Caribbean sunset.

Story 13: Seas of Titan (27th Century)

Salomon Ochoa remembered when he reached the surface up from the depths of the methane and ethane lake on Titan. The images of Titan's ice mountains, rivers, and lakes reminded him of Earth, and the sight of Saturn and its majestic rings reminded Salomon that he was alone, far away from home. It was his last moment of hope, joy, and awe. Now all of his happiness drained away into sheer despair.

Salomon Ochoa was in a space shuttle that doubled as a submarine. He was the only man who volunteered and qualified to go on the mission to Titan. The Dominican Space Agency was attempting to land a man on the farthest body in the galaxy yet to be explored. The farthest that a human being had traveled into space was when an astronaut sent by the China National Space Administration completed one orbit around Jupiter before returning to Earth. Salomon Ochoa brought glory to the Dominican Space Agency when he reached Saturn's moon Titan and remained on Titan as it orbited around Saturn, making Salomon the farthest space traveler to date.

It was an ambitious project, which also included researching Titan's soil and water. Salomon's starship soon malfunctioned, and his main magnetoplasma engines shut down. He could not fully power his backup engines, and he tried to troubleshoot the problem. Salomon soon beached his ship. Saturn's largest moon had a thick atmosphere covered in an orange-reddish haze. Titan was composed of an ice crust and a subsurface layer of ammonia-rich liquid water. He still had hoped to fix the problem back then, however, now, it appeared that he would die on Titan. A poetic death, Salomon thought as new tears flowed down the dried trails of the numerous tears he'd shed on Titan.

Titan was discovered by Christiaan Huygens in 1655, who is considered among the greatest scientists. Salomon studied the history of Titan's discovery years before he submitted his application for this mission. Ever since Salomon was a child, he dreamed of working for the Dominican Space Agency. He was born in Baní, in the province of Peravia in the Dominican Republic, to a working-class family. Although Salomon was not from a wealthy family, he was able to raise his wealth due to policies that were enacted during the Dominican Progressive Era. The Progressive Era of the second half of the twenty-second century brought numerous reforms to the Dominican Republic that greatly improved the lives of all Dominicans. The Dominican Republic created a world-class universal healthcare system, affordable education, and numerous careers in green energy, which transformed the nation into the pearl of the Caribbean.

The Dominican Republic improved technologically and soon joined other nations in space. The Dominican Space Agency advanced during the twenty-fourth century, leading to the first manned Moon landing and later the first manned mission to Mars within the Caribbean. By the early twenty-sixth century, the Dominican Republic began preparations to send a man or woman to the farthest reaches of the solar system. The United States, UAE, and China sent manned missions to Jupiter and Ganymede while China currently went as far as sending a robotic mission to Saturn. The Dominican Republic reached as far as Mars, however, the Dominicans now wanted to restart their space program with a bold new mission. The Dominicans desired to simply send a man or woman to the deepest part of the solar system, and they chose to target the Kraken Mare Sea on Titan.

Thousands qualified for the basic requirements after taking rigorous physical exams and tests in a variety of sciences. Salomon enjoyed sports as a youth, particularly basketball, but he spent most of his time learning the mysteries of nature. Salomon excelled in Physics, Mathematics, and Chemistry, and he earned two bachelor's degrees in Physics and Chemistry. After serving in the Dominican military for two years, he qualified for entrance into the Dominican Space Academy at the age of twenty-six.

During his time in college, Salomon met a young woman named Soraya from Cabral, Barahona. Soraya was a young elementary school Science teacher who caught his eye when he was visiting his grandmother in Cabral. She was a friend of the family, and he spotted her eating *kenepas*, after Sunday service one afternoon. She was wearing a long, white dress and her beautiful brown skin and brown hair caught his attention. She appeared to have a large amount of native Taino ancestry which manifested in her cheekbones and Asiatic eyes. They soon became a couple and married when Salomon entered the Dominican Space Academy.

Salomon and Soraya had two children after Salomon's first two missions to the Latin American Lunar Colony—a daughter named Estrella and a son named Arsenio. Right before Estrella entered preschool, Salomon applied and was accepted for the mission to Titan. Salomon was guaranteed that he, his wife, his children, and his grandchildren would receive a substantial increase in their basic income. They would receive free lifetime health coverage in the elite Dominican healthcare package and would also enjoy free college in all Dominican universities and the ability to attend elite international universities. They would also enjoy the benefits of cutting-edge technology, free housing, life-extending genetic treatments, and five free trips to the Lunar and Martian colonies. The offer was a great deal, and Salomon's concerns for the safety of his own life lessened while his thoughts on his family's well-being became his primary goal.

Salomon remembered everything the Dominican government promised his family, and he signed the contract. Soraya fought with Salomon, and through fits of rage and tear-filled eyes, she even threatened to divorce him if he chose the mission. Salomon begged his wife not to leave him and attempted to comfort her by saying that she and their family would live a life of luxury that very few would ever experience in their lives. Now Salomon remembered Soraya's tears and fears, and he felt that same fear which developed into despair as the Dominican Space Agency began to run out of possible solutions to rescue him. They attempted to contact any nearby Mexican space shuttles, but none of them could make the trip within the three years needed before Salomon's food stores would run out.

Salomon contemplated terminating his life. Salomon had never experienced this degree of sadness before. The last message that he transmitted to his wife was a detailed description of his ordeal and his plans to continue his search for solutions before ending his life. He instructed his wife on how to raise his children and sent her a detailed message that would be delivered to their children at the proper time. The message broke Salomon's heart, and he cried frequently until he had no more tears to shed.

Salomon delivered his plans of suicide to mission control in La Romana, and they advised him to wait for further instructions. They also advised him on various coping methods, including using THC vapor or psychoactive agents, which were only restricted to extreme situations. Salomon felt a deep hole in his soul—he might never see the Earth again, and he would never see the faces of his lovely wife and children. Titan would be the last thing he would ever know, and his depression deepened when he realized that his body would remain on Titan possibly for eternity. He thought about how his wife would handle the last message he transmitted to her. Salomon was nervous she would tell her children and his family. The thoughts tortured him, leading to nightmares whenever he slept.

He would sometimes have pleasant dreams about his childhood in the Dominican Republic. His joy at learning English and Arabic before his sixteenth birthday. It was required for Dominicans to learn a foreign language, and most Dominicans were encouraged to be trilingual at the minimum. Salomon chose English and Arabic, and he read many of the classic books of the Middle East. He dreamed of traveling through the Maglev trains to the northern cities of the Dominican Republic and through the skyways connecting the islands of the Greater Antilles. He remembered dancing with the beautiful women in Santo Domingo and his early training at the Dominican Space Academy. He thought about the underwater training at Lake Enriquillo that prepared him for long durations in space. These dreams brought Salomon brief respite from his nightmares and the reality of his dreadful existence in Titan—waiting to die through his design or by time itself. Tears and despair would envelop him once more.

The director of the Titan mission, Ramon Ortega, personally sent Salomon a message. "I am proud that you accepted this mission. I am overjoyed that you have been patient during this painful time. We are still trying to find a way to rescue you;

we can reach you in about two years, however, you will have to consume less, and it will be difficult. You will have to find strength within yourself and contact us if you are having a particularly hard time mentally."

Salomon said, "I will continue to maintain my hope during this time. You must find a way for me to get me home. I already made the dreadful decision of notifying my wife that I am considering taking my own life. Please send someone to my home to help her through this difficult time, and make sure the rest of my family members and friends do not know about my predicament. Rumors spread, and it could lead to more misery. Please make sure you follow through with our agreement and provide my wife, children, and possible grandchildren with all the rewards guaranteed by this expedition. Also, after all, I have been through, you should build me a small statue."

Salomon meant his last statement as a joke but after Ramon Ortega laughed, he seriously considered it. As time continued to pass, Salomon noticed his food stores were lower than previously estimated. He was disgusted by the genetically modified vegetables and fruits and the insect paste he survived on and was growing desperate. As several more notifications from mission control appeared that a rescue would not arrive, he began recording another letter to his wife.

This time, he was committed to taking his life, and the deepest despair surrounded him. To make matters worse, he'd recently received Soraya's response, and she was devastated. She reminded him that he was the best partner God could have ever delivered for her and that she would go to church and pray for his safety. She said she would soon inform her children about his decision. Salomon wondered how he would end his life. Perhaps it would be through the aerosol provided to him that delivered a cocktail of noxious gasses that would make him lose consciousness and eventually numb his nerve endings before stopping his heart. Or maybe he would inject psychoactive chemicals to slowly leave him in a state of bliss before he passed away.

He was debating whether to send his last message to his wife when he suddenly received a notification from mission control. Director Ramon Ortega slowly spoke in the message, "I am happy you have made it through this ordeal, and I want you to breathe deeply and relax before I give you the good news."

After a brief pause, the recording continued, "The Chinese have a secret manned mission to Saturn, and they promised to change their mission plans to help you. We sent them your coordinates several months ago, and they are on their way. They will reach you soon when the orbit of Titan is closest to the Sun. We have sent the updates of your rescue to your wife so that she will be updated long before you send her this information. You will receive a large bonus in pay, and you will be given two-year paid leave to spend time with your wife and children upon your return."

Salomon would maintain his title as the farthest human traveler from Earth. He would be rescued by the Chinese spacecraft Divine Horizon 5 and Captain Tang Mingmei. Salomon was excited to meet the famous Chinese captain and impress her with his basic Mandarin abilities. Perhaps he would visit the U.A.E. or China with his family during his paid leave. Or perhaps he would take his children to places they wanted to go to. Soraya and Estrella wanted to visit the Great Pyramids in Egypt and enjoy a vacation in Mexico. Salomon was interested in Mexico or Guatemala because he enjoyed Mayan history and culture and desired to visit the Mayan ruins.

Salomon Ochoa was scheduled to return to the Latin American Lunar Colony by October 2650, and after being debriefed by the Dominican Space Agency, he returned to the Dominican Republic by December 2650. The Dominican Space Agency would build a small statue for Salomon Ochoa in Bani, and he would be an instant celebrity after the full information regarding his ordeal was made public. He gained the respect of the Dominican people and people throughout Latin America and possibly the world. Salomon was grateful for what was to come to him when he returned to his beautiful Quisqueya, however, all he wanted was to kiss his wife and embrace his children once again. Later, he would remember his additional months of depression and sadness in the cold and deadly Titan as he awaited rescue. He also remembered that a small amount of hope had carried him through. Hope was all Salomon had needed and everything he would ever need in the future.

Story 14: Ace Boon (21st Century)

Maximo Garcia was everything a young Dominican man was supposed to be. He was tall, strong, tough, athletic, and good with the ladies. He was a B student and was on the basketball team. Maximo was one of the most popular seniors at Benjamin N. Cardozo High School and during his junior year, he dated a smart Indian young lady from Guyana named Priya, then during the summer, he began dating a beautiful Salvadorean student named Gloria, before beginning a romance with a stunning Colombian student named Marisol during his senior year. Maximo had many friends and the attention of many ladies at his school and was fun to be around.

In the year 2084, life in the United States was difficult, particularly in the inner cities. Despite some of the initiatives by progressives in Congress to lower the age of Medicare to the age of fifty, and despite the addition of a public option to Medicare, the quality of life for many people in the inner cities did not improve significantly. Maximo was the only child of his mother, Altagracia. Altagracia raised Maximo mostly by herself because she remained separated from her husband, Alejandro, who was currently in the Dominican Republic. Alejandro continued to send money to his Altagracia and Maximo, however, it only provided the basics. To supplement his mother's income, Maximo began work at sixteen.

During his senior year, Maximo was accepted to several schools, including Stony Brook University and Binghamton University, and due to his high SAT scores, he was also accepted to Cornell University and Tufts University in Massachusetts. Maximo desired to attend Tufts University and wanted to major in International Relations. His goal was to graduate from Tufts University and attend the Fletcher School where he hoped to learn the skills to become a Foreign Service Officer. His dreams required money that he didn't have, and although he was one of the best baseball players in Queens, he could not secure a baseball scholarship. Maximo's luck would change when he was presented with an economic opportunity during the spring semester of his senior year.

Maximo Garcia was approached by several researchers during a visit to the NewYork-Presbyterian Queens Hospital after reading his medical records. Maximo had recently turned eighteen in February, and they asked him if he wanted to participate in an experiment that would reward him with over 200,000 dollars. Maximo requested that he also receive partial tuition assistance if he chose to enroll in Tufts University, and they agreed. Maximo soon signed the contract after consulting with his mother. The research was performed by the Department of Defense and was held in several inner cities, including Philadelphia, Chicago, and Baltimore with a total of 100 test subjects. The government was secretly testing an advanced experimental technology similar to the neural link, which would mentally link strong individuals and depressed individuals. The device being tested was called the limbic ring. The limbic ring focused on the study and improvement of the behavioral system.

The neural link company was owned by the grandchildren of Elon Musk and helped improve the conditions of patients with neuromuscular injuries and genetic disorders. The Department of Defense desired to use the limbic ring to improve the PTSD of combat veterans. Paul Moretti was the lead researcher and inventor of the limbic ring, and his previous inventions had caught the attention of the Department of Defense. Paul Moretti was born and raised in Massapequa Park Long Island, New York. He was a seventy-year-old scientist and proud Italian-American from New York who became wealthy by his early thirties through his talent and hard work. The limbic ring would potentially be his greatest invention, and he worked hard to uncover the mysteries of the human brain.

Paul Moretti led a team of five scientists working to deliver the product for the military and possibly for citizens in need of mental help. The government was studying the impact of linking mentally fit individuals with depressed individuals. The suicide and depression rate in the year 2084, among middle-aged white males in the US, was rapidly increasing as joblessness and abuses of pharmaceutical drugs increased. The black and Latino suicide rates were constant and were lower than the white suicide and depression rates despite the Latino and Black communities living in comparatively worse socio-economic conditions. These observations fueled the interests of scientists and motivated the scientists to research the limbic region of the brains of the people that lived in the inner cities. The patients were paired with a partner, and some test subjects were informed not to have any contact with their partners while some were allowed full contact. Maximo was instructed to have minimal contact with his partner, named Javier Huaman.

Javier was a young, shy Peruvian who was the opposite of Maximo. He wore glasses and his clothes and was introspective. He wanted to go to Cambria Heights Academy because of the school's dress code. In junior high, he was bullied because of his choice of clothing and his awkwardness, but at Cambria Heights Academy, his limited sense of style was one less thing to be made fun of. Javier's older sister Monica graduated from Cardozo High School and was in her freshman year at Queensborough Community College. Javier confided in his older sister and good friend. Other than his sister, Javier had few friends at school and stayed mostly to himself.

Maximo soon met Javier at the hospital, and they were informed about the quick medical procedure and what they were to expect in the following months. Maximo didn't know who Javier was, but he knew his older sister, Monica, who had graduated from their high school the previous year. Monica was a respected young lady and was one of the few women who had turned down his advances. Javier recognized Maximo instantly due to his popularity in Hollis and his brief association with his older sister. Soon they were brought to the hospital and a small insertion was made into the skulls of Maximo and Javier and a specialized chip connected directly to the limbic regions in their brains. They belonged to completely different social circles, and they were allowed to exchange information, however, they were not to reveal their involvement in this experiment, and they were to be monitored at all times by the researchers. After the surgery, both boys were anxious regarding what they were about to experience, but their fears were assuaged by the scientists and doctors who operated on them and were tasked to monitor them in the following months.

For six months, both Maximo and Javier were connected and monitored by the researchers. The first few weeks went by, and the guys didn't feel any difference during their day-to-day activities. After about the second month, it was Javier who noticed a few differences. He participated a little more in class, to the joy of his teachers, and began talking with more of his classmates. Javier's teachers understood he was a brilliant student but they had previously advised his parents that he needed to get involved in more social clubs and develop friendships to have success in college. Now it seemed to Javier's teachers that their advice had come to fruition. He joined the science club and quickly outperformed the other members.

Maximo was enjoying his last few months as a high school student. Soon, he would have a ticket to his dream school and a new journey at Tufts University. Perhaps he could spend some of his money on a long vacation with his mother to the Dominican Republic. He could also spend some time with his father and inform him of his plans to attend Tufts University. The Saturday before Easter, Maximo was walking with Marisol through the streets of Richmond Hill, Queens. He wanted to introduce Marisol to Indian cuisine, and he invited her to his favorite restaurant. They both were seated, and Maximo ordered his favorite dish, lamb tikka masala. Marisol finally decided to order tandoori chicken.

They began to talk about high school and their future goals, and for the first time, Maximo began to miss Queens, his friends, and Marisol. Maximo looked at Marisol's light brown eyes, and beautiful blonde hair as he spoke, "I will be going to Massachusetts for school. I will be going to Tufts University. Everything seems to be moving fast suddenly. I am happy, but I feel some anxiety and some sadness."

Marisol was surprised by Maximo's words as she replied, "This is what you wanted, Maximo. You have to do what makes you happy and pursue your goals. I will probably go to Queens Community College. I want to stay close to my family and study to be a teacher. I am sad I was never your girlfriend, and I know you probably were not looking for a serious relationship."

Maximo looked at Marisol and within his heart, he did feel a deeper connection and realized he did want her to be his girlfriend. The timing was less than ideal, however, as he would be going away for school. Maximo decided to be honest with Marisol and he replied, "I like you, Marisol, and I considered asking you to be my girlfriend. I'm not sure we can stay together after I go to school, but we can always stay in touch. You are a nice girl, and whatever happens, I want you to know that."

Maximo felt a deeper affection toward Marisol, and he kissed her deeply after their meal. Attracting the attention of the opposite sex came easy for Maximo because of his charm and his physical size, however, he'd never developed a deep connection with a woman. Maximo had intimate relations with three girls before his senior year, and many of his classmates believed he had more sexual conquests. Maximo did not feel the need to exaggerate his status with the opposite sex as opposed to the other boys who felt they needed to do so, although they were inexperienced. What Maximo was yet to experience was a deep romantic relationship and the hard work and sacrifices needed to maintain one. Perhaps Marisol would become his first girlfriend. Maximo wondered how long it would last.

Javier was communicating more with his parents and participating more in school as he quickly rose to be one of the best students at his school. Javier even began to speak to girls that he was attracted to, and he began to walk upright. He was skinny and appeared smaller than he was, but now he stood at almost five foot eight but appeared six feet due to his increasing confidence. Javier was a little flamboyant now, and his personality began to manifest in his conversation and clothing choices. Javier attracted female classmates, the smart, conservative type of girls that Javier felt comfortable with. Javier ate and slept better, and he began to experience joyous dreams. Soon he embraced who he was and understood the man he could someday become.

Maximo was always respectful just as his parents taught him to be. He was sometimes careless with his romantic adventures, but he cared for the ladies he was with. Now, he thought more deeply about how his behavior impacted others, and he spent more time in self-reflection; perhaps he was maturing as he became a young adult. His dreams were not as pleasant as before. Some dreams were full of tension and fright; some involved various types of sexual activity that Maximo did not find appealing. Sometimes, he would have these odd dreams, and then soon it appeared they belonged to Javier. Maximo thought that they were part of Javier's subconscious thoughts and anxieties. Javier appeared to have feminine mannerisms; perhaps they contributed to Javier's shyness and depression.

These thoughts triggered memories from Maximo's past that troubled him, including a bad memory regarding his older cousin Vicente in the Dominican Republic. He was about eight years old, and he remembered leaving church on a hot Sunday in July. Maximo was in his father's hometown in Azua when he saw Vicente beaten up by some local boys who were jealous because he had the attention of some young ladies from the church. The bullies wanted Vicente to admit he was a homosexual, and he desperately denied this fact as he ran and called for help. Embarrassed at having a gay and cowardly cousin, Maximo never helped his cousin or asked his family members for help. With some negative thoughts resurfacing, Maximo received a call that informed him he would end the experiment in early September. Maximo was relieved.

In July, Maximo had graduated from Cardozo High School and was now preparing to leave for Tufts. He was spending most of his time with his girlfriend, Marisol, and he purchased a flight for him and his mother to the Dominican Republic for Christmas 2084. Director Paul Moretti personally contacted Maximo and Javier and informed them that they produced one of the best results and contributed data that would lead to the completion of the limbic ring for use in the military and veterans within five years and civilian use within ten years.

There would be changes to the limbic-ring system and they would continue to alter the technology. There were a few reported downsides, including extreme nightmares and a sort of subconscious leaking, which impacted the consciousness of users, however, none of the participants in the study experienced any serious side effects. Maximo would receive his money in two installments. One-half of the money would be sent in October, and the second would be sent in January 2085.

Maximo was informed that he would be legally allowed to speak about his involvement in this experiment in two years. Maximo was to have his implant removed in early September before he moved to Massachusetts. During the summer, Maximo would spend time in Queens and planned to visit his cousins in the Bronx. It appeared the limbic ring enhanced Maximo's life and made him more thoughtful regarding his future and empathetic toward the people in his life. Javier appeared to make the greatest gains during the last four months, which made Maximo happy with the experiment.

Maximo planned to purchase a used Japanese electric car in the following week. He wanted to buy a new car, but his mother advised him to save his money and build a future. Maximo's future was bright, and life was good, however, he was haunted by memories of his past. The limbic ring had changed his perspective on a variety of issues, and one morning, Maximo fought through tears as he picked up the phone to call Javier. Maximo wanted to talk with Javier and tell him everything would be alright.

Story 15: Bombero (21st Century)

Luis Estrada finished his first year as a prison firefighter. He qualified for the inmate firefighter program which gave prisoners a new opportunity in life. Luis learned that California Governor Gavin Newsom had signed legislation on September 14, 2020, to expunge the records of nonviolent offenders who had fought fires for the state while in prison, allowing them to pursue careers as firefighters and first responders once released. It was a great program for prisoners who wanted to change the direction of their lives. Luis desperately desired to change his life and become a good citizen. He wanted to prove to his parents and his girlfriend that he was the man they expected him to be.

Luis Estrada remembered that when he was helping his childhood friend, Raul, move his chemicals into a wooden shack nestled in the forests near Sacramento, Raul was manufacturing synthetic drugs, and Luis, who was desperate for money, agreed to help him move his chemicals and manufacture the drugs. Luis had agreed to sell drugs for a year or two until he saved enough money to enter a trade school. He had been desperate for money to provide for his girlfriend, Marlene, who was pregnant with their first child. One night, Raul had an accident that caused a chemical fire that spread through the forest during the particularly hot summer of 2028. Climate change worsened conditions in California and caused frequent fires throughout the state. Raul survived and was quickly jailed, and he and Luis were charged with arson. Raul was sentenced to over eight years in state prison while Luis was sentenced to five years in prison.

Luis remembered the shame that his arrest brought to his girlfriend and his family, and he promised them that he would turn his time in jail into a lesson learned. Marlene was a beautiful Honduran American bank teller who fell in love with Luis after his repeated advances. Marlene's parents disapproved of Luis due to his activities in the streets with people they considered unsavory, and Luis felt he had proven her parents correct. Luis also remembered the sacrifices that his parents had made for him. His father, Andres, was an immigrant from Leon, Nicaragua, who was a factory worker, and his mother, Margarita, was a Mexican American who worked in various grocery stores in Sacramento. Margarita moved from Yakima, Washington in search of better opportunities in California and soon met Andres. They were married and had two children, Armando who married a Puerto Rican woman, named Juanita, and moved to Los Angeles, and Luis. Luis was provided with the best life a lower-middle-income family could afford, and now he felt he'd betrayed his family and sought to rectify his past actions.

Luis enjoyed the outdoors, and he became interested in the inmate firefighter program. He was recommended to the inmate firefighter program and was assigned to the Growlersburg Conservation Camp in Georgetown, California. Luis excelled in class and field training, and soon he began fighting fires with his fellow inmates and earning $1.50 an hour. It was low pay, but he felt like a free man fighting fires in the California forests. The work was difficult, especially during the summer months when they wore two layers of clothing and carried close to fifty pounds of gear while cutting lines sometimes near raging fires.

During the summer of 2031, Luis was battling a massive fire ravaging northern California. Luis and his fellow inmates faced the devastating fire for five days. He did particularly well and saved two California State firefighters when they were trapped by two fallen trees and the flames that enveloped them. Luis carried the firefighters to safety, earning him the respect of his fellow inmates and the California State firefighters. Because of his excellent service, he was informed he would leave the prison by late 2032 and his criminal record would be expunged. Luis would also be offered a position with the California State Fire Department and possibly earn over 100,000 dollars per year if he gained experience and seniority.

It was the beginning of the summer of 2032, and the California wildfires worsened due to climate change. Luis' firstborn, whom he named Leonidas, was now two years of age, and he deeply desired to be a good father to him and a good husband to his wife. He spoke to Marlene on the phone about his desire to marry her and have a good and stable family life. Luis and Marlene were both twenty-two, and he desired for them to build a future together. Marlene and their child were living in her parent's home, and Luis promised her that he would be able to afford a down payment on a home within several years. He discovered a renewed determination, and it manifested in his performance as a firefighter. His performance caught the attention of other firefighters throughout northern California, including a native of the Yurok tribe named Steven Ray.

Steven Ray was a distinguished firefighter with an impressive record of performance and an advocate for environmental regulations. Steven was sixty-two years of age and had served the state of California for over forty years. He was a member of the Yurok tribe of northern California and was raised learning his native customs and philosophies. Steven married a woman named Ruby from the Hupa tribe, and they had two sons, Jason and James Ray. Steven saw a bright future for Luis, and he began to advise him before he was released from prison.

After another long day fighting fires, Steven Ray congratulated Luis and asked the correction officers if he could spend a few hours with him before he checked in for the evening. Steven shook Luis' hand and said," Luis, I am proud of the progress you have made. As you know, I am a native man from a people with a long history here in California. I am a member of the Yurok tribe, and we share a common history with the Karuk tribe. Our people live around the Klamath River, and I was raised fishing and respecting our environment. I was born in the 1970s and witnessed the economic downturn after the Reagan administration, and the cutting of environmental regulations that led to increasing temperatures due to climate change. My wife was an environmental lawyer, and she fought to make sure that the river flowed unhindered and there was no pollution in our lands. I have been fighting monstrous fires that are now increasing in intensity, and hopefully, you and the next generation will not only fight the fires but advocate for increased environmental regulations and conversion toward green energy."

Luis replied, "I do not know much about the tribes in the United States. I know my parents have indigenous blood from Mexico and Nicaragua. My girlfriend is also a *mestiza* from Honduras. She is a beautiful *Catracha* from a good home that took a chance on me. Her parents were born in Honduras, and they both arrived in California as children. They are upper-middle class now, and her dad is a banker. I was born in the United States, and I never took advantage of the opportunities that my parents provided for me. My girlfriend's parents did not approve of me, and I felt I proved them right by making the wrong decisions. Now I feel that I have a purpose and a future, and I am looking to become the best firefighter I can be. I feel I have a chance to become a great husband and father, and that gives me all the motivation I need. I also want to learn more about climate change and green energy. Anything I can do to contribute to the safety of my community, I will do."

Steven smiled and replied, "You belong to people rich in culture. The Latinos are a mixture of different races and cultures of people that also share a greater culture and speak various tongues, including the shared languages of Spanish and Portuguese. The Mangue-speaking people, which include the Chorotega people of Nicaragua, Honduras, and Costa Rica, as well as the Pipil-Nicarao, are part of your ancestry. You have a proud and rich central American history just like my people do here in California. Our bloodlines belong to the original people and societies of these lands, and we must provide for our families and our people. You come from a proud people, and you must find that pride within yourself so that you can be the husband and father that you strive to be. To be great in the career you are about to embark on, you must learn about nature and the forest. You must understand that fire is a natural part of life and learn about how to think ahead and respect nature so that you will not clash with it."

Luis nodded in agreement as he said, "I hope that when I am a man of your age I can also have your wisdom, Mr. Ray. I am ready to return to society and be a better man than I was before I entered the fire-fighting program. I am happy to start a new course in my life and my relationship with my family. I spoke with my mother last week, and she asked me if I was sure about my choice of being a firefighter, and I said yes, I want to be a *bombero.*

Steven Ray smiled and embraced Luis and said, "When I was a young man, I was full of doubts and sometimes anger that led me to make bad decisions, as you have. Depression and not knowing what paths you want to take in life can lead a young man down a road of peril. Many indigenous people have suffered from alcoholism and drug abuse, which is why I sought to counsel the youth and discover the potential within them. You made a mistake, and you learned from your errors. It is good that you learned from your mistake now while you are young so that you won't repeat the same mistakes when you are older. It is wise that you also learn from the mistakes of others and listen to the advice of respected elders. You are about to rejoin society, and your record will be expunged. You will have a high-paying career with benefits and make your family proud. You will also have new technology soon, including improved flame-retardant fabrics and new eyewear, which we are calling fire vision, that allows you to see through heavy fires and smoke. I wish you the best, and I am looking forward to you becoming a firefighter."

Luis was excited to start his new career, and he was eager to test the new technology. The technology was invented by Steven's younger cousin David, and other natives were working with him to develop other environmental technologies. The technology would improve the abilities of the firefighters in the ongoing trouble with forest fires. Luis returned to his bed later that evening after his conversation with Steven. In the following weeks, Luis would sign various documents that officially recognized his release and the expungement of his criminal record. Luis also was heavily recruited for the fire department and was expected to begin his career at the end of the year. Luis said goodbye to his fellow inmates and began preparing for his new life. He called his family and friends and later reassured his girlfriend that he was looking forward to an engagement and marriage. Luis smiled, and for the first time in a long time, he felt relief. Life was good.

Story 16: A Distant Twilight (28th Century)

Back on Earth, the year was now 2751. Various nations of Earth had averted disaster by choosing to enrich their planet through green energy. The nations of Earth had ended the dark centuries that followed the twenty-first century where the planet had suffered through pollution and harmful climate change that led to the deaths of over a billion people. Now, humanity, with its remaining flaws, has expanded throughout the solar system and beyond. The United States discovered a habitable moon orbiting a gas giant near a star similar to the Sun and soon sent a large shuttle to the moon. The moon and the gas giant were located within the Orion arm of the Milky Way galaxy. Soon companies sent their starships after the discovery of large forests covering most of the moon and the potential to make large profits. The moon was nicknamed New Amazonia by the colonists, and companies and profits fueled interest in its colonization.

Director Miller was a slender and athletic conservative from rural Alabama who rose to a leadership position after the accidental death of Rudy Johnson in an unexplored region of this alien moon. His lieutenant was a large man from Mississippi named Brian Johnson. The moon was the largest among the three satellites belonging to a warm gas giant that orbited a star similar in size and intensity to the Sun. The moon was nearly the size of the Earth and had a thicker atmosphere, a stronger magnetic sphere, with a higher percentage of oxygen than Earth. The moon had .95 percent of the Earth's gravity, and the laborers hardly noticed a difference. New Amazonia was covered in forests like the deciduous forests on Earth, with a climate a little warmer than the Mediterranean climate on Earth. There were higher incidences of dangerous wildfires on New Amazonia, similar to the hot Earth during the twenty-third and twenty-fourth centuries, because of the hot and dry weather.

Director Michael Miller increased the cutting of the trees on the habitable moon of New Amazonia to feed the hungry market on Earth for alien wood. The wood was hard, had a pleasant odor, and was highly sought after on Earth by the rich and powerful. The varieties of alien softwood and hardwood were more durable than their counterparts on Earth and were used for construction and art. The United States was the first nation to discover and successfully land humans on New Amazonia while the Chinese were preparing to arrive within the next ten years. Companies took the lead in space exploration by the late twenty-first century, and now various US companies were preparing to arrive at this alien moon. Director Michael Miller's primary job was pacifying any threats and preparing the alien moon for permanent human settlement and the extraction of its resources.

Due to recent mysterious deaths, the United States sent various scientists, including pathologists and astrobiologists, from their country and talented individuals from other nations and throughout the colonized solar system. Martian epidemiologist Elena Reyes from the Philippines and Daniel Francois, a sixty-year-old ecologist from Haiti, were among those chosen to travel to the US colony on New Amazonia. The first two colonies experienced few fatalities and diseases, and the scientists belonging to the logging company deemed the moon safe for humans despite the less-than-ideal atmosphere. Daniel Francois quickly arrived on the planet to lead a team of scientists to explore the mysterious causes of the diseases now impacting the colonists. After over two Earth years, Daniel Francois believed he might have discovered several mysteries of the alien moon.

Xeno-geologists found similarities to various earlier periods on Earth. The oxygen level was higher than on Earth but not enough to be extremely toxic to humans although prolonged exposure to the air would cause humans to get sick due to the different concentrations of chemicals. Some of the trees were larger than the largest giant sequoia trees on Earth, with some trees believed to be thousands of Earth years in age.

The natives of this moon appeared to be huge insectoids the size of large dogs. They were largely crepuscular, performing most of their activity during twilight. Their intelligence appeared to be equivalent to that of a human child of ten years old with the most intelligent of the species having an IQ of 90. The large insects had a language that they produced with their limbs and oral cavity that sounded like clicks. The insectoids called themselves what linguists roughly translated as the beings of the trees. They appeared to be peaceful beings that rarely clashed with their human guests. The colonists, however, treated these intelligent insects harshly sometimes and used the carcasses of the insectoids for dissection without the permission of their family members. Soon the humans started examining living insectoids much to the chagrin of their communities.

Daniel Francois advocated against the mistreatment of insectoids, and he called for a restriction of harmful pollution in the environment. His involvement in social issues raised the ire of numerous businessmen and leaders, including Director Michael Miller and Lieutenant Director Brian Johnson. Brian Johnson was an admirer of the now-defunct American Christian Patriot Party that existed through the early twenty-second century until the mid-twenty-third century, and he had a large ACPP tattoo on his right arm. Although Daniel kept his political views private, he had increasing confrontations with the boisterous Brian Johnson which led to heated exchanges between the two men that worsened over time. During Daniel's visit to New Amazonia, a vicious disease began to spread, and Daniel's most recent discoveries led him into direct conflict with the leadership of the US colonial companies.

The diseased patients were given radionuclides in aerosols through positive pressure pumps into their lungs. The semiconductor portable imaging machines were able to detail the path of the oxygen within the red blood cells and their distribution through the body. Daniel doubted that the insectoids were the most intelligent species on the alien moon and began to think that the giant trees might be the most advanced species. Daniel turned his attention toward the few dendrologists available and their research, which confirmed that the giant trees were much more advanced and older than the Earth itself.

The large trees communicated through numerous chemicals that influenced the vegetation and animals within the ecosystem. The exact mechanisms that influenced the relationships between the trees and the animals were not fully understood, however, Dr. Elena Reyes recognized that the trees were responsible for the activation of viruses similar but yet more complex than the coronaviruses on Earth. Various biologists also believed the trees were impacting the psychological chemistry of the brains of the insectoids, making them impatient and more prone to violence. With this information, he believed the colonists were in danger and might need to limit the cutting of trees and decrease the number of colonists until further studies could be made on the moon's ecosystem.

Daniel Francois walked toward the main administration building within the main colonial dome. Several scientists, including Elena Reyes, joined Daniel as he spoke to various representatives of the companies that were extracting resources on the moon.

Director Michael Miller quickly welcomed the scientists and remarked, "I welcome you all to my office. Mr. Francois, you previously informed me of a certain danger to us if we continue our current activities on this planet; do your fellow scientists agree with your hypothesis?"

Daniel Francois replied, "I am afraid to say that the colonists are in imminent danger. We believe that the trees being cut down are the most advanced lifeform on this moon, and although we do not know how to directly communicate with them, we have deduced that they are troubled by the number of trees being cut down and the pollution caused by the companies. The trees appeared to have sent alarm signals that activated viruses and influenced various organisms, including insectoids. I believe that the colonists will soon suffer a disastrous situation both from disease and a possible violent confrontation with the insectoids. I believe the companies should decrease the pollution and other measures should be taken to reduce the human presence here until we can understand this moon further."

Lieutenant Director Brian Johnson was visibly annoyed, and he interjected, "You were hired as a contractor by the US government to depart Haiti and travel here with another group of scientists to tell us to shut down our operations and go home?! What experience do you have to make such a bold judgment? You are an ecologist from Haiti, a land that was nearly a desert for so long because of deforestation. A nation where hurricanes and floods caused massive devastations."

Daniel Francois was annoyed and attempted to maintain his composure as he replied, "Yes, you are right; the deforestation caused many problems in Haiti, but I was one of the main scientists who improved Haiti's environment and fought politically to remove the corruption in my government, and today, we enjoy a cleaner environment with a larger and increasing forest. I also worked on improving the US Martian colonies and found ways to increase food production. This gives me the qualifications needed that encouraged the US government to offer me a contract to come to this alien moon to advise you on how to proceed regarding the environment on this moon. I believe the colonization of this moon so far from our solar system is a brave endeavor, however, I think the US should also have sent more scientists and government officials to regulate the companies here."

Brian Johnson informed his security to escort the other scientists and guests out of the director's office before he angrily replied, "You have challenged our scientists here, and you say that we are in grave danger, and now you come here to talk to me about your political beliefs? Industry and profits are what drive space exploration, and the owners of these companies were the people who put up most of their money to fund these expeditions. You were summoned only to help improve our knowledge of ecology here and help the other scientists find a solution to our situation with these diseases."

Daniel quickly replied, "Your company-hired scientists are only here to twist data and protect your business interests, Brian. My reputation and expertise in my field was the reason why I was requested to travel to New Amazonia. Your scientists have failed to deliver accurate reports regarding the lifeforms of New Amazonia and the impact and dangers relating to continued human colonization. It is like the scientists that lied regarding climate change to protect the fossil fuel industry centuries ago on Earth. Politics is always intertwined with colonization, business, and profits. You, of all people, should know this. You are a political person, and it is clear because you wear your views on your arm."

Brian tried to interject, but Daniel continued, "I know very well the history of colonization and the atrocities committed by Europeans in Haiti, the Caribbean, and Latin America. I also understand what happened to the indigenous people who live in what is now the United States. The colonizers mistreated, enslaved, and killed the natives, fueled by ignorance, greed, and hatred. Haiti was the first nation to break from bondage and declare its independence, and the Dominican Republic declared its independence, and our island became an oasis of freedom, surrounded by enslaved islands and slavery supporting the United States before Abraham Lincoln's presidency. You sympathize with the failed American Christian Patriot Party, which was a combination of far-right groups, including neo-confederates, and conservative Christian fundamentalists. The American Christian Patriot Party was the last gasp of white supremacy in the United States. That party hid its hate and ignorance beneath the cloak of Christianity and conservatism and managed to gain the presidency and Congress for ten years before making the standard of living in the United States worse through corruption and corporate greed. If you understand your history, then I can correctly assume that if you bring these ideologies to this alien moon, you will bring destruction upon yourselves. These organisms have lived far longer than humans, and perhaps we have worn out our welcome."

Director Michael Miller stopped Brian from physically challenging Daniel as he calmed both men down. The director then exclaimed, "We are men with different perspectives and opinions. Brian has served me well as my lieutenant, and he has been aggressive in helping maintain our colony and producing the raw materials that have brought profits for the United States and our citizens. We are in the process of ordering robots and androids to replace most of our human labor so that we can avoid a disaster. We have some investments in various companies here, so our adventure here must be a success. Do you understand what I am saying, Mr. Francois?"

Daniel replied, "I understand what you say. Your investments tie you and your lieutenant to the success or failures of some of the companies here. If you die here, then your profits will mean nothing. Studying New Amazonia's ecosystem leads me to believe that the most intelligent trees formed a mutualistic relationship with the insectoids. The insectoids brought them food from other environments, including from the few seas on the moon, and they also helped the trees reproduce. The trees appeared to provide the insectoids with food and various leaves that are the insectoids' food and medicine. When the humans arrived, the trees turned against the colonists as we rapidly increased the cutting of trees and pollution. The trees altered their relationships with other organisms on New Amazonia and are now actively killing you with various airborne viruses and possibly toxic substances that have attached themselves to the food you grow here on your farms. The relationship between the mega trees and humans can be defined as parasitic. My suggestion is that you reduce the number of colonists and halt production from all companies until further notice or you will suffer grave consequences."

A palpable fear entered the director's office as various representatives began to talk amongst each other. Daniel Francois, Elena Reyes, and other scientists prepared to board one of two large starships bound for Earth. To avoid a lawsuit, Director Michael Miller informed the laborers about the possible dangers in New Amazonia. Some colonists quit their work and asked for the cancellation of their contracts and boarded the shuttles. Director Michael Miller remained, and Lieutenant Brian Johnson also remained on the moon, awaiting an increased supply of robots and androids. Daniel quickly reported his findings to US government officials who agreed to send additional shuttles to New Amazonia on a future date.

Daniel and Elena soon departed the alien moon for Earth. Before they departed, the disease had hardly spread, and many colonists disregarded Daniel's findings as alarmism and quickly returned to their normal lives. Daniel had previously requested a video recording of the colony for an update on the progression of the disease. While watching the video a month after they departed from the moon, he and the other scientists were shocked at what they saw as the disease had become an epidemic. He watched as the skin of the afflicted changed color, the faces of the colonists became distorted, and they gasped for air as their organs began to malfunction. The once-peaceful insectoids brought the human cadavers to the trees as they fed on their decomposing nutrients. The few remaining survivors were frightened and followed the directions of the increasingly aggressive insectoids. One of the survivors was Brian Johnson. The look of confidence was long gone from Brian's face, and a look of fear and despair had replaced it. Daniel felt indifferent toward the fate of Brian Johnson, however, he felt immense sadness for the tragic fate of the laborers who had sought to work and provide a better life for themselves and their families.

Everyone cried, including Daniel and Elena, and they spoke about the horrors the survivors now faced. Daniel was eager to see his wife, Henrietta, his two sons, and his grandchildren. Daniel understood that most of the laborers would not survive to rejoin their loved ones. The moon would soon reclaim the buildings, roads, and domes the humans had built and reclaim its lost territory from the colonizers. Daniel closed his eyes and remembered the last time he'd left the alien satellite. He saw the green landscape disappear under the orange clouds. He thought of the last time he'd glanced at the moon and observed the distant twilight.

Story 17: Antillean Solastalgia (22nd Century)

Moises Santos moved to Orlando, Florida at a young age when his parents, Martin and Matilde, relocated from New York City. Now at age twenty-five, he could afford a beautiful three-story home with a two-door garage in Windermere, Florida. His fiancée, Alondra, from Barahona, Dominican Republic prepared to start a life with him in the United States. Moises met Alondra when he was fourteen during a summer vacation in Santo Domingo when she came to live in his grandfather's home to attend high school and university. Alondra had potential in science and was interested in chemical engineering. Alondra's family and Moises' family were close for several generations, and so Moises and Alondra spent time together as children and teenagers. Moises became enamored with Alondra when he returned to the Dominican Republic for spring break in 2105, during his sophomore year at Florida Institute of Technology.

In 2108, Moises began working for NASA and several private companies after he submitted his ideas for terraforming Mars. Moises' ideas were chosen as the best, and a scientist named Rajat Joshi was chosen for his ideas on creating the infrastructure for future Mars colonies. NASA accepted Rajat's methods and hired him, and they would apply his ideas in a project that would endure for several centuries. Moises earned a high-paying position as a NASA contractor with numerous offers for employment by several private companies.

In 2110, Moises was completing his ideas for terraforming Venus as he was pursuing his PhD in Planetary Science at the Florida Institute of Technology. Moises was employed to work for the Venus project led by the Egyptian-American Director Abdul Jalil Hassan. With the money he earned, he was able to pay for bionic eyes for his grandmother Valencia, who lost her vision decades ago. Moises was also able to help his cousins with school and purchased toys for the children. He was able to give many gifts to his family and friends during All Saint's Day, bringing joy to himself and those dearest to him.

Moises visited Barahona to see the parents of his fiancée in Vicente Noble, to help in preparations for their marriage the following year. During his visit, Moises observed the dangerous progression of climate change in the Dominican Republic. Seawater had risen, and the weather was hot throughout most of the year with frequent droughts. Hurricane season was particularly devastating with stronger and slower-moving hurricanes as the temperature of the Caribbean Sea continued to increase. The Dominican government had improved conditions in the Dominican Republic by switching mostly to green energy by the early twenty-second century, however, many nations including the United States, continued to use fossil fuels.

The population of over thirteen million Dominicans suffered from devastating floods and destruction during the terrifying hurricane season. The neighboring nation of Haiti fared worse due to its poor infrastructure and weak government, which led to continuous political turmoil. Puerto Rico was devastated by various environmental disasters and had suffered greatly from rising sea levels compared to the other nations of the Greater Antilles. Thousands of Puerto Ricans fled to the United States and the Dominican Republic. Other island nations, including the Bahamas and Trinidad and Tobago, suffered greatly from climate change, and some of their inhabitants traveled to the Dominican Republic, the United States, and other Latin American nations.

Some Puerto Ricans joined environmental movements in Puerto Rico, the United States, and the Dominican Republic that led politicians to enact additional protection laws. Moises noticed the impacts of climate change as a child and through his numerous visits to the Dominican Republic, however, now he began to focus more on climate issues. As Moises worked daily on improving the conditions on Mars and Venus for long-term human colonization, he witnessed the rapid degradation of the United States and the Caribbean through climate change. He thought about the dangers his family and friends faced in the Dominican Republic if climate change continued to worsen.

Moises was asked to join the Venus project as one of the main concept contributors, and he designed various ways to bombard Venus with refined magnesium and calcium to sequester carbon dioxide in the form of calcium and magnesium carbonates. A temporary solution was to build large structures that would rise from the surface of Venus where colonies would be constructed within the cooler layers of the Venusian atmosphere. Moises worked on several designs to build settlements in the atmosphere of Venus called the Mountains of Atlas.

During his work on the Venus project, he became depressed, possibly because he spent a long time away from his fiancée—or it was possibly something else. Alondra visited Moises during the summer at a time when he was suffering from a sudden onset of depression. He purchased a new electric car, and he traveled throughout Florida with Alondra. Moises tried to hide his struggles with depression by taking Alondra with him to Disney World and Universal Studios in Orlando. He enjoyed playing classic games, including Super Mario World and Super Mario 64, so he chose to visit Super Nintendo World at Universal Studios. Alondra and Moises enjoyed video games and roller coasters, and they had a fun time together.

Alondra particularly enjoyed the beaches of the gulf coast of Florida, and one evening, the couple traveled to a beach in Clearwater. Alondra enjoyed the fine, white-sugar sands of Clearwater Beach and gazed out toward the beautiful Floridian sunset. Moises appeared calm and temporarily removed from his daily stressors.

He was drinking a cold Heineken when Alondra said, "*Mi amor*, I noticed that you appear troubled. May I ask what is bothering you?"

Moises hesitated, but he wanted to be honest with the woman he planned to spend the rest of his life with, so he replied, "Yes, I sometimes think that maybe I should be doing something else. I am lucky that my parents encouraged me to focus on school. I was able to go to a great school and have the opportunities that led me to NASA. I designed a terraforming model that NASA and some private companies will adopt in the long-term, and I signed a contract to work in the Venus terraforming team. I feel financially secure and comfortable enough to start my life and a new life with you, and I am grateful. What I have noticed is that I work almost daily and spend many hours finding ways to make alien planets more habitable for human settlement, and yet I notice the pollution that corporations are causing here on Earth. It bothers me how climate change has damaged the Dominican environment and economy."

Alondra shook her head and held her fiancé as she replied, "Some people in the Dominican government have tried to stop the companies from polluting, and we have made some progress, but the corruption in the Dominican government has been there for centuries. We have only had a few politicians like Juan Bosch who tried to bring real change to the Dominican Republic. If you want to do something for society, then I will fully support you. There are groups in the Dominican Republic that are pushing for increasing green energy and environmental regulations. If you want to contribute and bring awareness, then I will join you."

The couple spent some time planning their future together. Alondra left several weeks later for the Dominican Republic, leaving Moises to continue working on the development of his ideas for the terraforming on Venus. In early 2111, a young Iranian student named Anahita Javadifar developed the most promising ideas for the settlement of Venus, and she was later employed by NASA. Moises continued working on Mars and Venus while also getting involved in local environmental groups in Florida. He would join environmental movements including various Native American movements for increased environmental regulations.

Moises researched the impacts of climate change in the Caribbean, including the bleaching of the coral reefs in the Caribbean Sea. He became increasingly active in Dominican politics, and he used his platform and popularity within the scientific community to support environmental movements in the Dominican Republic and the Caribbean. Moises also contributed toward politicians who challenged Republicans who supported policies to limit immigration from nations impacted by climate change. Soon the Dominican government would, once again, be led by a progressive administration that sought to increase green energy and agreements with the other Caribbean and Latin American nations, to restrict corporate power and pollution in their respective nations.

The Dominican government signed the Taino Environmental Initiative which led to increased environmental regulations and increased penalties for polluters. There was an increase in green-energy jobs and training for young Dominicans and increased talks with the leaders of other Caribbean nations regarding climate change. The Dominican Republic and the United States signed various agreements, which led to increased environmental regulations between the Dominican Republic and the United States. The Latin American nations also discussed plans for the United States to lead in green-energy projects in the Americas for their past contributions toward environmental degradation in the region.

Alondra became a US citizen in the summer of 2111, and Moises returned to Barahona, the Dominican Republic in November 2111, to arrange his affairs and marry Alondra. Before the wedding, Moises' grandmother Valeria pulled him aside to congratulate her grandson. She was proud that her son Martin had raised such a good young man.

Valeria kissed Moises and said, "I am happy that you have found direction again, Moises. God has given you a good family and health, and you have been wise in choosing your friends. You made a great choice in choosing Alondra to be your wife. One of the most important choices for a man is his choice of a wife. You have also discovered another purpose in service to others, which Jesus Christ taught us we should do. I know that you were depressed before because you needed another purpose in life, and I believe you have found it. Now, go start your life with Alondra."

When Moises questioned his grandmother about how she knew he had suffered recently from depression, she replied, "I am your grandmother, Moises. I have a way of sensing the well-being of those closest to me. There are some things that even a blind person can see."

Moises laughed and prepared for his wedding.

Story 18: Neighborhood Hero (21st Century)

Aramis Osiris Alfaro was walking down Dyckman Street toward the billiard hall. He was going to meet his friend Roberto for a few games of pool before they went to the bar and met up with some ladies. It was a cool October night, and so far, the year 2080 had brought Aramis good fortune. He'd received various endorsements from corporations, and his fame made him a local celebrity. Aramis was stronger than most men, handsome, and well over six feet in height. He rarely got sick, and his injuries healed quickly, making him almost superhuman. Scientists called him the first transhuman.

Aramis was diagnosed with neuroblastoma as a child, and he remembered the desperation in his mother Caterina's eyes when she reluctantly agreed to enter Aramis for the experimental genetic procedure at Jacoby Hospital in the Bronx. Caterina was a single mother, and Aramis was her only child. Aramis' father Patricio died of a sudden heart attack while working long hours as a truck driver. It was a stressful time for Aramis and his mother.

The experimental surgery proved to be successful, and Aramis was cured of his cancer. Aramis didn't notice his increased strength and coordination until he reached puberty. In 2075, as a sophomore, Aramis joined the senior baseball team of George

Washington H.S. and soon became the starting third baseman. Aramis could not outperform the starting shortstop, Raul Mendoza, but was able to display good instincts and agility at third base. Aramis began hitting for power in his junior year and soon led New York City in home runs and R.B.I.s in his senior year, leading various major league teams to pursue him, including his hometown New York Yankees. When Aramis chose to reveal that he was genetically enhanced, he was able to keep some of his previous awards but was not allowed to enter the Major League draft. It was devastating for him as he was given another opportunity in life, however, he would not be allowed to pursue his dream of playing professional baseball.

Aramis soon used his abilities to stop a few criminals in his neighborhood, and the news of his abilities spread throughout Washington Heights. The NYPD publicly praised Aramis, and soon he was hired by the police department to promote the NYPD and support peace and safety for the black and Latino communities. After doing several commercials and small roles on television, Aramis was able to pay for his education at Hunter College. He was close to completing his Bachelor's in Physical Therapy, and during his time away from school, he traveled to other schools to speak with scientists about his abilities. During one visit to Hofstra University, he met a beautiful young Iranian student named Shirin Ahmadi, and they remained in contact for several months before they began dating.

Aramis became a local celebrity, and some Black people in Harlem used his middle name to compare him to the Ancient Egyptian God Osiris. Aramis began to use the image of the Egyptian God Osiris and briefly dressed up in a superhero costume for a commercial and during comic book events. He enjoyed the attention and sought to use his growing fame to provide for himself and his mother. He paid little attention to the medical experimentation that enhanced his body until he noticed other patients speaking against the medical experimentation they were subjected to. Soon others filed lawsuits against the US government for subjecting them to illegal experimentation not outlined in the agreements signed by the parents when the subjects were children. Aramis hired a lawyer to discuss his thoughts about the possibility of filing a lawsuit and going to court. Soon he was offered the chance to settle out of court.

On Saturday night, Aramis just wanted to relax and have fun with his friend, Roberto. Roberto was his best friend since grade school, and Aramis confided in him and informed him about his lawsuit against the government.

Roberto met him downstairs near the entrance as he exclaimed, "Hey, Aramis, you made it! I already have a table for us, ready to go, we got some beers, and I just ordered some *tostones* which *chicharron.* So, what are you planning on doing about the medical procedures they performed on you?"

Aramis smiled and replied as they settled in to play some pool, "I was struggling with my decision to go to court because although I was given a second chance on life and I have earned a good living from my enhancements, this country has a bad history of experimentation with the minority community. I guess I will never find out if I could have made it to the major leagues without my genetic modifications, but I am also grateful that my life has been enhanced. I agreed to settle after talking with my mother, and the amount will change my life and my mother's life. I will be comfortable for the rest of my life, Roberto."

For a moment, Roberto tried hard to avoid asking how much money Aramis had settled for. "I understand what you are going through. It is horrible that the government is still experimenting on poor minorities. I thought we moved past that as a country, but I was wrong. Someone else will speak out, but don't be too hard on yourself, Aramis. We are poor people, and it is hard to turn money down, especially when it will change your life. Just relax and use your money wisely, my friend."

Aramis smiled and replied, "I did my research, and I discovered that after the proxy wars between China and the United States, scientists were trying to find ways to enhance the physical abilities of military men and women. They chose ill children from the Black and Latino community to experiment with. Some of the children did not survive, and I was one of the few who became genetically enhanced."

Roberto just stood and shook his head in disappointment. Aramis chose to change the subject as he continued, "Thank you for always being a good friend to me, Roberto. I will help you pay your college bills so you don't go into debt. It is the least I can do for a great friend."

Roberto laughed and said, "You have always been a great friend to me, but believe me, I have benefitted greatly from your fame. I have been with the most beautiful women and have been able to go to expensive events for free just because I am your friend. Maybe I will also find a beautiful girlfriend, not as beautiful as your Persian girlfriend, but we shall see."

The two men laughed and finished their pool game. Roberto won five games to three because he was the better pool player, a fact that he always reminded Aramis of. The two young men left for the bar for a night of dancing with some of the local young women.

During the summer of 2082, Aramis and Shirin were vacationing in Boca Chica, Dominican Republic. Aramis and Shirin graduated from their respective schools, and Shirin was pursuing a Master's in Pharmacology. Shirin kissed Aramis and said, "So Aramis, does your mother want to stay in New York, or will you buy her a house somewhere else?"

Aramis replied, "My mother wants a home in Florida. I will buy her a home in a suburb near Ft. Lauderdale, and I am thinking of buying my own home near her home. I am thinking of purchasing a home here in the Dominican Republic, as well. I just want to work and stay out of the limelight from now on. Perhaps you can come to Florida with us. You can start your career in Florida if you wish."

Shirin smiled, kissed Aramis and replied, "I think I may do that, my love. I have always loved Florida."

Later that night, Aramis turned on the news. He discovered that other genetically enhanced individuals had publicly spoken against the US government in New York City. Some of them had similar enhancements as Aramis, and two of them were flamboyant and embraced their abilities. They called themselves Captain Boricua and Ms. Quisqueya, and they mentioned Aramis as their reasons for speaking publicly. Shirin noticed a small smile manifest on Aramis' face before the couple ate supper.

Story 19: Gate of the Sun (21st Century)

Alejandro Quispe Mamani finished his long day as a union organizer in a lithium-processing company in Potosi, Bolivia. He was a proud man of Quechua and Aymara ancestry and the only child of Julio and Maya Quispe. Alejandro benefitted from affordable higher education, and he studied Environmental Engineering at Tomás Frías Autonomous University. After his graduation, he joined his father, Julio, at Aymara Electric, working in the extraction of lithium, and he joined his father's union which focused on worker safety and the minimization of environmental degradation.

When Alejandro was a child, he witnessed his father get arrested for protesting the coup against President Evo Morales in 2019. The United States supported the coup and the installment of the self-declared interim president, Jeanine Áñez. Julio was released in 2020 when Alejandro was five years old, and he remembered the celebrations of the native people when Luis Alberto Arce Catacora won the subsequent election. President Luis Arce was a member of the Movement for Socialism (MAS) party and served as the Minister of Economy and Public Finance during the presidency of Evo Morales. When Evo Morales was welcomed back to

Bolivia in 2021, Alejandro remembered the tears on his father's face, and he soon identified himself as a socialist by the time he was a teenager.

Alejandro read about the various forms of socialism, and he was particularly interested in the social democracy of the Nordic nations. He read the history of Lenin and the horrors of Stalin while also reading about Latin American leaders, including Fidel Castro in Cuba, Hugo Chavez of Venezuela, Jacobo Arbenz in Guatemala, Juan Bosch in the Dominican Republic, and Evo Morales in Bolivia. Alejandro was impressed with the success of the Nordic nations and the improvements during the presidency of Evo Morales.

Julio enjoyed history and taught Alejandro about his people and culture. Julio often spoke of the various gods, including the Staff God, also known as Viracocha in the Incan religion. Julio spoke about the importance of the *llama* in the Aymara belief system. Alejandro heard stories of the Heavenly Llama who is believed to drink water from the ocean and urinate it as rain. According to Aymara's eschatology, *llamas* will return to the water springs and lagoons where they come from at the end of time. The religions of the native people and the Catholicism brought by the Spaniards created a syncretic religion.

Alejandro was a young man of twenty. It was October of 2035, and Alejandro was working in a small Bolivian Lithium company called Aymara Electric, which began after 2025. Aymara Electric was partnered with a Chinese firm while other Bolivian companies were partnered with other European companies, including the German company ACI Systems. The largest salt flat was *Salar de Uyuni*, and lithium was also extracted from *Coipasa* and *Pastos Grandes*. Aymara Electric was a small company located in *Pastos Grandes* in the Sud Lipez region of Bolivia. The region was hard to access and was a part of the *Altiplano*, a high plateau bordered by the *Cordillera Occidental* and the *Cordillera Oriental*. Salts found within the salt pan included gypsum, halite, and ulexite. The brines were rich in boron, lithium, and sodium chloride, and the region brought various lithium and potassium mining companies.

Pastos Grandes was located in Potosi Bolivia, a mythical area of riches also mentioned in *Don Quixote* by Miguel de Cervantes. Centuries ago, the natives were conscripted to work in Potosí's silver mines through the Spanish *Mita* system of contributed labor. Today, many of the native people of Bolivia worked for various companies, including Aymara Electric, producing green energy and exporting lithium to various Latin American nations, Europe, and China. The standard of living continued to improve for the native people and all working-class people of Bolivia, and now, they had free time to pursue their passions. High literacy rates and affordable education helped teach working-class people how to read and write, and many advanced toward institutions of higher learning.

The standard of living continued to increase in Bolivia, however, members of the Bolivian elite funded right-wing and conservative Christian political candidates who desired to gain control of the companies in Bolivia and re-establish stronger ties with various corporate interests within the United States. Alejandro was aware of the growing tensions between the left-wing alliance and the smaller right-wing factions within the Bolivian government. Despite the liberal administration of President Joe Biden and Kamala Harris, the United States continued its foreign interventionist policies in Latin America, much to the dismay of the socialist parties in Bolivia.

Alejandro secretly monitored various right-wing officials with the help of his cousin Noah. Alejandro's father did not wish for his son to get involved in direct actions against right-wing officials because he feared for his son's safety, and he believed the right-wing parties could no longer be effective electorally. Alejandro, however, believed that right-wing extremists and racists posed a major problem to the Bolivian government because they were encouraged by the negative language of the United States toward the Bolivian socialist government.

Alejandro went to visit his girlfriend, Mariana Echeverría, a beautiful mestiza woman of native and Basque ancestry. Mariana was the daughter of two college professors, and she was taught to question everything around her and encouraged to seek intellectual pursuits. She had rosy cheeks and long, straight, black hair. Alejandro was a tall and athletic native man of six feet in height, and Mariana was nearly as tall as him. Her complexion was light brown, and her dark hair and rosy cheeks attracted Alejandro. Alejandro met her during his senior year of High School, and they began dating in college. Alejandro needed some time with his girlfriend to seek solace before speaking with his friend, Noah. After spending some time with Mariana, he returned to his father's home to read some encrypted messages from Noah.

Noah and his friends managed to gain information from the US embassy in Bolivia, including conversations and documents with various officials from the

Organization of American States in Washington D.C. and US officials in Bolivia, including C.I.A. members. The US officials were in conversation with various far-right Bolivian political figures and extremists who desired to foment division in Bolivia. Some members of the socialist administration and members of other progressive parties were offered bribes to cause public distrust in the Bolivian government, however, it appeared only a few socialists accepted the money. Most of the money was wired to top military officials and right-wing politicians as early as six months ago. Alejandro was angered at the conspiracy against the Bolivian government, and he and his cousin agreed to anonymously release the information to the office of the president and Bolivian intelligence.

Several days later, Alejandro met with his father after he had a long meeting on Friday with the owners of Aymara Electric company and members of various Indian companies that had recently arrived from their visit to Argentina and Chile. They desired to speak with Aymara Electric and smaller companies about new ways to extract lithium for the Indian market under the supervision of Bolivian environmental groups. The Indians desired to use lithium for their electric vehicles as well as their military equipment, including their new submarines, as tensions between China and India increased.

Julio was excited to inform Alejandro regarding some new international deals involving Aymara Electric. "Business is improving, and our shipments to the various European nations are increasing. We are planning on increasing lithium shipments to Mexico, Nicaragua, Honduras, and Panama. We are also scheduled to speak with electric car companies in Cuba and the Dominican Republic later this year. Our business is profitable, and I think you have been doing great within the mineral extraction and green energy unions. Soon, you can be a union leader and possibly join an environmental agency and use your intelligence to help improve social programs for the workers and the environment."

Alejandro hesitated to inform his father regarding the information his cousin Noah had uncovered, but he revealed it anyway, "Father, our government is being infiltrated once again by foreign entities. Noah and I discovered that diplomats in the US embassy and others within the C.I.A. are colluding with far-right politicians and high-ranking military members in an attempt to foment turmoil, once again, in Bolivia. I asked Noah to release the information he and his friends gathered anonymously. If people find out the truth, the conservatives and those right-wing Christian hypocrites will not be able to attempt what they did to Evo Morales."

Julio was visibly angered as he focused on his son's eyes and said, "I told you not to get yourself deeply involved in politics. You have one duty, which is to vote and support your issues, however, you and Noah possibly broke the law and could get yourself in serious trouble. You do understand that whenever we make deals with foreign companies, the United States is always observing those interactions? These negotiations are sensitive, particularly as tensions between India and China, as well as between China and the United States, are increasing. You simply cannot involve yourself in spying. You should let Bolivian government officials handle Bolivia's foreign affairs."

Alejandro countered, "Father, you understand that our socialist government's very existence is unwanted by the United States. Our business dealings with China and India have enraged our enemies both foreign and domestic. Natives have fought for centuries, and now, we have proven to not only thrive within our nation but also lead Bolivia successfully. We must always be alert because the people that have joined foreigners to halt progress for the poor and native people of Bolivia have not gone away. They are always here, plotting, and they sometimes use advanced technology against us. Perhaps it is time we negotiate a deal to bring advanced technology to Bolivia. The Chinese can help us develop quantum computers which we can use to run our society efficiently while also protecting our information from foreigners. We can also use our technology against our enemies."

Julio smiled although he still felt worried for his son's safety, then he replied, "You don't understand what it is to be a father yet, my son. You are my only child, and you won't understand the care I feel for you until you have a family of your own. When I was imprisoned, I was beaten and tortured in ways I never revealed to you or your mother. I was a vocal opponent of Jeanine Áñez, and after the coup that ousted Evo Morales, Jeanine Añez issued Decree 4078 to enlist the police and army to pacify the country."

Alejandro replied, "You taught me that our ancestors were fighters. We fought against the encroaching Inca Empire, and some of our people later united with them against the Spanish conquistadors and later formed our nations. After the death of the great liberator Simon Bolivar, our people continued to thrive. We continued to fight for our rights within our new nation of Bolivia."

Julio smiled and replied, "Remember when I took you to the Gate of the Sun? It was at the ancient ruins in Tiwanaku near Lake Titicaca. You were ten years of age, and you marveled at the beauty of Lake Titicaca and the statues at the site. You gazed in awe at the inscriptions written by our ancestors, and I explained the various gods that our people worship. Our family is Christians today, and I also taught you the words of Our Savior Jesus Christ. As you became older, I explained how people use the Bible for good but sometimes also to justify the pain they choose to inflict upon other groups they consider to be lower than themselves. You have learned those words well, my son, but please remember to learn not only from your mistakes but the mistakes of your father and others. I hope that your actions will only serve to increase the safety of our people and the nation of Bolivia, and as a father, I hope that you keep yourself safe and have a family of your own in a better Bolivia than the one from my youth. Let us have a beer, son."

Story 20: Departure From Eternity (23rd Century)

03/14/2270

Dear Octavio,

My dear grandson, I write to you because my day has come. Although this is a sad day, it can also be viewed as a day of happiness. I decided to write you a letter due to our mutual enjoyment of the art of penmanship and the lost art form of a handwritten letter. In this letter, I will summarize my thoughts on my life, my perspectives on issues important to me, and my hopes for you and the rest of my family. I sent private messages to my closest family members and finalized my will several weeks ago. I hope that you keep this letter with you and learn from my life and follow my advice.

At certain times, I have felt like a family relic. I became a living part of our history. I feel as if I am a breathing exhibit for others to learn from and admire, sometimes from afar. As you know, my dear grandson, these feelings are not a reflection of how you or my other family members have treated me. I have been treated nicely by all of you, and I have maintained a few friendships throughout my lifetime.

As you know, my father, Eugenio, was one of the most famous Cuban geneticists of the twenty-first century. He had many children, and I was his last and only child with my mother, Angela, from El Salvador. My mother was much younger than he was, and she met him in Washington D.C. before it became a state. My father experimented on animals in ways to improve the quality of life and longevity of human patients. His discoveries proved successful, and soon, human trials in Cuba began. My father was so confident that he allowed enhancements to be performed on his genes which soon were inherited by me when my mother became pregnant with me. I was born in the State of Washington Douglass Commonwealth in 2080 and was provided a good life through the financial support of my father and the good upbringing that my single mother provided.

I married your great-great-grandmother, Maria, who was a beautiful young Puerto Rican woman I met in 2119. I was forty years old, and she was twenty-five. My first son was Felix who was born the following year in 2120, and I subsequently had another son and a daughter. I returned to Cuba upon my father's request where they examined me for several weeks and improved my physiology. When I completed school, I became a research scientist and worked for various companies in the United States and earned a decent living. I was also paid by the Cuban government to maintain secrecy regarding the classified medical research in Cuba. Soon, my children had families of their own, and by 2145, I had my first grandson, Mauricio. I had celebrated a long and healthy marriage of eighty years with Maria when she passed away in her sleep in 2199. She wanted to see the new century in my arms, however, Jehovah had other plans for her.

My heart was broken because God had finally presented me with true romantic love, something that I'd never experienced before, and now, it was her time to depart from our life together. I suffered the loss of my family members, including the deaths of my mother and father who entrusted me with a copy of some of his major research before he passed away. He said that I was his greatest accomplishment. The death of my first child, Felix, in 2210, devastated me once again, and then the deaths of my other children and later grandchildren, brought a level of grief that was never meant for one human being to handle.

I also experienced joys that other people rarely experienced, including the births of my great-grandchildren and great-great-grandchildren. Now, I am one of the few people that can say they have seen the births of their great-great-great grandchildren. It was also revealed to me that I could now witness more generations of my own family come into this world. I feel a sort of deeper, more transcendent love for my family, and I observe you all as a sort of guardian angel. I have lived a long life, and my perspectives have shifted over time.

When I was young, I enjoyed partying, and in my twenties and thirties, I traveled throughout Latin America, the Middle East, and Asia. I enjoyed the company of beautiful women from all over the world, but soon fell in love with my wife and found a new purpose as a family man. When I became a widower, I did not seek the company of another woman for many years. I started dating, once again, soon after my 100th birthday, but I never married again.

My genetic enhancements hid my age until my late sixties, and my youthful appearance aroused curiosity at my local hospital. I later found out that doctors began to secretly analyze my anatomy and physiology for many years. The Cuban government continued to provide me with supplemental income until Cuban Intelligence realized the medical community of the United States was already aware of my condition. The US government has my DNA and has been developing its research, and the C.I.A. has been monitoring Cuba to study its medical advancements. I was approached by government officials to speak with them regarding my life and experiences at the research facilities in Cuba and to possibly donate my body for science in the event of my death, but I have declined.

I was informed that I could live beyond my 200th birthday by scientists here in the United States. Scientists made numerous discoveries after analyzing my lengthened telomeres and other genetic alterations, which have slowed down the lifespan of my cells. I have not been afflicted with cancer yet, and I am healthy and appear like a man of sixty years of age even though I am the longest-living human in recorded history. Unless you believe Biblical stories of men who have lived longer than me.

Some scientists now believe they can soon find the key to immortality, and perhaps, I can become the first man to have a chance to live forever. I must be honest that the idea of living forever frightened and slightly disgusted me. What is eternity? Can we live forever? What if I get injured or get an unknown disease and my quality of life decreases? Will it be worth living forever? I may live long enough to die violently or in an accident. Even if you live for many millenniums, the Sun itself is aging, our solar system is aging, and our universe is aging. Everything has a life span and expiration date.

Perhaps there is no such thing as immortality. Can we handle immortality as a society? Will birth rates plummet as people live longer and the Earth becomes increasingly populated? Will life enhancers, which are used mostly by the wealthy and powerful, lead to increasing inequality in society? There are numerous questions that life-extending procedures will raise, and those will be the conversations you will see become part of public discourse in the future.

My dear great-great-great-grandson, Octavio, I want you to know that I have been happy with my life although I have suffered greatly during certain periods in my life. If they can find the solution to mortality, I would like my life to serve as an example. I believe God never meant for us to live far beyond our time. When we are conscious of our mortality, we appreciate life and our loved ones, and it motivates most of us to pursue our greatness during our finite time on Earth. What I have found is that I have experienced periods of sadness and lethargy. These negative feelings have intensified with my prolonged life and now with the knowledge that my story has leaked to the public. This is an unwanted celebrity status that I wish to avoid.

I want you to live a full life and find yourself a good woman and start a family. I am happy to have found a friend and confidant among my descendants. It was a pleasure spending time with you and the rest of my family. I hope that I can be reunited with my family and friends who have passed away. I hope that when I meet God, he can forgive me if I have broken any laws of nature. May God also guide the scientists working to extend human life and on other scientific endeavors that can be both a blessing and a curse.

This is the year 2270, and I am now 190 years old, and I could see another century, however, I plan to see the next century with my wife once again. I ask you to cremate my body and to dispose of my ashes upon the Caribbean Sea. I have submitted my will, and you shall gain a small portion of my wealth as well as a copy of my research and those of my father. May you go with God all the days of your life.

Sincerely,
Anastácio Buenaventura

Story 21: Rendezvous in Roatán (22nd Century)

Miles was a shy but adventurous boy who was now fourteen years of age and ready to start high school. Miles lived most of his life with his mother, Judy, on Roatan Island located in the Caribbean, just off the coast of the nation of Honduras. Miles was his mother's only child, and he usually stayed to himself, choosing to spend most of his time exploring the nearby beaches of La Isla de Santa Elena on the eastern side of Roatan island. Miles found something remarkable just as he was discovering his attraction for girls. He discovered that some of his dreams appeared to have a connection with reality, a fact that at first frightened him but now intrigued him.

At first, he would dream of weird bright lights that would appear in the same secluded areas of Roatan. When Miles observed similar bright lights when he was awake, he became frightened. As the months progressed, his dreams slowly revealed the lights were extraterrestrial. Some of his dreams were lucid and he was able to speak with a strange entity that revealed his/her location in a mangrove on the island of Santa Elena. Miles experienced other dreams that appeared to predict actual events in his reality. Miles kept these dreams a secret for fear that his mother would think he was troubled.

Miles was studying Spanish after his father Diego asked him to move in with him in the capital city of Tegucigalpa in Honduras. Miles lived with his mother in Camp Bay on the island of Roatan and never traveled to the capital, and the farthest he'd previously traveled into Honduras was the city of San Pedro Sula. His father, Diego, was married to a Nicaraguan woman named Rosa Maria, and they often traveled to her home nation for vacation. Miles excelled in Mathematics and Science, however, his true passion was painting and photography. Miles would often spend time alone in nature painting or experimenting with different styles of photography. His father dismissed Miles' desire to become an artist and tried to convince his son to enter a good science program in Tegucigalpa. Diego believed the life of an artist, led to misery and poverty, and he instead wanted his son to focus on the sciences and build a career for himself.

Miles was happy to reunite with his father and have an opportunity to attend a good high school and university but was conflicted about whether he would pursue an art career or pursue a career in science. In the meantime, Miles would just be a kid and have fun this summer before he would be asked to make his first major decisions in life. Miles returned to Santa Elena Island early one Saturday morning when he dreamed that some lovely high school girls would be bathing at a nearby beach. His curiosity got the better of him, so he sneaked away, lying to his mother that he would be visiting a cousin.

On a secluded beach on Santa Elena Island, Miles saw the same beautiful girls from his dream. One of them was nude, just as she'd appeared in his dream, causing Miles to display a wide smile. She was a mixed young lady with light brown skin, dark nipples, a slim figure, and she had long, dark hair. When Miles looked at her face, he recognized her as the older sister of one of his classmates, named Jimmy. Her name was Clarice, and she was around eighteen years old. Clarice suddenly made eye contact with Miles, and his face displayed alarm. Miles tried to appear as if he was walking down that section of the beach by chance when Clarice smiled and seemed to laugh, causing Miles to turn around and walk away.

Miles walked toward a mangrove that he'd seen in his dreams. It was a particularly lucid dream that encouraged his curiosity. Miles saw a glowing orb near the mangroves—the same orb in the same area that he remembered in his dream. He never explored the glowing orbs he saw in his dreams, but today, he mustered the courage to do so. He nervously walked toward the mangrove and chuckled at his fright when suddenly the water changed to the color of the sky, which now appeared a sunset orange. An orb appeared, and his heart raced with fear fueled by adrenaline, however, he could not make himself run. A voice broke the silence, and soon Miles' fears and anxiety were mysteriously assuaged. The voice appeared to be of a male, with a local Roatan accent.

Time appeared to stop, and before Miles could ask his questions, the orb understood and quickly answered. "You have potential and a curious mind, Miles. Your mind is rich with ideas, and your subconscious is extremely active and somehow you tuned in to my presence and work here in Roatan. This is the summer of 2078, and I have been studying in this region of the Earth since the year 1405. I have returned over ten times and have seen societies fail or progress for close to seven centuries. I particularly enjoyed the Maya civilization and was tempted to interact with some of the Maya leaders from various historical periods. The Maya suffered a decline in their societies before the Spaniards arrived. I learned the various languages and writings of the people from these lands and discovered the marvelous history of the Maya. My initial research was based on the various cities in the League of Mayapan."

Miles managed to say, "You can live for hundreds of years? How old are you? What are you doing here, and what do you want with me?"

It appeared this being that had manifested into this glowing orb already understood what Miles would say before he said it, judging by his response. "I know you have many questions for me, Miles. I am a being from a civilization that originated in another galaxy from a planet nearly twice as old as Earth. My people expanded to different solar systems within our galaxy and some communities chose to become explorers, including my own. Life is a delicate thing, and intelligent life that can unlock the deeper mysteries of this universe is extremely rare. Some from my civilization can have longer life spans, however, my community rejected longer life spans, and we instead embraced the natural limits of our bodies. Some of my friends and family members have visited Earth and studied other civilizations, including that of Egypt and China. I chose this region, now known as Central America and the Caribbean."

Miles felt at ease and listened closely as the entity began to speak after a short pause. "I witnessed the arrival of the Europeans and their settling in the nation of the Dominican Republic and the creation of Santo Domingo. I witnessed the horrors that led to the fall of the Aztec Empire and then the ongoing wars between the Spanish and Maya and the conflicts that occurred when the other Europeans arrived in what they called the New World. Despite the horrors, I also witnessed the creation of new people from a combination of various peoples from other regions of the world. The African, European, Middle Eastern, Asian, and native peoples created interesting blends of people in Latin America and the Caribbean, and they helped me further my studies in human genetics and society. You are also a blend of various genetics, including that of African origin, through your Jamaican ancestors and from the native Ch'orti people. That is why your skin is dark brown and your eyes appear Asiatic in the style of the local natives."

After a brief pause, the entity continued, "Although I did not experiment on humans, I did experiment on some plants and animals and arrived at interesting conclusions. My community enjoys biology, and we seek to enhance our bodies by obtaining knowledge regarding the biology of other advanced beings. I soon traveled to Roatan island and observed famous pirates throughout the seventeenth and eighteenth centuries. The Paya people originally lived on these islands, and soon, this island was occupied by various groups, including the Spaniards and the English. The Bay of Honduras became a hub for various militaries, pirates, traders, and adventurers, and many conflicts occurred through the formation of various alliances. English, French, and Dutch pirates raided the Spanish ships, and eventually, Spain lost many of its Caribbean possessions, leaving Cuba, Puerto Rico, and the Dominican Republic as its main territories in the Caribbean. Buccaneers and other Europeans formed alliances with some native groups to protect their business interests, including the alliance between the buccaneers and the Black Carib people."

Miles was in awe of the knowledge the entity possessed and asked, "Is your research completed, and what is your purpose with me?"

The entity replied, "My research is nearly completed, and I am satisfied with the knowledge I have obtained. As to your second question, I do not have any purpose with you. I was just curious about your subconscious connection to my presence. I have learned greatly from your ancestors and have concluded that the future for humanity is dire. I believe humanity will not achieve the unity required to explore the cosmos with a deeper understanding. I have seen the damage humanity has caused the Earth in the last two centuries because interest in profits has made them neglect their interest in conserving their planet. The sea level has risen, and the water has become contaminated, causing many species to become extinct from these disasters. I would like to directly interfere and help humanity, but my people frown upon interacting with less developed societies. I cannot reveal the deeper sciences to you because I believe it will do more damage than good as your most advanced thinkers on Earth cannot understand the basic levels of our understanding. My last return to Earth will be when your grandchildren are old men and women, and then I will be satisfied with my contribution to my people. This will be our first and last meeting, Miles, and this is why I will make you forget about my presence and work here. I will give you a gift that will help you focus on your potential and reach a deeper understanding of yourself and the world you live in. You can use this knowledge for the benefit of your people."

The entity disappeared, and the sky suddenly turned dark as Miles woke up as if from a deep dream. Miles quickly used his smartphone to contact his mother, Judy, who had left many voicemails and text messages. Miles quickly returned to his home in Camp Bay and apologized for his absence, explaining that he fell into a deep slumber. He never fully understood why he had fallen asleep that Saturday afternoon in the summer of 2078, however, he believed he was given new gifts and opportunities which he now was determined to use in his life. He felt more confident and was determined to make positive choices in life.

Miles later accepted his father's offer to move in with him in Tegucigalpa. His future was full of opportunity, and he thought about studying art and science and using his talents in designing new communities on the Moon for the Mexican Space Agency. Miles also thought about using his abilities to possibly return to Roatan and construct new green-energy towns to uplift the people of his community.

Story 22: State of Puerto Rico (22nd Century)

Rodolfo Quiñones was beginning his dive for the fifth time during the second week of January. He had not seen his family since New Year's Day when he was home in Carolina, Puerto Rico. He was exploring the Caribbean Sea for what appeared to be a new species of Caribbean reef octopus. This particular octopus had edited its RNA within the axons of its neurons and could edit messenger RNA outside of its cell's nucleus. Most of this research began in Israel in the first half of the twenty-first century, however, in 2102, scientists in the state of Puerto Rico believed they could expand genetic engineering beyond the advances of Israel and Korea.

The leading geneticist in Puerto Rico was Margarita Olivo from San Juan who was leading the study of the octopuses and improving her genetic editing methods. Margarita had been a leader in her field for over five decades, and her research now led the world, and she began to receive funding from the United States government. Margarita worked with distinguished researchers from Puerto Rico and within the continental United States, as well as the best explorers on the island. The twenty-five-year-old Rodolfo Quiñones was not only one of the best divers in Puerto Rico but was also among the best young marine biologists on the island. He enjoyed swimming as much as he enjoyed biology and would spend most of his free time at the beach. Rodolfo sometimes played basketball with his friends and enjoyed 3D gaming, but his main love was swimming.

Rodolfo's father, Mario, was a native of Chicago, and he moved to Puerto Rico soon after the territory was admitted into the union as the fifty-second state. Many Puerto Ricans born in the continental United States returned to their ancestral island of Puerto Rico after the island achieved statehood, believing that Puerto Ricans would now justly gain a higher standard of living. Puerto Rican statehood had many enemies, including the Republican Party in the US mainland and the *Independentistas* who were Puerto Rican nationalists who desired full Puerto Rican independence. As the economy worsened and the island was battered by rising sea levels and an increased number of hurricanes and earthquakes, a faction of Puerto Rican progressives in the late twenty-first century believed they had the best chance to achieve independence.

Rodolfo's mother, Adelina, and her brothers were nationalists that were dismayed with the conversion of Puerto Rico as a state of the United States. One of Roldolfo's uncles was imprisoned after participating in a protest that turned violent in San Juan. Rodolfo sometimes thought about what independence might bring to Puerto Rico. He often admired the neighboring nation of the Dominican Republic which had endured hardships in the previous century and was now flourishing under good leadership that had improved its economy and standard of living. Maybe Puerto Rico would have done better as an independent nation, or perhaps the island could do better under a better US administration. Rodolfo was born in Puerto Rico when it was still a US territory in the late twenty-first century and remembered when Puerto Rico became a state before his tenth birthday.

Rodolfo sometimes pondered on the politics of Puerto Rico, however, all that mattered now was that he was successful in his mission that would help his research department gain extra funding from the US government. Margarita Olivo was close to greatly advancing genetic editing and neurological treatment and surgery in the next few years. Rodolfo was personally invested in the research because he was seeking help for his mother who had been recently diagnosed with amyotrophic lateral sclerosis or Lou Gehrig's disease.

Rodolfo began to prepare for his dive after the rest of his research team arrived and boarded their ship. He swallowed an anti-nitrogen oxide formation pill to help prevent the bends as the ship approached Culebra Island to the east of mainland Puerto Rico and west of the US Virgin Islands. The dive location was located near Playa Carlos Rosario Beach, and the octopuses were active as they were beginning their mating season. Mateo Solis was scheduled to dive with Rodolfo, and each man had various routes they planned on exploring and had ideas of new routes to explore today.

The men dove into the Caribbean waters in another attempt to find some octopuses. He placed his small diving visor and rebreather and put on his aqua skin that regulated his temperature. His visor lit up with a digital screen display that helped him identify exactly where he was under the Caribbean Sea and also allowed for clearer vision underwater. It was about mid-afternoon when the two men swam through most of their pre-established routes near the coral reef.

Rodolfo enjoyed exploring the coral reef and was part of several environmental groups in Puerto Rico. Much of the coral reef had been damaged due to climate change in the twenty-first century, however, environmental policies by the Dominican Republic, Cuba, Puerto Rico, and Jamaica had helped to preserve the coral reef and mitigate most of the damage by the climate crisis of the twenty-second century. Rodolfo was desperate to find the octopuses because Margarita desired a few more of them to examine before expanding her trials on various lab animals. Margarita planned on publishing several more papers this year and submitting her medical research and new genetic editing discoveries to the FDA.

Suddenly Rodolfo observed activity near a section of coral reef, and he zoomed in using his display. Alas, there were several octopuses, and four were mating. Rodolfo released chemicals that attracted the male octopuses and quickly released his smart cage from his side pocket, which quickly enlarged. In his excitement, Rodolfo did not see the small warning on his top, left display signaling that a large predator was rapidly approaching. By the time he realized he might be in danger, the shark was already close to him. Rodolfo's visor flashed red, and he panicked as the octopuses suddenly released their ink and darkened the view around Rodolfo. It was a Caribbean reef shark that was now swimming toward Rodolfo. Rodolfo tried to flee as the shark damaged his smart cage.

When he adjusted his visor to see through the ink, he saw other sharks rapidly approaching. He pulled his small electron gun and shot a dart that created a powerful electrical shock that disabled two of the sharks. Rodolfo started his electronic air-propulsion system on his lower legs and arms. One of the sharks bit his right leg as he screamed and began his rapid ascent to the surface. The boat was waiting for him at the surface as they tracked Rodolfo's location. The researchers pulled him on board and saw that he'd received a large bite on his right thigh. Rodolfo's heart was beating rapidly, and he was devastated that he'd failed to catch any of the octopuses yet again.

Rodolfo felt pain and disappointment as he thought about his mother who was at home suffering from the beginning stages of ALS. Margarita guaranteed that she was close to expanding her clinical trials and that within two or three years she could cure neurological diseases like ALS and also reverse nerve damage in patients that suffered accidents. The research was promising, and Rodolfo believed today was just a minor setback.

He exclaimed through his pain, "I tried my best and was close until those sharks attacked me. All my life I have swum in the Caribbean Sea, and only now do I experience a shark attack."

The scientists tried to lift Rodolfo's spirits, but his disappointment paled in comparison to his relief because he'd survived a shark attack. Rodolfo asked about his diving partner Mateo when the researchers notified him that he was about to surface. Mateo soon climbed on board with five octopuses in his smart cage. Rodolfo smiled when he saw that Mateo had —their mission was completed. He would spend some time in a hospital in San Juan, recovering but happy that his mother had been promised to receive treatment for her ALS paid for by the US government.

Things might turn out well after all, Rodolfo thought later that night in his hospital bed.

Story 23: The Others (24th Century)

Various South American nations were now united and were a regional power in the Americas. The United States was defeated in a sudden and shocking war that sent waves of fear through the nations of Earth in the late twenty-third century. This historical war saw the victory of an alliance between Chile, Argentina, and Uruguay, who were united in a temporary compromise with beings from another region of the Milky Way galaxy. The aliens unleashed atomic weaponry that was far more advanced than any human weapon created and quickly brought the surrender of the United States after only a brief display of power. The beings formed a prolonged alliance with the governments of Uruguay, Chile, and Paraguay, promising to introduce advanced alien technology and improve society in South America. These beings were called *Los Extrangeros* or The Foreigners, and later, out of fear, many people simply called them *Los Otros* or The Others. The alliance between The Others and the elites of Uruguay, Chile, and Paraguay soon became known as the Universal South American Alliance or commonly called, the Southern Alliance.

After the dissolution of the Organization of American States in 2305, many activists falsely believed that a new era of democracy and increased standard of living would occur, however, most of the wealth and power soon went to the Southern

Alliance. Officials of the Southern Alliance and The Others made public appearances. The Others appeared as reptilians and humanoids while others appeared slightly different with various-sized heads and limbs indicating that their home world was made up of several intelligent species that worked together. The public appearances by the aliens soon diminished until they were rarely seen. Officials of the Southern Alliance stated that they would enter a long-term partnership with the Others in establishing harmony in South America while building new lunar bases that would soon take humanity beyond the solar system. Despite the advances in technology obtained by the Southern Alliance, there were few advances for the working class and marginalized groups.

In Brazil, a large group of Brazilian and Bolivian activists was fighting the misinformation spread by the Southern Alliance. Government agents arrested some activists and their families causing an increasing number of rebels to join forces within the Amazon Rainforest.

João was a twenty-five-year-old activist who protested the increasing power and influence of the Southern Alliance in Central and South America. He was from a lower-class family that mostly lived in Morro da Providência between the districts of Santo Cristo and Gamboa in Rio de Janeiro. In the last few years, rebel actions against the Southern Alliance had led to Alliance officials calling the rebels anti-Republican and comparing them to the Canudos that fought the First Brazilian Republic in the War of Canudos from 1895 to 1890.

The Southern Alliance desperately sought to identify and prosecute the leader of the rebel movement, however, the movement was decentralized with several regional leaders. Now, João and almost 500 rebels within the Amazon Rainforest were awaiting information from hackers who believed they could infiltrate the alien computer network. The information the hackers revealed soon sent shockwaves throughout the various rebel camps in South America.

The only two nations in the Americas that openly challenged the Southern Alliance were Canada and Mexico. After the rebels began to organize against the Southern Alliance, the Mexican government began secretly funding various rebel groups in South America. The rebel attacks became bolder after The Others failed to make public appearances and only made seldom statements. Most of João's family that escaped Brazil fled to Bolivia and Peru, and they implored João to leave the rebellion and flee to safety. Native groups joined the rebellion and promised to join in the attack on the capital of the Southern Alliance. The rebellion soon called itself the Freedom and Democracy Alliance and was now ready to strike and awaited notification from leadership.

João's girlfriend, Selena, had left Venezuela just a few months ago after rumors had spread that the Southern Alliance would begin an offensive into the Amazon Rainforest and possibly into the northern reaches of South America. The two quickly formed a close bond, and they believed in similar goals for South America after the end of alien occupation and the Southern Alliance.

João observed Selena's anxiety and kissed her before saying, "My love, just stay close to me, and I will make sure to keep you safe. The time is coming to see if we can finally bring an end to the Southern Alliance and experience true freedom. We can then start our life together with peace of mind."

Selena laughed as she replied, "It seems people like us never fully had peace in our lands. Between the foreigners and the elites, they always seemed to keep us distracted with just enough hope to continue squeezing us. In Venezuela, we have oil that could have been used to fund social programs, but it instead hurt our people in the past due to corruption and foreign intervention that desired to maintain an order of exploitation. Fossil fuels and greed also caused climate change leading to the increase in renewable energy. Countries like Bolivia soon became wealthier but under the wrong administration—the wealth only helped improve the lives of the elite. We had our hopes lifted with the Southern Alliance, but they have not brought all the changes they promised, and now, they threaten us with their alien allies. I am scared, but I know I am safer with you, João."

After a few more hours, as midday approached, João, Selena, and the other rebels were notified that a large group of rebels had uncovered sensitive information regarding the South Alliance and their alien allies. The Southern Alliance was vulnerable and not as strong as it portrayed itself to be. A force of over 5,000 rebels moved toward the Southern Alliance base in Santiago, Chile, and another offensive led by thousands of rebels advanced in Uruguay and Argentina. The rebels were happily surprised at the rapid fall of various bases of the Southern Alliance and of the capture of various exotic weapons factories where alien weaponry was replicated and produced.

One of the main leaders of the rebellion, named Claudio Oliveira, was stationed within the Amazon in Brazil. Claudio informed his camp that he'd received important information regarding the initial rebel offensives. João listened as Claudio explained, "We received important intelligence regarding the Southern Alliance and their partnership with the aliens. The Others had visited other planets before with minimum conflict, however, when they arrived on Earth, various nations, including the United States, attempted to establish communications with South American government officials. The United States was alarmed by the devastating technology that The Others brought to South America, and they secretly sent nuclear warships near Chile and Argentina which caused an incident when the United States fired upon an Argentinian fighter jet, leading to a small strike by the Argentinians that eventually led to warfare.

The United States bombed various military bases in Argentina and Chile, leading Uruguay to enter the conflict because the aliens had secretly spoken with Uruguayan government officials. Many of the aliens died during the initial stages of the war before the aliens unleashed devastating attacks on the US mainland, bringing an end to the war. The elites soon used their friendship with the aliens to install puppet leaders in Uruguay, Argentina, and Chile, and after a few years, the aliens dwindled in number to disease and assassination by government officials."

The rebels stood silently as Claudio destroyed years of propaganda by the Southern Alliance. Claudio continued, "The elites soon controlled the aliens and forced them to break communication with their societies. They formed the Southern Alliance which mostly served to increase their wealth and power and used the aliens to keep us subservient to them. Now that we know the aliens are no threat to us and we have acquired some of the alien technology, my superiors informed me that the government of Mexico was notified, and they will send their military to help us. The Southern Alliance is fractured, and they will be sending some of their forces toward us, but we shall have reinforcements from the Mexican government as well as help from the nations of Central America."

The rebels were overjoyed and more determined to face the Southern Alliance. João and Selena gathered their few personal items, including hygiene products, food, and printed pictures of their families, as they prepared to move to a northern location of the Rainforest in an attempt to stretch the remaining Southern Alliance forces until they received military support from Mexico and their Central American allies.

Selena looked into her lover's eyes and said, "Finally we might see the day when we and our families taste true freedom."

João replied, "I hope we will truly discover Simon Bolivar's dream after we are victorious. I hope our leaders deliver on their promises so that we can truly rejoice in all that our land gives us and have the freedom and security to also venture into the stars."

Story 24: Garbage Disposal (22nd Century)

Raquel Aguero attended the Guadalajara International Book Fair in Jalisco, Mexico. It was her first time at the largest book fair in the Americas and a welcome break from her waste-removal job in the Mexican Space Agency. She had not visited a book fair since she left Paraguay and arrived in Mexico for training and work almost two years ago in early 2128. She loved romances and developed an interest in sci-fi novels and interactive graphic novels. Raquel was with her friend, Jaime, whom she was interested in as a potential romantic partner before she was informed that he was gay. Raquel enjoyed her time with Jaime, and they shared an interest in comic books and gaming.

Raquel was focused on obtaining a high-level position in the Mexican Space Agency so that she could support her parents, Martin and Beatriz, and their family restaurant in Paraguay. Raquel worked hard in her contract job in space recycling and removal for the Mexican Space Agency, and she quickly earned the respect of her superiors. The Mexican Space Agency recently surpassed the Japan Aerospace Exploration Agency in debris removal. Japan was a leading nation in the space debris removal business for most of the twenty-first century, and Mexico had improved upon the Japanese removal techniques. Raquel understood that becoming successful in Mexico would mean a long and successful career.

At just twenty-two, Raquel was among the youngest workers in her position as a recycler within the Geostationary Earth Orbit. Raquel controlled five removal units and was now being considered for a role within the Low Earth Orbit. The space junk was usually recycled by various orbiting stations belonging to the Mexican Space Agency or they were shipped to the Mexican Lunar Base where they were used to build satellites or used in the base. Small unwanted parts were redirected toward Earth's atmosphere where they would burn in Earth's atmosphere while larger pieces were transported to the Moon.

The removal units or recyclers used various methods of capturing debris, including magnets and robotic arms. Raquel's duties were mostly the removal of small space junk and the transport of the junk to the various orbiting recycling stations, however, she desired to be promoted to capturing non-functioning satellites and transporting them to the Moon for maintenance. A promotion guaranteed Raquel a career in space recycling with a great wage and benefits which would help her and her family move up to the upper-middle class.

Raquel Aguero returned to her apartment in Mexico City, tired and eager to see her messages. Raquel had recently moved out of her dormitory for foreign contractors and began renting a small apartment in Colonia Roma in the Cuauhtémoc borough of Mexico City. The apartment was a little expensive and so Raquel split the rent with a young Mayan student named Izel from the Yucatán Peninsula in southern Mexico. Izel was studying to become a teacher and was interested in teaching Art History, particularly indigenous art and culture.

Izel notified Raquel that she had received sensitive electronic mail. Raquel had a personalized computer given to her by the Mexican Space Agency to use whenever she had to complete work from home. The email notified Izel that a mysterious interstellar object had entered the solar system. The object was oblong and the size of a small building, and it appeared that it would enter the orbits of the inner planets. The interstellar object was over 1,000 feet long and close to 400 feet wide and almost appeared to be manufactured. The object appeared to have a trajectory heading toward the Chinese Lunar Base, and the Chinese were discussing possible actions against the object to divert its path.

Raquel received a private message from her friend and an older man, named Arturo, who informed her that the interstellar object was mostly made of precious metals. It appeared the Chinese government was attempting to deviate the object from its path toward the Moon and wanted to send robots to harvest the metals. The mysterious object was approaching the Moon quickly, and it appeared the Chinese government did not have an organized plan of action. Raquel wondered about the interstellar object and how much it would be worth. She wondered what it would be like to come into possession of such a precious object. Of course, if anyone came into possession of this object, the value of the precious metals it contained would decrease. She smiled at the thought of coming into the possession of even part of the mysterious object.

Izel noticed her smiling and remarked, "I haven't seen you smile that big in weeks! What is the good news? Did you get a promotion at your job?"

Raquel smiled again and revealed the information. "Some people believe that the interstellar object that entered our solar system may be made of valuable metals like titanium and gold, and it may be heading toward the Chinese Lunar Base. Nobody knows what the Chinese government is going to do, and soon this information will be leaked to the public. The United States, Canada, and several European countries already know about this object and its possible worth, and I think they are going to move quickly to mine it."

Izel's eyes opened wide as she exclaimed, "You have access to orbiting machines. Can you find a way to catch parts of the object if the Chinese destroy it?"

Raquel laughed as she replied, "The chances of me catching anything if the Chinese choose to destroy the object is very slim. I think I have a better chance of winning the lottery."

Both ladies laughed as Izel invited Raquel to join her and her boyfriend, Emmanuel, for an evening dinner at a popular restaurant.

Two weeks later, Raquel was working the night shift as everyone spoke about the interstellar object that was possibly heading toward a direct impact with the Chinese Lunar Colony. The Chinese had released a statement several days ago that their attempts to deviate from the object without a large explosion were not successful, so they were about to send several explosive devices. At around three in the morning, Raquel received a message that the Chinese had fragmented the interstellar object, sending about forty percent of the remaining object toward the Sun and fragmenting the rest into small pieces that would mostly burn up upon reaching the Earth's atmosphere with some of the material impacting the Lunar surface without damage to any Lunar colonies. The smaller fragments that were now on a direct path to Earth were expected to burn in Earth's atmosphere.

Some of the Mexican space-recycle units had been damaged with two falling through the Earth's atmosphere. One of the damaged units was being monitored by Raquel's friend and coworker, Ruben, who at first, was not aware of the reason one of his recycling units fell in Luzon province, in the Philippines. When Raquel learned about what had transpired, she informed her roommate Izel. Izel correctly predicted that there would be a worldwide hunt for pieces of the object that had made it through Earth's atmosphere. When Raquel contacted Ruben to see if he saw the video and trajectory of the unit that was struck and fell through the atmosphere, he stated that he'd observed the unit fall in the Philippines before the unit stopped processing information. Ruben's access to records soon ended, and a message from the Mexican Space Agency informed all their workers that the agency would lock access to any video or sound files until further notice. Izel suggested that Raquel contact her second cousin, Paco, a computer hacker, to see if he could temporarily access the files of the downed recyclers. The two ladies debated Izel's suggestion the entire night before Raquel agreed the next day.

Within the next few days, Paco hacked Ruben's computer after Raquel asked to link her computer to Ruben's. Paco was able to see the small segment, a quarter of the size of a small car, strike the space recycler, and calculated its deviated path and fall into a wooded area in Sri Lanka. Paco deduced that the Mexican government was trying to locate various segments that had fallen through the Earth's atmosphere before other governments located them, including the governments of Russia, China, and the United States. Raquel and Paco believed the Mexican government might know that the object landed in Sri Lanka, however, they most likely did not know the exact location.

Paco made sure that his infiltration into the computer systems of the Mexican Space Agency was not tracked, and he went to his apartment where he attempted to hack the computer system belonging to a police station in Nilaveli, Sri Lanka. The police station had active drones in the area where the object crashed. It appeared a piece had crashed near a wooded area and another had landed in the sea less than a mile offshore of Nilaveli Beach. Paco and Raquel quickly traveled to Sri Lanka, and Paco rented a small submarine and eventually located the object. They booked a flight to Sri Lanka the following weekend, and after Paco secured a loan, he bought a small submersible used to recover small fragments from wreckages.

Paco soon located the object near the beach, and he returned with Raquel at night to recover the object. Paco and Raquel embraced and laughed with tears in their eyes, when they observed the numerous precious metals, including iron, nickel, gold, and platinum, that made up the alien object. After agreeing to split the money from the object, Paco paid to smuggle the object to Raquel's native nation of Paraguay. He promised to smuggle the item after breaking it down into smaller pieces that could fit into suitcases. Roughly half of the pieces were to be smuggled into Paraguay, and Paco would later help her further extract the metals in Paraguay.

Raquel made sure to keep her activities a secret from her coworkers and continued to work as usual. She helped her roommate Izel financially and began helping her parents in Paraguay. Raquel also helped her friend, Jaime, with his university tuition and bought him some graphic novels and pre-ordered exclusive interactive graphic novels from China and Japan. Raquel was soon offered a permanent position with the Mexican Space Agency, and she was now working within Earth's low orbit. She soon had enough money for her and her parents to live comfortably for a lifetime, and with the right investments, Raquel could start real generational wealth for her children and grandchildren if she chose to have a family. Raquel began preparations to invest in her parents' restaurant and help improve the family business.

On Christmas Eve, 2132, Raquel was spending time with her family in Villarrica, Paraguay, enjoying the festivities and speaking Guarani with her loved ones when she was notified by her mother about breaking international news. Various nations, including China, Russia, the Philippines, Bhutan, Laos, and Sri Lanka had captured some fragments of the interstellar object with the remaining few believed to be at the bottom of the Indian Sea. The largest fragments had landed on the Moon and were mostly gathered by the Russians and Chinese. The Chinese government speculated that the interstellar object may have been part of a larger object, and rumors spread that it might have been a technological device. Perhaps the object was a communication device. Raquel had a sharp, cold feeling within her but laughed to herself. If the speculation was true, the civilization that sent this object was most likely no longer in existence. Raquel dismissed these deeper questions and enjoyed her time with her family and grinned as her future was now full of possibilities.

Story 25: Dream Dance (22nd Century)

Plutarco Machado left his home and traveled to a secret location in La Vega, Dominican Republic where he was studying a new communication technology. The experimental technology was tested on patients who were lucid dreamers, and the research was funded by the Dominican Health Agency. The study had been built upon an earlier study performed by researchers from various nations, including the United States in 2019. Now in 2091, Dominican scientists were advancing communication technology to help people with depression and other disorders as well as creating a new form of entertainment. The study attracted the entertainment industry, particularly Dominican Electronic Entertainment.

Plutarco was spending more time in the lab to the dismay of his wife, Indira, who now spent most of her time alone in their home after their daughter Elif had left home and relocated to Seattle, Washington. Elif had completed her Ph.D. in Comparative Literature and soon became an assistant professor at Washington University and married a Jordanian-American man named Omar Saleh who was a professor of literature at the same university. Plutarco's son, Morfeo, was currently studying Computer Programming abroad in Germany. Despite his reservations with

Dominican Electronic Entertainment, Plutarco thought researching for a gaming company would bring him and his son closer together.

Before he left, Plutarco's wife warned him once again, "My love, be very careful with allowing your studies to be used for entertainment purposes. Companies usually care about profits. It is important to understand that human psychology is important and should not be manipulated. The body is only as healthy as the mind. I have studied psychology since I was a girl, and even as I have reached the heights of my profession, I never fail to learn something new every day with my patients. Please be careful."

Plutarco nodded in agreement, and he left for work. Plutarco was currently in the last month of a six-month study on ten subjects. One of the patients that the Dominican scientists were most focused on was a young Guyanese-Dominican woman named Sunita Romero, who was born in the Dominican Republic to a Dominican father and a Guyanese mother. Sunita Romero also gained the attention of Chief Technology Officer Vicente Pujols of Dominican Electronic Entertainment. Vicente Pujols desired to combine current psychiatric technology and Plutarco's study to create various forms of entertainment using lucid dreams—creating an enhanced dream that could be enjoyed by the dreamer and perhaps another person. The new technology would be called Dream Dance. Dream Dance would tap into a player's conscious and subconscious minds to provide a fully immersive experience.

Plutarco and the other scientists were working to improve the current technology that tapped into a person's subconscious to improve the quality of life of people that had suffered from a traumatic event. This technology was used most often in a hospital setting for patients with mental trauma, and now, various innovators and businessmen were seeking to use the technology for entertainment purposes. Vicente Pujols was one of the most vocal supporters, and he asked to observe the study and analyze patients who could manipulate their dreams to the highest degree.

Pressured by Vicente Pujols and interested in gaining a new contract as a researcher for Dominican Electronic Entertainment, Plutarco advised Sunita to participate in additional trials for Vicente that would guarantee her additional money after just one more week of tests. Sunita agreed, and soon they began additional studies for Dominican Electronic Entertainment. As soon as Sunita's six months were completed, she began an additional week of studies with Plutarco and scientists who were recently hired by Dominican Electronic Entertainment. The studies would resume in the following months at another facility in Puerto Plata, and Plutarco was invited to be part of these extensive studies.

For the first few days, Sunita was observed closely as she slept, and when she reached rem sleep, she was attached to the new Dream Dance technology. As soon as Sunita was engaged in lucid dreaming, she signaled to Plutarco through electrical signals that she was ready. Plutarco started a beta program of the Dream Dance technology, and soon images formed in Sunita's dreams, complementing the images her subconscious had already created.

Various surroundings were generated of lush, green fields, snow-capped mountains, and pristine lakes appearing as if Sunita was in Switzerland. Soon Plutarco linked into the Dream Dance program, and he also influenced what appeared on the screen, including interactive views of historical monuments and locations, including the Statue of Unity in India, Timbuktu in Mali, the religious structure of Angkor Wat in Cambodia, the Great Pyramids of Egypt, the Great Pyramid of Cholula in Mexico, and the Genghis Khan Statue Complex in Ulaanbaatar, Mongolia. Perhaps it was Plutarco's love for history and culture that influenced the Dream Dance to produce these images which increased Plutarco's enjoyment of the study. Several games were created, and both Sunita and Plutarco agreed to play some of them, and they partook in sports like tennis and basketball, while also participating in futuristic and ancient sports like pok-ta-pok in a Pre-Colombian and Mesoamerican ball court.

Plutarco understood the potential of the Dream Dance in the Dominican Republic and internationally. He believed the Dream Dance could also be used to enhance sexual dreams for adult entertainment. On the fifth day of the initial studies of the Dream Dance technology, other interactive worlds were recreated as Sunita slept. Horror elements were added, including dark rooms and an abandoned location near a river. Suddenly, the Dream Dance triggered an unexpected reaction within Sunita, leading her to wake up with tears in her eyes. Sexual images appeared on the screen connected to the Dream Dance, as well as a visor that Plutarco was wearing. Plutarco's heart was also racing after this traumatic experience.

Sunita reluctantly revealed to Plutarco that she had suffered a violent and shameful experience as a young girl with a relative but refused to explain further. She had not revealed any prior trauma before agreeing to the initial six-month medical study, and she wanted to continue the studies with Dominican Electronic Entertainment. Tears flowed from her eyes as what was previously occult was now revealed. Sunita also revealed that she saw images of Plutarco in inappropriate acts with a younger researcher that worked with Plutarco, named Sadira. Plutarco didn't deny his secret relationship with Sadira but stood quietly as his deepest secrets were revealed. Sadira, who was nearby, was alarmed and wiped her tears as she looked to Plutarco for guidance.

Plutarco embraced her patient and was alarmed at the harm the Dream Dance technology could inflict upon Dominican society if it were to be used for entertainment. The technology could also be stolen by foreign governments and be used to inflict harm. Plutarco now found himself in agreement with his wife and the Dominican activists that spoke against Vicente Pujols and his company. He decided to not accept Vicente's proposal to continue his research for the benefit of Vicente and the Dream Dance technology.

Plutarco was driving home after several days of talking with CTO Vicente Pujols regarding the possibility of researching for Dominican Electronic Entertainment. Plutarco was offered a substantial amount of money, but he felt the company was unethical and decided he would not participate in the studies. Plutarco felt shame and sadness at the secrets he'd kept from his loving wife, Indira, and at his unprofessionalism in his duties as a scientist. Plutarco should have listened to his wife and the activists who spoke against the usage of the conscious and subconscious mind for entertainment. Dominican Electronic Entertainment possibly could improve the Dream Dance technology for safe use, however, the human mind was a complicated organ. The Dream Dance and its manipulation of the brain would pose ethical problems for any scientists that sought to exploit the mysteries of the brain for entertainment.

Plutarco continued his drive home. As the sky darkened and he approached his home, he dried his tears. As he entered his home, Plutarco promised himself to spend more time with his wife. He breathed in and exhaled deeply before opening the door.

Story 26: Panda Down Under (22nd Century)

Djalu was an old man nearing his seventieth birthday. When he was a young man, he'd believed he would never live to see thirty years in his beloved Australia. He was in a joyous mood after celebrating Christmas with his children and grandchildren and welcomed in the year 2138 with good health and a happy spirit. Tonight, Djalu was meeting up at a local sports bar with his childhood friend Christopher. Christopher was in town visiting some relatives, and he thought it was a good opportunity to spend some time with Djalu.

Pubs were now cleaner and were filled with a mixture of tourists, aborigines, Asian, and white Australians. Pubs and lounges were larger with television, music, karaoke, card tables, and billiards. Family-friendly establishments were constructed during the brief Chinese occupation. The Australian draft was initiated during the first year of Chinese occupation as Aussie rebels continue to destroy roads and bridges to halt the Chinese advancement toward the capital city of Canberra.

Djalu spoke to his childhood best friend, Christopher, about their lives growing up and a matter of contention between both men regarding the Chinese-Australian war in the late twenty-first century. The two men were childhood friends who had lost touch after the war but they'd rekindled their friendship later in life. Both men were war veterans with different opinions of the war and its outcome, and they rarely spoke about their experiences to their family members and friends. The old friends were ready to speak openly about their feelings about the war and their feelings about their roles in the conflict.

Djalu was stocky and had dark brown skin and blond hair that was not turning gray with age. Christopher was tall and slender with lighter skin and his features displayed his mixed native and white ancestry. Both men remembered the progression toward warfare on the Australian mainland. China had annexed Taiwan by the late twenty-first century, initiating a regional conflict, and had continued to aid Russia during their war in Europe. Russia had annexed eastern Ukraine by the mid-twenty-first century and threatened to annex the entire Ukrainian territory.

Western sanctions destabilized the Russian economy and offshore properties, and the money of the Russian oligarchs was frozen. China increased its economic power during the early part of the Russian-Ukrainian War and aided Russia while expanding its influence in Southeast Asia. Inflation weakened the United States while the United States continued to support its allies against Russia and China. The United States threatened to initiate a direct conflict with China during the Chinese invasion of Australia. By the late twenty-first century, China reached the Australian mainland.

The Chinese Communist Party supplied aid and technology that improved the standard of living for aboriginal communities throughout Australia. The Chinese military promised to withhold an eastern military advance in Australia if the United States discontinued its military and financial aid to Australia and its allies in Southeast Asia.

The two men drank, and after several hours of playing pool, Christopher said, "I was always confused as to why many Aboriginal people, including you, did not join the war effort until you were drafted into service. I remember vividly how the Chinese military advanced through the Australian mainland and occupied Sydney, and how my family had to flee. The Chinese appeared like an invincible juggernaut that would soon capture the capital of Canberra and the city of Melbourne. I remember there were conversations about holding a government in exile in Tasmania."

Djalu replied, "After the British buccaneer, William Dampier, explored the Australian coastline from 1688 and 1699, and the subsequent arrival of James Cook, the native people of Australia suffered greatly. The Europeans called our homeland New Holland and began to colonize our ancient country. Our people have been abused for centuries and continue to be abused today. So, the other Aboriginal people and I asked ourselves what the purpose was of fighting and dying for white Australians and wealthy people who'd never cared for us before the conflict began."

Christopher shook his head in disapproval as he replied, "You understand history well, my friend, but things are complicated during wartime. The Chinese government was emboldened after Russian aggression in Ukraine and Europe. Russia and China believed the United States was weakening, and China began to expand its influence in the Pacific. The conflict between China and Australia worsened and led to the Chinese invasion of Australia. I joined the military a year before the invasion when the Chinese positioned weapons in Papua New Guinea and their warships began patrolling the Australian coastline."

Djalu replied, "Australia joined the United States in sanctioning China and increased the presence of the US Army and Marines in Australia. Many of us in the outback never wanted this conflict nor the US and Chinese presence in Australia. All we wanted was equal rights and good programs so that our families could enjoy the same benefits that white Australians enjoyed. You had a great upbringing in Sydney, and you had an easier time getting accepted because you have a white family, and through your family connections you were able to include yourself in upper-middle-class society."

Christopher raised his voice as he interjected, "Yes, I was lucky to have good parents that were financially secure. But you don't fully understand my world, my friend. You are not aware of the difficulties in being half-white and half-Aboriginal. I am of European and Torres Strait Islander ancestry, and I sometimes struggled to understand how to identify myself growing up. I am both, yet I am considered apart from both the Aboriginal and white people. Despite my upbringing, I understand that the Aboriginal people have been and continue to be mistreated in Australia, and that is something we need to improve on in Australia. The Chinese are not the saviors of the Aboriginal people, however, because they are only trying to sow conflict within Australia for their benefit. China has a long history of ethnic abuses within its nation, including the mistreatment of the Uyghurs. The most important thing we can all do is fight for our sovereignty as Australians and then fight for those deeper and more nuanced issues."

Djalu replied, "When the Chinese occupied Australia, they began occupying Western Australia and then rapidly occupied the Northern Territory. The Chinese quickly constructed smart roads and smart towns in the Australian outback. They helped build schools and create jobs in the outback. The Chinese officials sent diplomats to Canberra to negotiate a peace treaty with the US and Australian governments to remove US nuclear submarines from Australian waters. After negotiations fell and the Australians attacked, the Chinese marched toward the capital, and the draft was initiated. Many Aboriginals, including myself, entered the military and fought the Chinese bravely and helped to stop their advancement toward Canberra. I killed Chinese soldiers during the fight for Sydney and celebrated the end of the war. Now that the war is over, perhaps the Australian government can build infrastructure in the outback like their enemies once did."

Christopher sighed. "The Chinese built those smart roads and smart towns mainly for the support of their military vehicles and drones. I understand your point of view, my friend, but we must be careful with propaganda from Chinese media that is used to divide us."

Djalu laughed as he said, "Propaganda is everywhere, old friend. Everyone has an agenda to push. Things are improving now for the Aboriginal people, and we have more opportunities. We have more Aboriginal people entering higher education and higher-income jobs, and we have more representation in our government. We have a higher quality of life and fewer deaths due to alcoholism and drug abuse. We are making progress, my friend. Sadly, it took a major war to make some progress in Australia. The United States, Russia, and the major powers of the previous century are now less powerful, but China still has some influence in Asia. If the Australian government wants a stronger and more united Australia, they must include all Australians, particularly the Aboriginal people that have lived on this continent for thousands of years."

The two men stopped playing pool and took their beers outside to enjoy the Australian night. The outback was more developed with many Australians and foreigners coming to live and work there.

Christopher smiled at his friend and said, "I understand your perspective, old friend. I think it was foolish to argue when we were younger men. You are strong-minded and confident, and no matter our disagreements, I always admired those qualities that you possessed. I always second-guessed myself, but you always seemed confident with your decisions even if your opinions and actions were not favored by the majority. We lived long, married great women, and we now have children and grandchildren. I hope that they live in a better Australia than the one that we grew up in. I pray that our grandchildren don't have to go to war and only experience happiness through hard work and the fruits of their labors."

Djalu laughed and said, "Thank you, Chris, for your kind words. I must admit I have had times when I questioned my choices, as well. Before the war, I asked myself if I should join the raids on Chinese bases alongside Aboriginal rebels. I initially saw the conflict as only between global powers in the eastern Australian cities. I believed the conflict would be resolved quickly. After the war, some white Australians shifted their anger away from the Aboriginals toward the Chinese and ignorantly toward any Asian Australians. I met my wife shortly after the war. She fled Cambodia with her family as a young girl during Chinese expansion in the region. You married a white woman, but I wasn't sure if I should marry a Cambodian woman and have Aboriginal and Asian children. It seemed they would face double the prejudice. I combated my doubts and followed my heart, and now my children carry my spirit and have become successful Australians. I hope Australia improves conditions for all Australians, and I hope the panda and the kangaroo do not fight again and find a way to coexist."

The two men laughed and spent most of the night speaking about their lives and long friendship. They sang songs and spoke with the townspeople about their own stories during the war and life in the outback. There were many stories told and lessons learned, and the two friends looked at their lives from different perspectives. Good friends are rare, and both men enjoyed their night together. Nights like these were less frequent as the years went by.

Story 27: The Artificial Melancholy of Ana Rosa Wagner (22nd Century)

Hola, *Mariana, how are you? Thank you for coming here to San Cristobal. I still don't know what happened to Ana Rosa. It has been weeks, three weeks to be exact. She has not responded to my calls or text messages. At first, I thought someone had hurt Ana Rosa, but then I started thinking that she might have fallen into a deep depression. I did not notice the signs of her despair until only a few* months *ago.*

Ana Rosa Wagner is everything that every young woman wants to be—confident, sexy, beautiful, and independent. I met her three years ago, in 2107, when I went to see an opera at the Eduardo Brito National Theater in Santo Domingo. I was surprised to see Ana Rosa, the heiress of one of the largest Dominican companies, in attendance. Ana Rosa was more beautiful in person. She wore an elegant white-and-red dress and her long, blond hair complemented her beautiful fair skin and hazel eyes. Ana Rosa's family was an old German-Dominican family that had originally lived in Puerto Plata and later settled in Santo Domingo. I remember that day I was twenty years of age and Ana Rosa was twenty-five. We spoke, and one of her friends told her who my father was, and she seemed interested in getting to know me. At that time, she was dating the famous Dominican-American director, Ulises Serrano.

Ana's grandfather, Rodolfo Wagner, enhanced a language-deciphering artificial intelligence that was originally developed at M.I.T. in the United States in 2021. The improved language decoder was used in the Dominican Republic to decode and expand the Taino language, and soon the technology was used throughout the world. Ana Rosa's father further enhanced the A.I. through the use of quantum computers which he also used to improve Dominican infrastructure—this made her family wealthy. Ana Rosa was born into a life of luxury and comfort, and it was exciting to become her friend. I traveled to so many countries with her. We flew in her private electric jet to various nations, including India, China, Japan, Dubai, and Italy.

Our families were rich, but the Wagner family was wealthy. The difference between rich and wealthy is night and day. I think she befriended me because my father Mario Cespedes was a recent celebrity with his new fertilizer which had enhanced Dominican farming in the last ten years. Ana seemed to gravitate toward people who had achieved a high level of celebrity status. I think she kept me around because I am honest and didn't simply agree with everything she said. I began to notice months ago that Ana was not as happy with herself as she appeared to be. I believe she experimented with psychoactive drugs whenever I wasn't around and she was around her other wealthy friends.

One afternoon, I overheard a conversation between her and someone else. She was speaking about illegal memory insertions. Usually, people use positive memories in some Asian countries but some use temporary sad memories to give them a feeling of gloom. This was usually used by people who seem to have everything they wanted in life. It was a silly notion because even wealthy people suffer through tragedy and emotional pain. I noticed that she became more depressed, and she stop wanting to travel or go to events.

I found out that Ana's romantic relationships usually failed, including her relationship with Ulises. I found out that Ulises broke up with Ana, but she never mentioned the reasons why. Ana also seemed unhappy when her Jamaican best friend, Nicole, married a wealthy businessman from the Democratic Republic of Congo. His family owned a company that processed tantalum from coltan mining in the eastern side of the nation. Nicole just moved from Jamaica to the Congo last week.

Ana had a Dominican suitor named Radames who was a great person. He was a self-made man who created an advanced medical imaging machine. Dominican hospitals were purchasing his machines, and although he was not as rich as the men Ana was used to dating, I think he would have been the best man for her. Radames tried to gain her interest for many years, and he finally gave up, and soon he began dating the famous Dominican violinist, Amina Abadi. Ana told me he'd proposed to her last month, and although she'd tried hard not to care, I could tell she was hurt that the man she'd rejected had found love.

I think Ana was aimless and hadn't found something to give her meaning. Other members of Ana's family had carved their paths, for example, Ana Rosa's younger brother, Otto, is an archeologist who used language technology to make discoveries about ancient societies in the Caribbean and other countries in Latin America. Since Ana enjoyed fashion, I suggested she create her clothes. When I spoke to her about this, she replied to me in a bad tone. Ana then became cold toward me, and I knew our friendship was over. Several days later, she disappeared, and no one has heard from her for weeks.

After Esperanza informed Mariana about what had happened, they pondered the possible whereabouts of Ana. The next day, a Dominican detective named Esperanza explained that he had informed Ana's family that they discovered Ana unconscious in her luxury boat. The Dominican Navy had intercepted Ana's boat before she'd reached US territorial waters north of Cuba. Doctors were working to try and revive her, and there was a chance she would live. It didn't matter to Esperanza if her friendship with Ana Rosa was over; all that mattered was that Ana survived and that she could find lasting peace within herself. Mariana and Esperanza spent most of the day crying and praying and crying and praying. Then they cried and prayed some more.

Story 28: Electric Currency (21st Century)

The debt had ballooned to over 200 billion in Puerto Rico while climate change and natural disasters had led to thousands of Puerto Ricans leaving for the US mainland. Many Puerto Ricans had settled in Florida, the Carolinas, and the East Coast. The Puerto Rican government had trouble restructuring the debt and was forced to cut on social safety-net programs, further impoverishing the Puerto Rican people. During this time, many wealthy crypto investors moved to Puerto Rico, enjoying tax breaks while raising property values and increasing the number of Puerto Ricans leaving their native island.

Ashley Santiago was the lead prosecutor against Ramesh Rajkumar and his company. She'd endured years of abuse and defamation, mostly at the hands of right-wing businessmen and politicians. Some even labeled her a radical and a communist when she began to speak against corrupt capitalism and unregulated digital currencies. Despite this, the fierce *morena* twenty-five-year-old prosecutor continued forward with her case.

Ashley's father had previously supported Rubén Berríos and the Puerto Rican Independence Party for most of his life. The Puerto Rican Independence movement had subsided, but now in the year 2035, it was resurgent and dangerous to the Puerto

Rican establishment. This case would be a major turning point for Puerto Ricans, either toward independence or statehood, as the case for the status quo had declined in the minds of most boricuas.

Ashley fought for over two years as the case gained national attention. Today was the day of judgment. Judge Miguel Osorio would read the verdict in front of numerous news outlets. Reporters with cameras swarmed outside the courtroom in San Juan, eagerly awaiting the verdict. After a long speech in which Judge Osorio explained the dangers of unregulated currency and scams directed at poor working people, he finally read the verdict of guilty. A crowd of activists outside of the courtroom erupted in cheers.

Ramesh and several of his business partners faced jail time and millions of dollars in lawsuits. Documents revealed that he used money from investors as his slush fund and manufactured a computer-hacking scandal that manipulated his blockchain to cover up his fraud. Ramesh had also paid several Puerto Rican politicians to help support deregulation and additional tax exemptions for his businesses and the businesses of his friends. Ramesh claimed he was innocent and angrily protested the ruling before he was removed from the courtroom by police officers.

Ashley spoke to various news outlets outside the courtroom. "Today was a victory for the people of Puerto Rico against the scam of deregulated currency pushed by extreme right-wing libertarians. I read history and support traditional socialist libertarianism that protected the rights of the working people. These harmful ideologies from the United States have spread throughout Latin America and particularly in the territory of Puerto Rico which still exists in limbo between independence and full integration as a state of the United States. Some of these people, who exploited the laws of Puerto Rico, raised money and ran for political office in the United States."

Ashley paused for several seconds as the crowds of activists chanted her name before she spoke. "The concept of freedom means different things to different people. Freedom to me is living in a society where a working person doesn't have to struggle for the basics of life. Where everyone from the wealthiest to the poorest can expect fair judgment within the justice system. Where people can have a chance to reach their potential through hard work and their skills. Where people can enjoy a government that is transparent, democratic, and truly represents them and their desires. This is what it means to live in a society. We have freedoms, but we also need to work together so that our freedoms do not restrict the freedoms of our fellow citizens. Where we have a more equitable society, cleaner environment, affordable healthcare, and education. This is true freedom to me, and I suspect it is true freedom for many others, as well."

After the verdict, numerous companies faced class-action lawsuits throughout Puerto Rico and the United States. Numerous class-action lawsuits were brought against many social media influencers that were involved in insider trading. The cryptocurrencies relied heavily on celebrity support, and their value was easily manipulated and dangerous for people that could not afford to invest their hard-earned dollars.

Other nations in the Caribbean and Latin America enacted regulations on cryptocurrencies to protect people from scams. Various forms of digital currencies remained that were heavily monitored by software programs to mitigate fraud and promote transparency. Later, laws were enacted to increase regulations and taxation on the wealthy while restructuring Puerto Rico's debt. Social programs were increased to help working people, and small businesses received tax incentives to help lower the unemployment rate. It was one step forward and the start of another long journey.

Story 29: Eco-Phantasm (23rd Century)

Surgeon General Daniel Santos reviewed his notes before his public address. It was now the year 2135, and the United States was in the second year of a devastating pandemic. War was imminent as China expanded its power throughout southeast Asia and threatened an invasion of Australia. President Vincent Ureña was taking questions from the news media during the press briefing. He made a passionate speech, as he attempted to hold the nation together, regarding the need for all US citizens to work together despite their real or imagined differences. The president cited Abraham Lincoln and his call for unity as the nation declined into civil war. President Ureña warned that the United States would not survive a second civil war.

President Vincent Ureña was disliked by the progressives in Congress and was hated by all far-right groups and a desperate Republican Party that was attempting to gain control by exploiting the anger and fear caused by the ongoing pandemic and a potential world war. Climate change exacerbated inflation, and government spending escalated due to damage caused by the increased occurrences of natural disasters. Political violence surged as income inequality and divisions continued to rise throughout the United States.

Daniel was motivated to address the US public and was prepared to counter the misinformation from the Republican Patriot News Network. Far-Right media outlets sought to undermine the weakened Democratic Administration. President Vincent Ureña was of Puerto Rican and Mexican descent, and his push for mandates enraged far right-wing groups and the Republican Party that saw him as the outcome of an increasingly diverse population and white Americans losing their majority status in the late twenty-first century. The Republican Party was on the brink of collapse and openly calling for increased border control and an attack on China.

Daniel was speaking with Vice-President Neera Nahar, the Bangladeshi-American former junior senator of Georgia. Neera was a popular progressive figure and Daniel's first choice during the Democratic primaries. Neera's position as vice president was the reason that Daniel accepted his appointment as Surgeon General. Daniel rarely spoke publicly regarding his socialist political leanings, but he privately supported Neera Nahar and her environmental regulations and her support for affordable healthcare and medicine. Daniel voted for President Vincent Ureña during the general election, primarily to avoid the election of a far-right Republican president.

Vice-President Nahar whispered to Daniel just as the president was finishing his speech, "Thank you for your hard work through this difficult time. I understand you supported me for a long time, and we both share similar visions for this nation, but now we must support the president and fight against the misinformation campaign throughout social media. Far-Right media is pushing these conspiracies. We are facing war and a worsening pandemic, and we need to decrease hospitalizations because our healthcare system is on the brink of collapse. If we can survive the political storms, I promise that I will continue to fight for our progressive ideals. Remember, I nearly beat the president during the primaries, and now the House of Representatives consists of over forty percent of progressives with increasing numbers in the Senate."

After President Vincent Ureña completed his address, he welcomed Daniel to the podium. Daniel wanted to believe in Nahar's words, but he felt deep anguish and despair as if a dark cloud had now permanently settled upon the United States. As Daniel approached the podium, he could feel the tension in the room as everyone focused on him. He'd become a major villain due to a massive misinformation campaign that had painted him as a part of a pharmaceutical plot that had desired to experiment and strip the freedoms that US citizens enjoyed, even though, throughout his life, Daniel had fought for affordable drug prices and against the pharmaceutical lobbies. Daniel's Dominican ancestry, his brown skin, and wavy hair, which gave him a Middle-Eastern appearance, only served to further anger the far-right groups.

Daniel walked to the podium as the President of the United States stepped to the side and observed him as he made his speech. "My fellow Americans, we have suffered greatly in the last two years. Many of us have lost friends and family members and have witnessed the hardships their loss has left behind. Young children have been orphaned and must live with other family members or are now part of the foster care system. We are facing a pandemic that can be worse than the black plague if we do not take vaccinations and safety precautions seriously. I advise everyone to continue practicing proper safety protocols and get vaccinated. We all enjoy our freedoms, but now, entering the second year of this pandemic, we have lost over 25 million people, and we have a population of just over 400 million people. This means we lost over six percent of our population to this pandemic in just over two years. This is the worst pandemic we have faced in the history of the United States, and it will continue to worsen if we don't get vaccinated. We can mitigate the harm of this pandemic, and we believe we should keep our borders partially closed while pushing international efforts to provide medications for poorer nations. We must work together as we face economic turmoil as well as a possible war. Because of the dangerous consequences we potentially face, we believe we should institute mandates throughout the United States to help secure our borders and get as many of our citizens vaccinated and abiding by safety protocols."

Daniel finished his statement as the entire room raised their hands. There was a growing distrust in government and many questions for Daniel. Daniel was dismayed but determined to try to get the most accurate information to the American public, and he was focused on disseminating his information in an accurate, simple, and concise way.

Daniel pointed at a reporter from Cable Information Network. "Hello, this is Nicole So with CIN. Does President Vincent Ureña plan on investigating the fungal spores that have exacerbated the pandemic in Asia? Do you have measures to stop the fungal role in the ongoing increase in the death rates from this coronavirus?"

Daniel replied, "We are investigating these fungi, and we are taking every measure to make sure that this deadly fungal and viral combination does not wreak havoc here in the United States. We are already developing a successful vaccine and anti-fungal combination of drugs that will help us if Dark Lung arrives in the United States. The important thing for people is to follow safety protocols and remain safe but calm. If you fall victim to conspiracy theories, fear, and anger, it will cause panic, and that is the last thing we need."

Daniel answered as many questions as he could before turning to Richard Jeffries, a Conservative reporter for Patriot New Network that had asked him loaded questions in the past. Richard Jeffries also had several channels in social media and was one of Daniel's major enemies in the war of disinformation that now enveloped the troubled nation.

Richard Jeffries raised his hand, and Daniel reluctantly pointed at him, "Hello, Richard Jeffries with Patriot New Network. Surgeon General Daniel Santos, many people feel your administration is mishandling this pandemic. Americans believe you are not exposing the true information regarding the Chinese Communist Government and their involvement with viral and fungal experiments. It seems convenient that this pandemic is occurring while China is threatening the Philippines and is preparing for a land invasion of Australia."

Daniel quickly replied, "We are facing many challenges at this time with the economy, impending war, and a worsening pandemic that threatens to cripple our healthcare system. We are facing increasing Chinese aggression in Australia, and our allies need our help. We are studying fungi that cause diseases in the human body while at the same time researching fungi that can help us eradicate viral diseases. We are working hard to understand these fungi and to catch up to other cultures, including China, that have studied and have had a better understanding of fungi for thousands of years."

Jeffries interjected, "There are reports that China developed a biowarfare program involving fungi that can transmit deadly respiratory fungal infections. Your administration appears weak and has not retaliated against China."

Daniel focused on Jeffries as he replied, "I will remind you, Mr. Jeffries, that the president is taking all intelligence regarding China seriously. We are increasing our economic sanctions against China and trying to discuss a peaceful resolution to avoid further conflicts. We have to work together to improve conditions in the United States as well as improve our foreign policy so that we can avoid possible warfare that could devastate the world economy."

Jeffries replied, "The CDC has given contradictory reports regarding the pandemic and death rates. Deaths are still increasing in nations that have achieved high vaccination rates."

Daniel shook his head in disagreement and replied, "The people in your network have agreed to mandatory vaccines and safety protocols, Mr. Jeffries. Data can be manipulated to push an agenda, and your network and misinformation from social media now create a synergistic relationship in spreading false information. Scientists and epidemiologists agree that the upper-respiratory virus has killed many millions of people throughout the world, and the United States has the most deaths even though we have the technology to decrease hospitalizations and deaths. Some fungi transmit spores that have significantly increased the possibility of death, particularly among unvaccinated people who have contracted the virus and Black Lung or have survived the coronavirus and later contracted Black Lung disease. There has been a massive disinformation campaign, particularly from far-right Media, including the Patriot News Network, that has further confused US citizens. Your network and others have not improved conditions but have worsened them during the pandemic. We must follow the science and safety protocols and unite as Americans so that we can survive through these tumultuous times and thrive afterward."

Daniel received loud applause from the room, and he walked away from the cameras. The president smiled at Daniel and asked him to accompany him to the Oval Office. Daniel observed the seriousness in President Vincent Ureña's eyes and believed the United States was now facing dire consequences. The meeting at the Oval Office continued late into the night before the president dismissed Daniel just before midnight and he continued speaking with his military advisors. Daniel left the White House and entered his electric vehicle and finally drove home.

Daniel's wife, Milagros, was sleeping in the bedroom. She'd left dinner covered on the table—a Dominican dinner of rice and beans with oxtails—just what Daniel needed after this long, cold December day. Milagros was positioned with a pillow beneath her legs, her caramel skin shining in the star-filled night, her long, black hair covering most of her hands, and her left arm outstretched, waiting for her husband to share their bed.

Daniel changed his clothes and took a warm shower. He thought about the noticeable anxiety he heard from the president's voice as he said that China was about to invade Australia. Australia could not withstand a land invasion by China, and the United States would have to counter China. The president would publicly call for a nationwide mandate, something he tried to avoid but which was now necessary as many millions of people would die from the pandemic during the potential war against China.

Daniel felt a sharp pain in his head, and he suspected it was another migraine. Daniel had begun to suffer from migraines just over a year ago, and he'd begun to have frequent nightmares. Sometimes, it appeared that images from his dreams would bleed over into his daily life. Strange faces appeared, familiar ones, and sometimes, familiar faces and voices would appear foreign. In his dreams, he began seeing scenes from previous generations or sometimes bleak images of the future. Daniel had checked himself into the hospital several times, but he'd never contracted any viral or fungal diseases. Perhaps it was just the mental strain of becoming a controversial public figure.

Daniel felt he was losing control of his emotions, which embarrassed him. He was raised to be a strong Dominican man and professionally perform his duties, but he now felt like giving up. He wiped his tears although they were concealed by the shower he had just taken, and he went to bed. He tried not to awaken his wife, but she felt him as he covered himself with the sheets.

Milagros told the home computer to turn the light on dimly before she said, "*Mi amor*, you seem troubled today. Before you agreed to take this job, I warned you that you might become a controversial figure during this pandemic. People are nervous, angry, and scared, and millions will love you and millions will hate you. You made your choice, and I supported your decision just as you supported my decision to become a physician's assistant after we had our son, Aurelio. Now we are grandparents and have a good life, and you must continue to fight the good fight and help this wounded nation. But if you feel you do not want to move forward in your role, I will also be here to support you."

There was so much he wanted to say to his wife, and he went to the bathroom before his tears revealed his deep anguish. He walked slowly to the sink to wash his face, but when he looked in the mirror, his face did not seem like his. His vision became blurry, and he felt a sense of conflict within his soul. He splashed cold water on his face and breathed deeply before returning to bed. Tomorrow he would wake up determined and take on his days. He would take time to explain the dire situation the nation was in, the fact that war was imminent. He would try to provide the best service for his country and be the best husband and protector to his wife, and the best father and patriarch to his family.

Daniel awoke a little confused; his bedroom appeared different, and his wife was no longer there. He heard strange voices nearby and strained to hear their conversation.

A young man spoke quickly, "I believe he has awakened, General Luna. The surgery and treatment have been a success, and we believe we have cured Daniel Santos. I think he can maintain his consciousness and return to his formal self before the tragedy that inflicted him and his family members."

Suddenly, two men entered the room, and Daniel realized he was no longer in his condo in Washington D.C. but somewhere in the south. It was no longer cold but hot, and he was wearing a hospital gown. The room had smart walls that portrayed the island setting of coconut trees and a sandy beach, perhaps to remind Daniel of his Caribbean origins. A smart window became transparent, revealing a vast wilderness with plants and wildlife and enlarged fungi. There were workers and people with smart pads documenting what they observed. Daniel was in a room about four stories above ground level.

Before Daniel attempted to ask questions, the young man said, "Hello, Mr. Santos, we are happy that you have awakened from your medically induced coma. My name is Roberto Hernandez, and I am a scientist working for the Mexican military. You are now in a Mexican military base in our northern territories within the former US State of Arizona. The year is now 2205. The former United States collapsed after the ongoing pandemic crippled the US economy and extremists from the Middle East and the former nation of North Korea detonated a nuclear weapon in the middle of the United States. The United States now consists of twenty states on the east coast. Several northwestern states were acquired by Canada. The southwest and west coast are now inhabited by numerous advanced fungi and wildlife that thrive under radioactive conditions and are now part of Northern Mexico. We have discovered several advanced fungi that are medically beneficial to humans. Our scientific discoveries allowed us to eradicate most cancers and extend our life expectancy. The Mexican government has now settled the former wastelands with communities that can live under high radioactive exposure.

Daniel paused and attempted to gather his thoughts as he began to recover his memory. "Did the United States lose the war? When did I arrive in Mexico, and is the pandemic over?"

Roberto Hernandez replied, "The United States was near economic collapse when China attacked Australia, leading to the last major war in the previous century. The war between China and the United States began in 2136, and by 2139, the Chinese retreated from Australia. In 2140, several extremists from the Middle East and North Korea were able to launch a nuclear warhead toward the US Midwest, killing millions of people. The United States launched nuclear warheads at China, ending the war, however, internal turmoil fragmented the United States between the united leftist front and several far-right paramilitary groups. These conflicts continued until just a few years ago, in 2202. Close to fifty percent of all Latinos fled the Midwest and west coast of the former United States and migrated to Latin American nations. Some migrated to Canada and Europe, and about thirty percent migrated to the current United States on the east coast. Almost twenty percent remained in the wastelands of the west coast, including your family.

Daniel began to remember the nuclear devastation of his youth in New Mexico. He remembered his father moving from Arizona to New Mexico to flee the pandemic and increasing political violence. After the death of his mother from breast cancer, Daniel became a biologist, but after the US government lost control of most of the United States, he moved to Mexico. Daniel's father remained in New Mexico and lost his life in a church when a bomb was detonated by a far-right group that was angered by the political activities of one of the pastors. Daniel remembered meeting a Mexican scientist named Milagros and getting married to her at the age of thirty in 2167. They had their first child, Aurelio, in 2170 and their daughter, Esperanza, in 2175.

Daniel asked, "Were the vaccinations successful? What happened with the fungal Dark Lung infections?"

Roberto replied, "The conspiracies were partly correct. China was researching deadly fungi that could be weaponized, but there was no evidence that the Chinese Communist Party would use them for biological warfare. Mexican intelligence discovered that US operatives infiltrated a Chinese lab and were able to take several of the fungi, and they were brought to several military facilities in the Midwest. After the nuclear attack, some of these fungi survived and Dark Lung and the viral pandemic killed millions of people."

Roberto paused to allow Daniel to process the information before he continued, "In the late twenty-second century, Mexican scientists learned about several advanced fungi in the wastelands that could help end the pandemic. These fungi communicate with other fungi and a variety of plants through info chemicals that also influence animals. We have genetically modified some of these fungi to produce anti-viral medicine and other agents that have extended human life.

"Before the last world war, the Chinese held supremacy in quantum computing, but after the war, Mexico and several other Latin American nations now have advanced quantum computers, and Mexico is now the leader in biocomputers and bionetworks. With this knowledge, the pandemic is now over in Mexico, and the rest of Latin America, Europe, the Middle East, Africa, and most of the United States have substantially lowered death rates. Our research of fungi will improve society on Earth and has applications in our Lunar colonies and future Martian expeditions."

Daniel became anxious as he interjected, "Why am I here, and where is my family?"

Roberto paused and collected his thoughts before saying, "You were among several thousand people that suffered from a devastating parasitic fungus. This advanced fungus made up nearly twenty percent of your biomass, and we have successfully removed about 95% of the fungus within your body. The fungus impacted your psychology, and you became increasingly conspiratorial and erratic. You began spreading far-right propaganda against the Mexican government and far-right US pseudo-history which was supported by several remaining US far-right groups at a time when the Mexican military was engaged in several conflicts in Oklahoma and western Tennessee."

General Jose Luna interjected, "We believe we have restored your personality, and your memories should fully return within a week. You suffered greatly these last two years, and you are a respected scientist that began to push misinformation. The former United States collapsed for a variety of reasons, particularly the spreading of false information leading to the deaths of most US citizens. More than sixty percent of the remaining far-right groups in the mainland have died due to the respiratory virus or Dark Lung. We do not want misinformation to spread in our nation, and we need you to strengthen the resolve of our Mexican citizens. We are launching a final campaign to defeat the remaining far-right groups and establish our northeastern border in western Tennessee. We have promised to subsequently end the war and sign a final peace treaty with the United States next year."

Roberto continued after the general spoke, "You suffered a psychotic break in the previous year, and your thoughts merged your present with your ancestral past. We believe we can use some of these fungal chemicals to retrieve, not only a person's memories but memories linked to family members. Your most recent thoughts involved your grandfather, Simon Santos, who once served as the Surgeon General of the former United States. Your memories somehow merged with your grandfather's, and you saw yourself as him. Your wife in your dreams is a combination of your wife, Milagros, and your grandmother, Altagracia. Your son in your visions is not the son of your grandfather and your father Generoso, but your actual son, Aurelio, who unfortunately passed away along with your wife last year. Your wife and son caught the disease from you, and their conditions deteriorated rapidly."

Roberto paused as Daniel began to weep and rub his head in distress before he continued, "It appears your life events have merged with your grandfather's and other family members in your mind. Your grandchildren are now under the care of your daughter, Esperanza, who is living in Jalisco, Mexico."

"You were in a medically induced coma for two months, and you awakened several times this week. We, unfortunately, have had similar conversations with you three times in the last two days."

Tears streamed out of Daniel's eyes, but the two men appeared to have seen this reaction before. Nevertheless, the two men consoled Daniel and continued to explain his reality. A Maya nurse, named Gloria, entered the room and provided Daniel with comfortable clothes and a warm Mexican dinner. Gloria wiped away Daniel's tears and promised to return after Daniel finished his meal and showered. As more of Daniel's memories returned and he relaxed, the two men continued to speak with him. They explained world events, including how Japan and Unified Korea were now the two powers in Asia, and how Russia was now weakened after its involvement in the last war. General Luna explained how a new era of peace was of utmost importance and how a potential conflict between Canada and Russia should be avoided.

A few therapists were now allowed to enter the room to take care of Daniel. Daniel remembered the pain he'd felt the last several years—a pain that had existed in his family for several generations and which was shared by millions of people in the Americas and billions worldwide. Daniel only remembered fragments of the false life he'd lived that stood against everything he represented, and he felt disgusted as well as relief that his mind and body were reconnected. It was time for Daniel to welcome the pain of his reality and the determination and hope of trying to do what he felt was just. He thought of his family and asked for his daughter.

Roberto smiled and said, "Your daughter, Esperanza, has just been notified that we were successful in the operation, and we invited her here to see you."

Daniel wiped the tears from his face and said, "I will do my best to help the Mexican government and, most importantly, the working people. I want to do the best that I can, reverse any wrongdoings of my past, and finish the last days of my life well. But first, I want to see my grandchildren. I want to see Esperanza."

Story 30: Reflections in St. James Park (22nd Century)

Adam Cisneros was enjoying his Saturday afternoon in the Bronx. It was a hot July day, and Adam's girlfriend, Jenny Sok, was with her parents in Pelham Parkway. Adam shared an apartment with Jenny in the building located on the corner of 192nd Street and Jerome Avenue, across the street from St. James Park. Adam originally lived by Sedgwick Avenue and West Kingsbridge Road before he moved in with Jenny after meeting her at Bronx Community College. Adam subsequently transferred to Lehman College with a Physics degree and graduated two years ago in 2098. Adam worked at Montefiore Hospital for several years as a physicist in the imaging department. Jenny was a nursing student and worked part-time at a clinic to help Adam pay rent.

Adam received a call from his friends, Jesus Soto and Rodney Nichols, to spend some time at St. James Park. Adam picked up his basketball and met his friends at the court where they played a few games of full-court basketball before stopping by the *bodega* and picking up some cold beers. The friends had grown up together in the same building, and they'd gone to the same elementary school, junior high school, and they'd all attended John F. Kennedy High School. Rodney was currently attending Lehman College, and Jesus was taking a break from school and was currently working with his father in Hunts Point in the South Bronx. The guys realized that as they aged, it would be harder to spend time together like when they were children, so they made the most of today.

After the basketball game, the guys walked toward the benches and watched the kids ride their bikes and play tag. It was strange to see kids playing as most kids these days stay indoors playing video games. In previous decades, St. James Park would be filled with kids running, playing handball, basketball, and stickball, having their first kiss, and getting into trouble. Throughout the twenty-first century, an increasing number of kids would stay indoors glued to the internet, however, Adam's parents tried to limit video games in the home and encouraged him to get into a little league and play outside. Adam grew up playing stickball and baseball in Crotona Park. He remembered walking down to St. James Park and Devoe Park to play basketball with his cousins and friends.

As the sun began to set and the temperature began to cool, the three friends walked over toward a more isolated part of the park. David and Rodney were talking about the basketball game as Jesus prepared a vape. The vape had specialized cannabis oil, and Jesus wanted to share it with his friends. Rodney sometimes vaped, but David had stopped vaping various recreational drugs since he'd graduated from school. Marijuana had been legalized throughout the United States several decades ago thanks to pressure from various left-wing groups and in Congress, however, it was still prohibited for those who were underage and for people in certain professions, including the health field.

Jesus passed the vape to Rodney and looked at Adam as he said, "Adam, you have to give this a try. I know you need to unwind a little from all the studying you do. I know I need to relax after working all week at the warehouse."

Adam hesitated but finally agreed. "Alright, just a couple of hits. I'll be off from work next week for a little vacation anyway, and I'm only working a couple of days this week, so I guess I can relax a little bit. I'll try to visit you sometime at Hunts Point; my father drives trucks there. I hope I can earn enough to help my parents, so they won't have to continue working these jobs. Truck drivers and factory workers develop health problems as they age."

Jesus laughed and replied, "That's true. Many poor black people and Latinos work these jobs and suffer the consequences. Remember the last major pandemic?

The Covid-19 pandemic that started in 2020 killed over half a million people in the United States alone. The poor black and Latinos that worked essential jobs in that pandemic suffered the most, while the wealthy became wealthier. Even with some of the reforms and automation, our people continue to work these jobs. I guess some things never change. So much for essential workers."

Rodney laughed and said, "That is right, but all we can do is work hard and look out for ourselves and our loved ones. Most people don't have time to get into politics and think far into the future. They are just trying to survive day-to-day life, and that is how the elite wants us to be—worried more about where we will find our next meal instead of analyzing how they are all robbing us blind."

Adam laughed before he said, "You are completely right, Rodney. This is why I'm ready to move and find a good opportunity. I applied for a few jobs at some hospitals in North Carolina and Florida that are paying well. Thinking of taking things seriously with Jenny and moving as soon as she finishes nursing school. I'll help my parents move, too."

Jesus smiled and spoke as he exhaled after taking another hit from his cannabis vape. "So, you are finally going to take things seriously with your Cambodian girlfriend, huh? That's good, Adam; I wish you the best. You have to invite me so I can visit you when you do move."

Rodney smiled. "Jesus, you should get serious with that Indian girl from Guyana—Rajkumar's sister—I think Sonya is her name, right?"

Jesus laughed. "Yeah, that's Raj's sister. We have been seeing each other for a few months now. Maybe I will get serious with her after I get my life together. You know how things are. Sometimes life can be crazy, and it's hard to get the ball rolling the right way."

The guys nodded in agreement as the sun dropped below the horizon. After a few minutes of silence, Jesus spoke again. "I've been thinking about a lot of things. What if everything we have been through—the wars, pandemics, personal problems—are all a setup? What if our government set us up to fail or helped spread disease to research how our bodies react, and the pharmaceutical companies cashed in? What if some of these diseases come from outside of our planet?"

Before Jesus could continue, Rodney interrupted him, "Jesus, my man, you got to slow down on the psychoactive stuff that you like to do, my friend. You are talking that crazy shit again. You got to concentrate on the here and now, my friend, and leave those thoughts alone."

The friends laughed as they left St. James Park. Adam enjoyed spending time with his friends, and the thought of leaving the Bronx saddened him, but he understood that he needed to take advantage of the few opportunities he had in life. He desired success for his childhood friends and knew they would do well in life because they were of strong character. Adam said goodbye to his friends as he crossed the street back to his apartment. His girlfriend would arrive later that night, giving him time to shower and prepare dinner before she returned home. Adam thought of proposing to Jenny in the following year and planned to start saving money for an engagement ring. He smiled as he thought of a better life for his parents, his friends, and particularly for Jenny and himself as he poured some Scotch and opened the window. He gazed outside and looked down 192nd Street as he took a sip and waited for Jenny.

Within the solar system, in a location unknown to humanity, there was a higher intelligence with complex technology. They were patient, listening, and observing. Sometimes exotic thoughts can easily be reality.

Author's Note

Science fiction has always interested me since I was a small boy. I watched *Star Trek* with my father and, soon after, became interested in the *Star Wars* series. I remember the excitement of going to the movies with my father and friends to watch films like *Total Recall*, *Predator*, *The Fly*, and *Stargate*. As a teenager, my love for science fiction was reignited by films like *The Matrix*, *Event Horizon*, *Demolition Man*, *12 Monkeys*, and *Independence Day*. As an adult, I discovered *Blade Runner* and subsequently went to see *Blade Runner: 2049*, *Arrival*, and *Dune* in December 2021. I am also anticipating *Dune 2* and the adaptation of *Rendezvous with Rama.*

I soon began to read the science fiction books that inspired some of the movies I saw at the theater. I enjoyed reading and seeing the visions of the directors and writers of how the future might be if we make the wrong decisions. I wrote this collection during the Covid-19 pandemic from the fall of 2020 to April 2021. I noticed the anti-science culture coming from mostly right-wing circles in the United States. The anti-vax misinformation was mostly adopted by the far-right. The far-right continued its history of climate-change denial, anti-vaccine sentiments, and propaganda that helps to continue the rise of inequality. As the omicron variant spread along with ignorance, Covid-19 deaths in the United States passed one million in 2022. This experience further shows the importance of spreading factual information.

Although I enjoy cyberpunk, I decided to write stories that leaned into the genre of solarpunk. I placed most of my stories in the Dominican Republic, the Caribbean, Latin America, and the inner cities of the United States. These communities and nations suffer most from the negative effects of decreasing representation in government, de-regulation, and anti-science policies. I wanted to imagine a more positive future for working-class people and people of color. The challenge for me was creating adversity within the genre of solarpunk that depicts a more positive future.

I hope that these stories can be entertaining for those who read them. If some of these stories can inspire the young people who read them to find ways to improve health and technology to benefit their communities or nation, then I have accomplished my goal. I hope you have as much fun reading these stories as I did writing them. Thank you for taking the time to read my stories!

About the Author:

Rafael Morillo was born in the Bronx, New York. Rafael studies history, and he is an avid reader of history and historical fiction. He enjoys sports and studying different cultures and their history. Besides reading historical fiction, he enjoys reading alternate history, science fiction, and writing historical fiction from different points of view which are not traditionally explored.

Other Books by Rafael:

The Kiskeyano: A Taino Story

The Lion of India

Might of the Phoenix

The Crimson Sands of Eden

Santo Domingo 2437

Kindle Vella Stories:

Historical Fiction:

Song of Magadha

Emancipation of Quisqueya

Sci-fi:

Exotic Equinox

The Antillean Candidate

The Chronicles of Agent Machado